T0157381

The Last Egyptian Standing

The Last Egyptian Standing

The Great Egyptian

Story and Written by,

Mo Nassah

authorHOUSE®

AuthorHouse™
1663 Liberty Drive
Bloomington, IN 47403
www.authorhouse.com
Phone: 1-800-839-8640

Published by AuthorHouse   10/30/2015

ISBN: 978-1-4670-0067-3 (sc)
ISBN: 978-1-4670-0068-0 (e)

Print information available on the last page.

This book is printed on acid-free paper.

Chapters & Index

In loving

Memory of my father

The STORY

To you!

&

To everyone in my family, with love, I love you all, and consider us as one, so I thank you all for the love and life we have all lived together.

&

To the Super Special Creation in life, with love always, know my heart is true, and for you the inspiration will always remain.

&

To the Special One/Female, I pray we meet some day, for thy love remains true, as above, as you.

&

Mr. Mystery & Mr. Super Mystery for all the positive and special words and super energy towards the story, and the inspiration given that has developed this story. Thank you for believing in and with me!

&

To all those that did and may still not believe. Well, thank you too.

&

I thank God.

&

I Praise to God.

For everything, including creating you, thank you!

AUTHOR *CHAPTER INTRODUCTION*

An Author Chapter Introduction for this story, to me personally, would feel best kept short for a book, and from the angle of the main character MN80M. THE AMAZING ONE/MALE, is always best, and a touch of my fantasy as the Author to his reality too with a smile, right.

The Last Egyptian Standing: The Great Egyptian is pro—duced herein as a written format of a story based around events before, during, and following, the Egyptian Revolution in the year 2011 from the eyes and angle of one very special young man. The written text herein is in the same/similar nature as it was true in the physical form, herein allowing this book to be, as is. This is one of the reasons that the book(s) main focal points are very vocal, with a lot of speech from each character instead of certain descriptions of the day-to-day extra atmosphere and/or surroundings that may at times take away from the true essence of pure energy and closeness that all of these CHARACTERS and more have combined.

Friendships and special connections that they have nurtured in real life with one another in the day and age of the year 2011 that continues into the year 2012.

The Last Egyptian Standing: The Great Egyptian, although mainly always based around MN80M. THE AMAZING ONE/MALE's version of events, finds matters unfolding excitedly in full truth as everything is already revolving mainly around his personal as well as business relationships from within Cairo, Egypt and London, England as well as several other International locations around the World.

From before the moments of chaos and rioting began and then hit peak, MN80M. THE AMAZING ONE/ MALE finds his spirit suffering between heart and mind whether or not to accept the life as it is in this day and age and continue with his chosen normal life, or to just join-in with everyone on and off of the streets of Cairo, the main city in Egypt, during the 2011 Egyptian Revolution. At the same time, a window of opportunity opens for the possibility to follow his emotional instincts that have been restraining his heart and mind for such a long time now, especially before the January early start into the 2011 Egyptian revolution. Or, also the simple possibility to just sit back and watch everything un-fold from the Television at home like the majority of the year 2011 near seven billion Human population.

He said, she said, is exactly what happens in this version/ book, and over eighty (80%) percent of this book is a true story, hence, a reason the words of each character (to the Author) was/is more important for the first book to be writ—ten in exactly this way and form for the reader(s) of each book to truly appreciate, and understand at-least some of that to come in the second book, third and possibly fourth book of this part of the entire MN80-M story series starting as, *The Last Egyptian Standing: The Great Egyptian.* This also a reason for privacy, original (Human) people names, company names, certain brands, have all been extracted and replaced with new fictional character names created by the Author. The locations set out in BOLD CAPITAL LETTERS is to allow the reader to comprehend the rapid switches in locations and things that occur at the exact same time, and/ or co-inside with each other from City to Country, during, before, and after the January 2011 Egyptian Revolution.

Imagine then a true story, a miracle, with real events, in our life-time . . . 2010/2011/2012. And/or then turn that into a book, like here, or a fantasy film, from the real life event(s) true life CHARACTERS in BOLD, real words and actions from real life (Humans) people.

From the outspoken and brilliant start until the end of this entire true story, the author allows us the readers to enjoy the read as we enter a new World here, a whole new dimension with real life CHARACTERS and Personalities that capture the heart of each reader from the first chapter when all the chaos begins. Full of excitement, passion, adventure, love, envy, fear, betrayal, success, possible murder, untold mystery and much more; As sad, and as happy, as some of these events may be to some, this is inspired from a true story, and a part of Mankind now, the History of you, and I. Especially with the main character MN80M. THE AMAZING ONE/ MALE alive and the majority of those connected within the stories.

An Example of what to expect;

CHAPTER ONE ZERO:????—Now it begins . . .

INTERIOR OF LOCATION: UNKNOWN / DAY:??—
TIME:??:?? (GMT)
NOVEMBER 2011 & MARCH 2012

MN80M.
(Quoted)

"The date this second is supposed to be November 2011, as written above, and well, publishing wise, that be the truth on the first edition, yet at this moment while adding this in, the month is March 2012, and I find myself no longer the same location, so that be four or five months after this was originally written and published, for the reasons being as it be. Only the creator of all creations would know what time and date you the reader shall willingly read any of this which I share, but when you do manage to have time to read, then feel free to each time Imagine a true story, a miracle, with real events, in our life-time . . . and/or, then turn that into a super fantasy film while reading with your own imagination this inspired true story written within the books."

". . . So you see, to me, to me personally, everything is simple in this life we live. I am a firm believer in that, *'If you understand the languages of the World, you understand the stage'(s)"*

CHAPTER ONE: When it all began . . .

{9 or 10 MONTHS before
November/December
2011}

EXTERIOR OF LOCATION; TAHRIR
SQUARE, CAIRO, EGYPT—
DAY?? TIME:??:?? (EET)
The 2nd February
2011.

The chaos and rioting has begun right next to the Museum entrance towards the heart of the Liberation Square. We hear screaming as rocks and stones being thrown from several angles. MN80M—THE AMAZING ONE/MALE (30 Years Old) unharmed, is running fast past Egyptian Army Tanks situated on the front line of the battles to make his way back towards the secondary line of people holding

PRELUDE

INTERIOR OF LOCATION; LONDON, ENGLAND,
UNITED KINGDOM
DAY {??Unknown??}—TIME: {??Unknown??} (GMT)
MONTH: NOVEMBER—YEAR: 2011

MN80M. THE AMAZING ONE/MALE (31 Years Old) speaks out in a gentle but soft and bold tone as if a voice-over (VO) In his mind in the Japanese Language, *"In the name of God Most Gracious Most Merciful . . ."* he said gracefully.

A moment of silence is heard as a gentle wind sounds. MN80M. THE AMAZING ONE/MALE continues sharing his thoughts in the most subtle manner to himself in his mind now in English,

"As time goes by, and lives are lived, how can one share and/ or express what I want to say to you all now in the best angle to debate and possibly end the entire great Nature-Nurture debate while sharing events of the 2011 Egyptian Revolution and more.??. I wish in a feature film, as 80% of this continuing blessed true story is real, as to date, I swear to God. And for those that may not believe in God, then well, this is a true story, based on real events in the year 2011, you can easily verify that yourself, even some of the 10% Imagination & 10% fantasy. Today being a different

publish date to when the entire story was First published by myself while sending to Sir Mystery and then later on in this book format via Author House [09/16/2011] copyright secretly. I chose not to share this story to the public until a later date for a reason, also allowing me the Author, the possibility to do last minute corrections and/or adding information like these past 69 or 70 words. The 11th of November 2011 is supposed to be the authorized publish date for this first of many within the book series. One reason was a love for the date 11/11/11, another was that it is also my step-fathers birth-date as well as the birth date of Mr. [Must fill in name] I think, or maybe I got the days and date wrong, God knows . . . Yet I decided at the near end of publishing to re-set the date, to a different date [11/26/2011 or 12/02/11] for the public to be able to read. To this, I thank God. Let me think, let me think . . . . Maybe a quote, and how does that quote go again by that one American President many did and still do love . . . "Those who make peaceful revolution impossible will make violent revolution inevitable." said MN80M with a smile as a gentle wind gushes past him louder than the English Hip-Hop music playing in the background. MN80M. THE AMAZING ONE/MALE continues speaking in English,

"John F. Kennedy said that quote, I think, and all rights there reserved with own proprietor, and well, this is how things are to me through my eyes, as if you yourself can now, walk 1 to 8000 miles or more, in my shoes, and see how you feel to continue." Another gentle wind sound breezes past as MN80M. THE AMAZING ONE/MALE continues speaking his mind,

"Would you? Could you? I guess I am going to have to break one or two ancient writer's rules while publishing to allow you and I, the possibility to take our minds into this reality and fantasy of mine, ours, and imagine being here, and there with us and me among Hundreds of Thousands of other Brave Egyptians that turned out into the Millions, all standings strong together during our history

in Humanity that will always mark the early January 2011 evolution (many others titling as a revolution) as the paramount part of Egyptian, African, Middle Eastern & Universal turning points for our growth as Humanity into the newest of ages. (God Willing)— The book layout is as it is, for a reason. Just like life is I guess. And this being mine, so would you continue to . . . Could you? Do not look at what you have lost . . . . Look at what thee have gained . . . ."
MN80M. THE AMAZING ONE/MALE said while breathing out softly and smiles as the sounds of the keyboard typing now stops and the written story now begins. Egypt.

CHAPTER 1: Where it all began . . . Egypt *THE DAY.* (14 or 15 MONTHS AGO)

EXTERIOR OF LOCATION; TAHRIR SQUARE,
CAIRO, EGYPT—
DAY??—TIME:??:?? (EET) The 2nd February 2011.

The chaos and rioting has begun right next to the Museum entrance towards the heart of the Liberation Square. We hear hundreds of people screaming as rocks and stones are being thrown from several angles. MN80M—THE AMAZING ONE/MALE (30 Years Old) unharmed, is running fast past Egyptian Army Tanks situated on the front line of the battles to make his way back towards the secondary line of people holding . . . .

The Story

CHAPTER ONE

When it all began . . . Egypt 'the day'
{14 or 15 MONTHS AGO . . . . }

EXTERIOR OF LOCATION: TAHRIR SQUARE.
CAIRO, EGYPT—
DAY 9: TIME: 15:32 (EET)
2nd February 2011—

The chaos and rioting has just begun right next to the Museum entrance towards the heart of the Liberation Square. We hear rocks and stones being thrown from several angles. MN80M. THE AMAZING ONE/MALE (30 Years Old) unharmed, is running fast past Egyptian Army Tanks situated on the front line of the battles to make way back towards the secondary line of people holding ground as others coming into the square continue to fight and push through the front-line. MN80M-ALI & 12 ASSOCIATES are in battles against an evil force of men next to an Egyptian Army tank situated just ahead of MN80M THE AMAZING ONE / MALE, also known to some as MN80-M.

MN80M. THE AMAZING ONE/MALE continues running fast past hundreds of wounded people and near rock attacks, while also praying in English.
"God help me. God help me. God help me." He said to himself as he continues running fast.

[MN80M-EMPATHY LEVELS INCREASE]

MN80M. THE AMAZING ONE/MALE continues to run fast while pulling out his sling-shot quickly from his back pocket and taking out from his inside pocket with his other hand a small pouch, to then quickly pour out the space-marbles into the palm of his hands, load three into the sling-shot and fires multiple marbles within seconds towards the direction of the evil force.

{[UNIQUE SPACE-MARBLES CONTINUE FAST TOWARDS IMPACT]}

The sounds of the helicopters above combined with the screaming of thousands of people within the Liberation Square is by now blocked out by MN80M, but then shouts out as he notices the flag has fallen from one of the wounded men on the front-line. Others next to the man that falls to the ground start to run back in fear towards the secondary line of brave young Egyptian men. MN80M. THE AMAZING ONE/MALE shouts out in Arabic and English,
"Hold your positions . . . Hold your positions . . . Keep the flag up high . . . Keep up the flag . . . The flag has fallen . . . The flag has fallen." he said.
MN80M. THE AMAZING ONE/MALE pulls out more special space marbles from his pouch, loads into the slingshot

and fires again multiple shots in the direction of the evil force as he runs fast towards one of the Egyptian Army tanks just past those running back leaving the flag on the floor unmanned near the front line. MN80M. Does a forward front-flip landing perfectly on his toes and then leaps into the air over several people landing smoothly on his feet near the flag on the floor and picks up the flag quickly with his right hand.

[MN80M. EMPATHY LEVELS INCREASE]

MN80 M. THE AMAZING ONE / MALE is now holding the flag up high in the air as he continues to run forward towards MN80M-ALI & 12 ASSOCIATES that remain standing strong in battle-mode on the front—line. The sounds of screaming intensifies as men are being sliced up by knives and machetes in battle, as well as the sound in the distant of those tens of thousands of men and women remaining in the inside of the square or running for his or her life. MN80M. continues to run fast past many wounded individuals bleeding heavily from the battle. MN80M-THE AMAZING ONE/ MALE starts to shout out loud In-Arabic & English,
"Egypt! Egypt! Egypt! . . . God is the greatest. God is the greatest. Men!! Hold your ground . . . Hold positions . . ."

[MN80M. EMPATHY LEVELS INCREASE]

MN80M. holds the flag up higher as he continues to run faster towards those still in battle on the front-line. MN80M. THE AMAZING ONE/ MALE reaches just before the front-line and hands the flag to MN80M-ALI that is also close to the battle near the front-line. MN80M—THE AMAZING ONE speaks out In-Arabic,

"Where is he??" he said in a hurried voice.

MN80M-ALI responds quickly in Arabic,

"We do not know. He just vanished . . ." his friend said.

MN80M-THE AMAZING ONE/MALE now looking around quickly at the hundreds of faces is annoyed and slightly out of breath, says back to him In-Arabic, "Vanished. Where to?!?? Anyway . . . Hold control of the front-line and the flag, keep it raised high . . . What-ever happens. Keep the flag up high. I will be back, God willing. Stay strong."

MN80's look at each other and shake heads in agreement with a smile as other men only a few meters' behind continue in arm-to-arm combat, many weapons being utilized in this horrific battle scene on the front-line.

[MN80M-EMPATHY LEVELS INCREASE]

MN80M THE AMAZING ONE/MALE turns and runs back fast towards the secondary line. Sounds of rocks hitting metal can be heard as well as people screaming and shouting while MN80M. continues to run fast past and luckily through Molotov Cocktails being thrown from the other side of the Egyptian Army Tanks situated on the front-line.

Tens of thousands of people can be seen from afar stuck in the inside of Cairo's Liberation Square, and only a couple of hundred people are holding both first, second and third defense lines while majority of others stand in fear inside the centre of the square. Most of the Egyptian people are either frozen from shock and disbelief, and/or about to start running out from the square's back-end exit like thousands of others now seem to be doing. MN80M continues to run fast past others that have blood pouring from faces and body parts that have been cut deeply from machetes and blades. MN80M reaches the loud chanting secondary line of men that are all holding arms linked together to strengthen the secondary line from the possible onslaught, and is asked a question by one of the young men that stands nervous, scared and out of breath. The YOUNG Egyptian MAN speaks out In Arabic,

"What is happening? We cannot see. What is happening? Shall we move forward now sir?" The YOUNG Egyptian MAN said brave, but nervously.

MN80M-THE AMAZING comes to a halt, takes two steps closer to the young man, looks him in the eyes, and then closes his eyes for a quick second before he speaks. MN80M-THE AMAZING (Says loud in mind In English)

"Spartans/Egyptians . . . What is your profession?" he said in hope that obviously no one but he heard.

MN80M THE AMAZING ONE/MALE opens his eyes quickly as the continuing sounds of thousands chanting intensifies, looks the brave young Egyptian man in the eyes as he places his right hand on the man's left shoulder.

MN80M says back to him in Arabic,

"Stay here. The same situation, and they fighting through, more people are needed, but no. Stand in your positions. Stay here."

[{{{MN80M. EMPATHY LEVELS INCREASE}}] [{{{EMPA-THY LEVELS INCREASE}}]

The young man at the front of the line, as well as many others next to him continues listening attentively to MN80M-THE AMAZING ONE. Yet, as soon as he finishes saying what he does, MN80M. moves on past the brave men in-towards the heart of the square, while the men continue on chanting

and standing firm among hundreds of other brave Egyptian men holding the secondary line of the battle. The MEN CHANTING In Arabic,
"The people, and the Army, are one hand. The people, and the Army, are one hand. The people, and the Army, are one hand." continued. The sound of the crowd intensifies as people continue to chant while MN80M-THE AMAZING ONE/ MALE reaches the Middle of the Square, and apart from noticing the massive amount of people that are screaming and in fear, he also notices that after all this happening in a rapid moment, he needs to use a toilet to urinate from all the beverages he had hours before at lunch-time with his sister, and so he looks around before he recalls a small shed type building at one of the other entrances that was possibly utilized as a toilet, so he heads in that direction, quickly.

[{{CROWD SOUND INTENSIFYS}}]
[{{MN80M-EMPATHY LEVELS INCREASE}}]

MN80M. THE SPECIAL ONE/*FEMALE (Unknown Age*—Possibly 20's/30 Years Old) dressed in a unique attire, with an Egyptian flag bandanna wrapped around her face to disclose her true identity, brushes past MN80M THE AMAZING ONE/MALE shoulder slowly and he does not notice. MN80M—THE SPECIAL ONE/ FEMALE comes to a halt and she watches as he walks away into the screaming crowd of thousands unaware of her existence as of yet.

[CROWD SOUND INTENSIFYS]
[EMPATHY LEVELS INCREASE]
{{MN80M. THE SPECIAL ONE/FEMALE EMPATHY LEVELS INCREASE}}

[{{MN80M THE AMAZING—EMPATHY LEVELS INCREASE}}]

MN80M THE SPECIAL ONE/FEMALE *(Age: Unknown— Possibly 20's-30)* smiles under her bandanna, and then moves in stealth mode in the same direction as MN80M THE AMAZING ONE/MALE. The sun shines down from the pale blue hot skies as if an invisible beam of light towards her bandanna. The stunning Golden body of Jesus Christ necklace hidden beneath the bandanna around her neck continues to shine bright, and then brighter, she smiles more as she continues to walk and then places her right hand up towards the necklace on her chest area, and with hand now firmly pressing on necklace,
"He must be the one . . ."
She said as she continues to walk with her smile now even happier than moments earlier.

[MN80M-THE SPECIAL ONE/FEMALE—EMPATHY LEVELS INCREASE]
[MN80M THE AMAZING ONE/MALE—EMPATHY LEVELS INCREASE]

CHAPTER TWO

Where it all began,
Egypt!
8 MONTHS EARLIER to love poem.

EXTERIOR OF LOCATION: KING SALEH
STREET, OLD CAIRO, EGYPT.
MN80M's FAMILY AREA; NIGHT:
May 2010—02:11 AM
(EET)

MN80M. THE AMAZING ONE/MALE (30 Years Old)
and MN80M-ALI (35 Years Old) are in conversation about
life in general as they both have done as best friends since
childhood. MN80M-ALI is sitting comfortably in his
chair, wearing his MN80-M-60's-STYLE/SUIT and his hat
on his knee while MN80M remains wearing an MN80M-
UK-URBAN-SUIT and an MN80M-CAP on his head.
MN80M. THE AMAZING ONE/MALE says out softly
yet in a bold way In-Arabic,
"I have to tell you something." He said as he looks at his
friends face.

"Tell me." MN80M-ALI responds quickly in-Arabic, eager to hear the coming words.

MN80M then continues in-Arabic,

"I will travel, to the special place again. I have had enough. I cannot take it anymore." he said while still looking at his friend. Surprisingly while still sitting on his chair calmly, and continuing to smoke his roll up cigarette MN80M-ALI responds in Arabic saying,

"So imagine us then . . . This is your country MN80M your father, his father, their wives and all above them lived here, Old Cairo."

MN80's look at each other before looking away at the surroundings; The moonlight continues to shine down light from above as if the Old Cairo streets have always had the same warm and tender bright light shining down from the moon above in the dark night sky. Both remain silent for a brief moment as they continue to smoke cigarette before one decides to speak.

"I know . . . I know . . ." said MN80M. as he looks towards his best friend to hear MN80M-ALI say back to him with passion,

"You were doing so well. What happened? It is that girl right!?! She ruined everything . . . Right!?!?" said his friend as MN80M THE AMAZING ONE/MALE Then responds instantly In-Arabic saying,

"My heart is torn. Apart from MN80M SUPER SPECIAL CREATION leaving my life, it's more than that . . ." said MN80—M.

MN-80's both look to the floor and then at each other as the moonlight remains strong. MN80M-ALI then asks in a slow trembling tone in the Arabic language, "You can feel something, right!??!" he said.

MN-80's look at each other quickly before THE AMAZ-ING ONE/MALE says.

"What do you mean??" MN80M. said in a low tone as MN80M-ALI quickly responds,

"Don't play games with me MN80M. I know since 1991 when you used to come to Agami to be next to paradise beach. You only came back from Los Angeles in 2005 . . ." MN80M-ALI said while he turns his body slightly away as if upset and agitated. "I know you can feel things before they can happen . . . You did it every year summer time in Agami and helped us to be free and enjoy special times finding girls and playing football on the beach. Times that could have gone wrong, tell me MN80M. What's wrong!??! What is going to happen?? Is that why you let MN80M SUPER SPECIAL CREATION go??" he said, while making sure to slow down on the last few words and just as he finishes and MN80M-ALI turns to face MN80M. In a quick response, MN80M-THE AMAZING ONE/MALE replies in Arabic saying,

"MN80M SUPER SPECIAL CREATION has nothing to do with anything, or anyone. Even though what she did as her first reaction was spectacular. This has nothing to do with her, or anyone as I said before already to you." said MN80M with a stern look on his face and his mouth and jaw closed together, but then smiles.

MN-80's look towards each other in a stern look as MN80M-ALI then asks,

"So what is it then?? Others like you have done OK here, some others maybe could not survive here because they are used to the lives they live, like millions of other half Egyptians or part Egyptians around the World, but they can still try, you did and are doing good for many years here brother against all odds. Even others like thousands you already know from over the years with your travels and studies many of them all doing great, at-least a few hundred of them at the very least. Even if you choose to be like MN80M-THE AMAZING SECOND/MALE you can be like those doing very good here." MN80M-ALI said, with his last words injecting about other personalities that may have had success.

MN80M THE AMAZING ONE/MALE replies with,

"I am not MN80M-THE AMAZING SECOND/MALE, or like any other half Egyptian, or creation of my kind, and you know that. And it's not that anyway." MN80M said while turning to look up into the night sky. A moment of silence comes about as they both take in the atmosphere.

"So what is it then . . . ???? It is us isn't it?? Is something going to happen to us?" MN80M-ALI said asking quickly as if preparing himself for shocking news.

MN-80's look to the floor, and then up at each other quickly before MN80M. THE AMAZING ONE/MALE says In-Arabic,

"I am not sure of the feelings or vision. I just feel something is about to happen soon. And with everything I have been through the past four to five years here in Egypt. I am not sure I can continue at this time with the nation, the people are too much, most think backwards and are moving back. On top of this all, rumor has it that MN-80—THE EG PRESIDENT 1's son seems to be the strongest candidate now right!??!" MN80M said as they both continue to look straight at each other.

A longer moment of silence as only sounds of the minimal background atmosphere combined with one or two vehicles and a few people passing by up near the main road is heard while MN80M-ALI continues to smoke and instantaneously responding in Arabic, "Of-course . . . No question about it . . . We not know what worse can come, you hear the rumors of how people are killing each other for practically nothing, and someone is keeping those people off of the streets, even if many of us say we hate the life how this is for us here. We are stuck like this. Nothing we can do about it. Life gets worse. I am blessed to have the restaurant that my father gave me to learn to work very hard in life, and his father gave to him. We work so hard and still struggle." MN80M-ALI said nervously as MN80M. THE AMAZING looks around him before he says,

"Something very bad may happen . . . and I am not allowed to say, because it could change the course of History, and you know I am not allowed to do that, and even if so, I do not want to speak about it." MN80M said quickly.

MN80M-ALI looks on listening attentively near the edge of his seat,

"Can you at-least tell me something in-case I need to tell people something to prepare. Anything?" asked his friend.

"I wish I could brother." MN80M responded quickly.

MN80M-ALI eagerly wanting to know more details continues questioning for an answer, "Even if one person will die." MN80M-ALI asked as MN-80's look at each other while MN80M-ALI continues, "Then I think I should know something . . . Remember about that time and days in your apartment/flat in the City, I told you about the rumors going around of the Mountain or Mountains of Gold found in Egypt, and how the rumors also say that possibly MN-80—THE EG PRESIDENT 1, his teams and possibly the government with men in power positions may have also kept a secret from a nation the wealth. Or that we hear minimal to nothing of this . . . and you went on your computer system and found the company abroad in Australia managing things with an Egyptian company, then said to me if they those Australian professional are involved managing things, then there should be nothing to worry about, but we have still not heard anything, and we all still feel so much of the nation's wealth has been stolen from us!??!?! You have to tell me something MN80M." said his Egyptian friend.

MN80M looks to floor.

"In the name of God, most gracious, most merciful . . ." MN80M said in his mind in English.

MN-80's look at each other before MN80M THE AMAZING ONE/MALE continues to speak out now verbally in Arabic,

"How many people do you know we have here in Old Cairo??" he said.

MN80M-ALI moves his chair closer and asks,

"Do you mean in and around MN80M. King-Saleh Road?"

MN80M THE AMAZING ONE/MALE responds with,

"All of Old Cairo. You know more than I know how far things go. Is there 10.000, or 20.000 in this community?" MN80-M said.

MN80M-ALI quickly says, "More . . . may be 50".

Another moment of silence before MN80M—THE AMAZING ONE/MALE asks.

"More . . . how much more? What do you mean??" asked MN80M.

"More . . . If you add the other locations of our area of Old Cairo, and other areas too, then maybe one or even two million of us easily in all the surrounding areas." his friend said with a smile.

MN80M looks at the floor slowly as he continues to smoke and blow the smoke out fast through his nostrils and mouth at the same time.

"Tell me . . . I know you MN80—M." said his friend in Arabic.

They both look to the floor, and then up at one another.

"Just get ready, 50.000 is an army, not a community."
MN80M said while looking at his Egyptian friend through
the smoke being blown out from his mouth.
MN80M-ALI nervously responds,
"Ready for what?" he said.
MN80M. THE AMAZING ONE/MALE then says slowly
in his mind as if a voice over in English.
"War . . . ."
MN80M looks towards the floor, at the same time as his
friend says out loud,
"War!!! When????"
Both MN80's look to the floor first.
MN80M THE AMAZING shrugs his shoulders twice as
MN80M-ALI continues speaking in Arabic,
"How many will die? One or some." he said while MN-80's
look at each other face-to-face.
"More . . . ??? How many MN80M?? Tell me . . ." MN80M-
ALIsaid persisting in an attempt to get to the truth.
MN80M THE AMAZING ONE/MALE sheds a tear as he
lowers his head slowly towards the floor and shakes his head.
MN80M-ALI continues speaking in Arabic while seeking an
answer, "Two Million, Ten Million . . ." he asked.
MN80M THE AMAZING ONE/MALE sheds a tear. Two
tears then follow and fall from cheek onto the floor.
"I do not want to leave now. I swear to God I will come if it
starts." MN80-M remarked decisively and reassuringly.
MN80M-ALI lowers his head, *"May God have mercy on us
all . . ." his friend said, as he too sheds tears.* MN-80's look at
each other slowly, then back to floor. MN80M-ALI continues
in a demanding manner asking,
"Can you not do anything? You know all that computer stuff
and Internet. You can tell the World the truth. How *about
all of those famous people, even that Woman [Must fill in*

name] could she not help, anyone, someone . . ." his friend said with the last sentence sounding most desperate.

MN80M THE AMAZING ONE/MALE responds In-English with,

"As you always say to me and we both know, only God can help us all. Plus, I am not the one that makes problems remember, one fixes problems. I cannot do anything about this. We don't know what evil force may come. It's just a feeling and visions remember. That I cannot just write and tell *[Must fill in] or anyone else so to speak, no one cares about us* MN80's. But just to re—*assure you, I already tried to write to [Must fill in name] via her* on-line website, you already know how much I love her and how many times my family watch her television shows, I tried my best many times to help many people and many situations, I tried direct to her representatives, but the email response say she is busy, but I know my story or even our story to come next year in 2011 is just not as important to her, as other stories may be, not that I think anyway, otherwise they would respond to us, she is one of the most busiest women in the World, she has millions of others to help as she always does anyway, same as many other legends alive that can help. And also, just because I was living in *Los Angeles and Hollywood does not mean I know [Must fill in name] and [Must fill in name] and [Must fill in name] now does it!?! No. I was just blessed by God to work alongside some of the stars and celebrities and legends like Mr. [Must fill in name], Mr. [Must fill in name], Ms [Must fill in name] and [Must fill in name] to name a few, that is all, anything else I have done in my* life has just been from the love of what I do. I cannot share with anyone my true *Skill' Ohako',* is this understood brother? Said MN80M

"Yes but, what about the special MN80-M. ANCIENT SCARAB BEATLE RING, the White Golden Ring you are blessed with for us all, and what about life even, out there, are you forgetting when in 2005 and 2006 you came back from Los Angeles you was telling everyone about "Social Network 1" and "Social Network 2", you was teaching people how to create an account on Social Network 1 and saying not to go onto the other one as it was boring and not as positive as the other one, and you showed many people how to do things on-line. You are good at this too. Can you not help tell the World our rights? Our lives . . . .?????" MN80M-ALI said back quickly in an innocent tone.

MN80M THE AMAZING ONE/MALE takes in and breathes out air before he lights the cigarette now in his mouth and says,

"I am not God. I am only human like you MN80M-ALI. Plus, come to think of it also, on-top of everything you ask me about the MN80-M. ANCIENT SCARAB BEATLE RING, you know this ring is not to be spoken of or even used unless we truly need to, that includes all of Humanity, and the near seven billion of us today is not like 200 years ago now is it!?? No!. Not just the two of us now is there, MN80M THE AMAZING SECOND/MALE is the lucky one he can run around and have fun all he likes and I have the responsibility on when and where to use it, not you, or anyone else. Is this pressure not enough on me? I don't even have time for women in my life, I have no life, and it's not fair on me too. I need that special one female to love me like any man does in his life. Plus, just so you know. Those social networks and websites will not last for much longer too. There is something else coming in a Time-Line and not what most thinks. There is something new to come on line for the nation of all nations God willing." MN80M THE AMAZING ONE/MALE said in a bolder tone.

"So you see. You can do something . . . ?? Help us then . . . ."
MN80M-ALI said slowly.

"How can I help us, when I could not even help MN80M-SUPER SPECIAL CREATION the way I wanted??" said MN80M

A silent pause for a moment before his friend asks,

"Yes but you could change that when you want to MN80M."
said MN80M-ALI in an up lifting an inspirational tone.

The look on both faces could slice a lemon in two before you at the dinner table. MN80M. THE AMAZING ONE/ MALE then says In-Arabic,

"I do not want to change anything. I want to evolve with everything . . ." said MN80M

MN80M looks at MN80M-ALI as his friend points with his right hand, and index finger straight and then says,

"Do you see that Mosque there??" he said.

MN80M THE AMAZING ONE/MALE looks around the old paved cemented road and up towards the Mosque before responding with,

"Yes of-course I do. I feel it." said MN80M with a smile now on his face.

MN80M-ALI asks back in Arabic, "Because your grand-father built it . . ." with a smile as he raises his head up high and his chest out. MN80M THE AMAZING smiles before saying,

"Yes. And because it is part of Masr and Planet Earth . . ."
MN80M said.

MN80M-ALI then asks calmly,

"You see this street here . . . and that pavement there . . . and where we are sitting now." said his friend.

MN80M THE AMAZING ONE/MALE looks around at each location the index finger is seen quickly pointing at as he then responds with, "Yes." and looks back on towards the Mosque before back at his best Egyptian friend since childhood. The moon light from the night sky remains bright even on the Mosque. MN80M-ALI moves his chair closer placing his right arm on MN80M's shoulder.

"I think I remember you once telling me some radical notion that I asked and found to be possibly true, that our fathers, their fathers and all, fought, lived, laughed at, sat, played and walked past these roads all their lives, and you know this for a fact. Plus, you too are here, walking, sitting and playing on the same streets and pavements that we both remain here tonight as the last ones standing here now. This is your country by heritage MN80M. THE AMAZING ONE/ MALE remember!?! . . . Don't worry about what everyone or anyone in this day and age says because you are half Egyptian. Your father was Egyptian, his father Egyptian and mother Egyptians, and all of their parents Egyptian before them and you know this. You know that right!??! And even if you were not Egyptian by heritage, in your heart MN80M, you are an Egyptian. You know that right!?! Your father was the one to break the tradition and marry a non-Egyptian in the family, we all love your mum." said MN80M-ALI with a massive smile now on his face and his hand now slowly coming off of the shoulder. MN80M. THE AMAZING ONE/MALE smiles,

"She loves you all too. You know she is an Egyptian at heart." he said in Arabic.

MN80M-ALI smiles, "From her cooking." he said.

Both laugh out loud while nearly falling off of their seats. MN80M—THE AMAZING ONE/MALE smiles saying back in Arabic.

"At-least she cooks like an Egyptian."

MN80M-ALI smiles back, "The best Basbousa cake, Orange and Carrot cakes tasted in my entire life."

Both smile, as MN80M. THE AMAZING ONE/MALE agrees,

"True." he said.

Both move sitting now with back to the chair in an upright position. MN80M-ALI takes out his packet of cigarettes, opens the packet and then takes out two and offers one over, "Stay with us brother." he said.

MN80M THE AMAZING ONE/MALE lowers his head for a moment and then raises it up high as he responds with,

"I am always with you brother. All of the nation, you know that in your heart. I always said, if Egypt goes to war, even if across the oceans and no flights/planes to get back. I would walk . . . I would swim. I will God willing. You just prepare for our safety in heart. God willing nothing will happen anyway."

MN-80'S stand and embrace with a brotherly hug and then look around before back at each other. The warm night in Old Cairo has a gentle breeze come through the narrow side road. Both smile, as if content to just resume back to the normality of the life within the systems they are within and/or choose to be. MN80M-ALI smiles and says In-Arabic,

"Keep your head up. Remember, you are Egyptian . . . This is your land, your country MN80M, like all of us Egyptians" said his friend. MN80M THE AMAZING ONE/MALE then whispers in Arabic.

"You too, you too, stay strong." MN80M said as he continues to smile.

MN80'S both smile.

MN80M-ALI lifts his chin up higher than it is,

"Always . . ." he said in an honorable tone.

"One more thing I need you to do with me and for me brother." MN80-M asked.

"Anything, just say it." his friend responded quickly.

MN80M THE AMAZING ONE/MALE pulls from under his shirt, tucked away in the side-pocket of his MN80M-URBAN-COMBAT-TROUSERS a sling-shot, wooden, looking very old.

"Brother, look after this for me please . . ." MN80M said.

"What is it? I have never seen it before . . . or is that the . . ."

"Yes, my usual weapon of choice physically if needing to use one in war." MN80M said quickly before his friend could finish his sentence.

"We still do not know why you choose to use this, or how even, it's Old."

Both friends smile as the conversation continues,

"At-least it works." MN80-M said as if coaching his friend.

"Where and when did you get this wooden piece of thing anyway??" his friend asks.

"One of my secret locations and a long time ago, most of that story is a secret." MN80M said quickly as if not wanting to let out too much information about his weapon of choice.

"Yes, but this wood is not Egyptian, and we have the best wood, where is it from then?" MN80M-ALI asks in Arabic.

"Spruce, Norway Spruce, but this special one here is from Sweden, and this is very special and has more of a softer-touch so to say." MN80M THE AMAZING said in English with a smile on his face.

"Can you say that in Arabic please?" his friend said back. "Special wood, from a special land, located on a mountain I once visited in Sweden. Called Dalarna I think." MN80M said in Arabic.

"Sweden . . . ?! When did you go to the Sweden MN80M." his friend asked back.

MN80M THE AMAZING ONE looks at his MN80M-SPECIAL SWISS WATCH on his left hand for a moment. "Long story brother . . . Long story, let us just focus on what we spoke of just now, I can tell you more about Norway and Sweden another time. This Egypt vision matter that may become a problem in the future needs us, all of us, together as one combined if anything positive will come of this all, ok. We must all stand together and be the Last Egyptians Standing, even if all of us fight, one will always be the last one standing. Is this weapon of mine safe with you until I return God willing??" MN80M said out quickly in hope to end the unnecessary questioning.

"Yes brother, of-course. Feel free to ask for it any time." MN80M-ALI said back quickly, this time not waiting to hear a reply, yet suddenly, out of nowhere.

"Thank you. Oh and brother. It has a name, my sling-shot that is, I give her a nick-name, she is called 'Okiko-Ohako', 'Special-Skill', her true origin, this one here in my hand, yes, is from Sweden, from before Sweden was Norway, and from before that, she was really found along the main belt in the time I was doing MN80-M-Universal Research, and the straps attached around the Swedish Wood, that is special from Japan. Just like this pouch I have here in my hand is too. Please keep these safe, my Japanese special pouch, keep them all wrapped safe together please ok. No more questions please for now, the pouch only has a total of 33 special MN80-M-SPACE-MARBLES inside and I cannot take all of this to the place I am going to now, ok." MN80M Said to his friend as if a final request before continuing. ". . . and above all brother, we must keep peace, we must always, as much as possible, be neutral, because all of these wars from mankind selfishness and greediness is no good, we must be the Equilibrium within everything, and try to maintain calmness with all, this is very important, positive words are by far greater than negative words and negative actions, please always remember me saying this to you, ok."

Both MN80-'s smile.

MN80M THE AMAZING ONE/MALE hands over the sling-shot wrapped in a piece of old cloth together with the material pouch, filled with only 33 large marbles. His friend as he smiles back at him lifting his chin up high as his friend accepts the pouch and hand-made wooden sling-shot into his hands.

"Thank you brother, there is only one God . . ." MN80M said in Arabic.

"And the Prophet Muhammad is the Messenger of God." MN80M-ALI instantly said back as they now both turn and walk away slowly in separate directions. The moon light remains shining down onto the Old Cairo Street. MN80M THE AMAZING ONE/MALE continues walking straight and then slightly to the right towards the Mosque. He comes to a halt, placing both palms together slowly while touching the MN80-M. ANCIENT SCARAB BEATLE RING on his finger with one of his thumbs and then places palms together as if in a prayer mode. "Bism Allah." said MN80M before he takes in a deep breath of air while looking up towards the moon and then blows out cold air from his mouth onto the ring on his finger.

MN80M, now standing in-front of the Old Cairo Mosque in King-Saleh Street, has a smile on his face as the White Golden ring on his finger shines. The engraved letters 'MN80-M' glows first in bright Orange, and then the letter 'O' and then the letter 'M', and then the letter 'B' starts to glow at the same time in a blue color back-and-forth. MN80M smiles as he closes his eyes and whispers the special words while turning the ring anti-clockwise, opens his eyes and looks towards his right hand side to the Abu-Gamous Shop and building entrance, and then back to the Mosque his grand-father and family constructed before he looks at his MN80M-SPECIAL-SWISS-WATCH on his left hand for a moment then smiles and says,

"In the name of God . . . Masr to Mars . . . God Willing . . . Show me light . . ."

An MN80-M-SUPER-SONIC LIGHT appears in under two seconds. MN80M THE AMAZING ONE/MALE smiles as he raises both arms slowly from his side, and vanishes with the light.

Unnoticed of this occurrence, MN80M-ALI continues walking in the opposite direction of the light as he moves slowly towards the MN80-M vehicle parked across the road to Estabina, the Traditional Egyptian Liver and Brain food restaurant for a few moments. MN80M-ALI then turns around looking back to notice all of a sudden, MN80M THE AMAZING ONE/MALE has already gone, vanished, as if turned right into the next road, or already into his MN80-M vehicle and gone, leaving him standing all alone on the bright light street. MN80M-ALI smiles before he says,

"God be with you brother. God be with you. Where-ever you may choose to be, thank you for sharing with me. God be with you. God be with us all God willing." he said as he smiles and continues standing.

CHAPTER THREE

Confusions & distractions . . .
Britannia . . .
{14 or 15 MONTHS AGO . . . . }

A Dedicated Poem
INSIDE OF LOCATION; MN-80 M. APARTMENT,
LONDON, ENGLAND:
DAY??: TIME:??

MN80M. THE AMAZING ONE/MALE is sitting down
on the bed mattress while he types on the PC keyboard.
The bedroom has Victorian High Ceilings, and wooden
floors anyone would adore. The Victorian pulley-system
window is still intact and the view from the bedroom is the
garden area at the back of the house leading onto the garages
and the three or four bungalows that are also rented out
by the same freeholder remain hidden at the back of the
house behind several oak trees. The un-kept garden seems to
have over-grown, and the atmosphere is silent apart from the
gentle wind outside the window. MN80M. continues to type
as he thinks of what to say.

"OK M . . . What to say?? What to say? A Poem . . ." MN80-M said in English as he starts to type on the keyboard.

A Dedication Poem—
"California knows how to party."
January 9th 2011

—Some say, 'Merit can be bought. Passion Can't.'
—So I ask, what type of passion does one need to pass.

—In California I truly learned how to dance.
—First on my feet, and then in my heart.
—Learned ISLAM truly from the start.

—Like being in Tokyo, away from mum.
—All alone, you realize the sum.
—Sum of true love, and that there is only Allah.

—How is it that my passion has grown for her.

—She yes a she, knows who she is.
—Blocking out love, as if it a sin.

—Wondering to herself, "Where will I begin"

—Take a step back and may be your own fresh start.
—Like me in California, learning how to dance.

—I allowed myself to love and be loved again.
—Even if in the end I was stabbed in the heart.

—Said to myself, Allah is greater.

—May be another day, the ocean will not break my heart.
    —May be another day, someone for me to say,
        "I love her"

MN80M-THE AMAZING ONE/MALE stops typing on the keyboard and has a smile on face.

CHAPTER FOUR

102b: Confusions & distractions . . . Britannia . . .
{14 or 15 MONTHS AGO . . . . }

INSIDE OF LOCATION; MN80M APARTMENT,
LONDON, ENGLAND;
DAY?: January 2011—TIME: 11:08 AM (GMT)
{Months later}

MN80M-THE AMAZING ONE/MALE, also known as MN80M and/or MN80-M is sitting down calmly, back straight while sitting on the bed typing away with his fingers on the keyboard a new poem. MN80M. smiles. "How many subscriptions on-line do you have for your poems M . . . ?? and how many of them are Egyptian?? OK, M. type away, you just heard from your friend in Alexandria that what happened and tension is boiling. I think it is about time since considering those on line groups are not going in the right direction, that a new group and/or new poem is created to allow people to know their true Humanitarian rights . . . What is the Universal Declaration of Human rights again!? All this tension from things in life like religious beliefs and ancient conflicts between Muslims onto Christians, and even the Jewish community, and Buddhism and all those atheists and more, and vice-versa in a circle eating away at the true essence of Humanity, Life. All this negative vibrations need to stop. Every one negative must stop. Stop being negative now. And learn while we evolve together as one Insha Allah." he said in English with a smile on his face.

MN80M THE AMAZING ONE/MALE starts to type on the key board as the tapping sounds is all that can be heard in the entire apartment, well, that and the clicking sounds from the heating pipes under the floors from the Victorian house. MN80M THE AMAZING ONE/MALE smiles as he says in mind while typing and reading,

"Poem Number 14 "the Universal Declaration of Human Rights" so far, on similar posts I read 111140 Impressions · 108.43% Feedback that on January 8 at 6:05pm more or less . . ." he said with his smile now enlarged.

MN80M continues to type on the pc with a big smile, takes in a deep breath and continues to type on the keyboard fast with his fingers, repeating every word thought and said while typing.

"Title: The Universal Declaration of Human Rights / Part 1"

Apart from Allah
No other I feel fright
Please do remember
I use several languages to write

The truth day and night
The Universal Declaration of Human Rights

MN80M THE AMAZING ONE/MALE stops typing before saying, in mind in English,

"May be I can start a new group for the 22nd; help people to start speaking in Egypt together on-line . . . . But then again, maybe not . . . Some people may try use the group in an evil way. Who am I to speak for nearly 100 million Egyptians? I am a nobody . . . The poem should be enough for now God Willing, to make some open their minds and allow me to express myself freely with how I personally feel, instead of creating a group speaking for others that could be considered trouble making. A poem is more peaceful than a group that could turn violent for an entire nation." he said reassuring himself.

MN80M THE AMAZING ONE/MALE then continues typing on the key board.

"Alhamdulillah, Praise to God, it's just the poem for now. I'm coming off line for a while." MN80M said as he continues to smile.

CHAPTER FIVE

103: Promises . . . Universal . . . .
10 Months Ago . . . .

INSIDE OF LOCATION; MN80M APARTMENT,
LONDON, ENGLAND;
DAY 1: 25th January 2011—8:08 AM
(GMT) London, England
—*17 days later from that poem. "The Universal
Declaration of Human Rights / Part 1"*

MN80M-THE AMAZING ONE/MALE comes out of the shower naked and walks into his bedroom and switches on his Television while he changes into his clothing. A tattoo of what could look like an Eagle or a Dragon, with numbers near the claws like a bar-code is noticeable on his right arm as he turns around drying himself, yet too many details within the patterns deter any one that looks at the tattoo from afar to truly understand what it is exactly across his inner-right arm area between his elbow and hand. He continues to hold the towel around his waist and dry off the remaining parts of his wet body. The television sounds continue in the background,

MN80M-THE AMAZING ONE/MALE looks on as he takes in deep breaths, praying in his head saying, "God, please make today a good day for me Insha Allah." he said as he continues drying himself.

The TV sounds of the News continues and you can hear the loud hyper tone of the TV NEWS BROADCASTER speaking, "Current unrest in Tunisia has seen a rise in the regions tension towards dictators that have been ruling with an iron fist for several decades. After the uprising of Tunisia and the president fleeing from the country, it seems that Egypt too have now begun." she said.

MN80M. looks up towards the TV surprisingly, listening as the TV NEWS BROADCASTER continues speaking. "Today in Egypt, protests in Liberation Square known as Tahrir Square, has begun. Thousands of protesters have taken to the streets to demonstrate. We aim to bring you an update within the coming hour." she said.

MN80M presses a button on the remote control and switches off the TV. Now dressed fully in his urban attire, MN80M-THE AMAZING ONE/MALE walks over to the five drawer dark wooden dressing table and opens a drawer to then take out a black praying mat with golden stitching noticeable all over. MN80M lays the mat on the floor in the direction towards the Holy City of Mecca in the Kingdom of Saudi Arabia, and places his praying cap on his head, then starts to commence a call to prayer before starting to pray. MN80M-THE AMAZING ONE/MALE starts a call to prayer In Arabic,

"Allahu Akbar (x4)
Ash-hadu Al-la ilaha illa llah (x2)
Ash-hadu anna Muhammadan rasulullah (x2)
Hayya 'ala-salahh (x2) Hayya 'ala 'l-falah (x2)

As-salatu khayru min an-nawm (x2) Allahu akbar (x2)
La ilaha illallah (x1)"

MN-80 M. continues with the prayer alone. "Allahu Akbar."
he said as he raises his hands up behind his ears and then joins
together on his chest area.

[MEANWHILE AT THE SAME TIME
IN A DIFFERENT LOCATION]

EXTERIOR OF LOCATION: TAHRIR SQUARE,
CAIRO, EGYPT—
DAY 1: 25th January 2011—10:10 AM (EET)
{17 days afterward from that poem. "The Universal
Declaration of Human Rights / Part 1"}

The demonstrations have begun within Liberation Square
with a feisty passion. The sky is filled with helicopters as the
clear blue color and white clouds seem non—existent next
to the level of voices being heard by Hundreds of thousands of
very brave Egyptians, both male and female. Hundreds and
possibly a couple of thousand individuals in one section are
chanting out loud the same anti-government slogans n-sync.
CROWD CHANTING,
"The Army, and the people, are one hand. The Army, and
the people, are one hand. The Army, and the people, are
one hand."

[MEANWHILE IN A DIFFERENT LOCATION]

INSIDE OF LOCATION: MN80M's APARTMENT
LONDON, ENGLAND; DAY 1: 25th January 2011—
8:18 AM (GMT) London, England

MN80M-THE AMAZING ONE/MALE continues with the prayer, and then once he finishes, stands up, places the praying-mat back into the set of drawers, and walks over towards the area where the shoes and jackets are located. Once ready, MN80M-THE AMAZING ONE/MALE walks into the hallway, sets the apartment alarm, and walks the five steps towards and out of the front door just before the alarm sounds.

[MEANWHILE IN A DIFFERENT LOCATION]

EXTERIOR OF LOCATION: TAHRIR SQUARE, CAIRO, EGYPT—
DAY 1: 25th January 2011—10:20 AM (EET)

The demonstrations continue within the Liberation Square. Hundreds and possibly a couple of thousand individuals continue chanting out loud anti-government slogans. MN80M-THE SPECIAL ONE/*FEMALE* is noticeable among the crowd on her own, silent, with an EG bandanna wrapped around her face. The CROWD CHANTING continues peacefully.

[MEANWHILE IN A DIFFERENT LOCATION]

EXTERIOR OF LOCATION; UK SHOP/
SUPERMARKET 1, LONDON, ENGLAND; DAY 1:
8:34 AM (GMT) London, England

MN80M-THE AMAZING ONE/MALE walks up to a cash machine at the front of the local super—market to check his account balance before he walks in to purchase some food. As he approaches slowly as if the sky has already bloomed, MN80M-THE AMAZING ONE/MALE says to himself in his mind in English, "Please God, I now know why yesterday I had the feeling within my gut to just get on a plane and go to Egypt today. Now I understand. But I do not think I am prepared for this again right now." He said quickly.

MN80M-THE AMAZING ONE/MALE then steps up closer towards the cash machine inside the wall, places in his cash card and presses the security code while saying with a smile,

"Please God, please." he said as he now has a serious look at the screen that shows the amount available.

Annoyed and looking slightly frustrated,

"Seventy pounds. What! Oh yea, the food shopping and sweets last night, and a packet of cigarettes cost like seven pounds into the early hours of the morning. But it was £111 pounds I got paid from the thing this week. Anyway, let me take some more out in case." he said half mumbling the last few words.

MN80M-THE AMAZING ONE/MALE pushes a button and awaits his cash to be dispensed, it does so with him placing straight into his pocket and then walks into the supermarket.

[MEANWHILE IN A DIFFERENT LOCATION]

EXTERIOR OF LOCATION; TAHRIR SQUARE, CAIRO, EGYPT—
DAY 1: TIME: 10:37 AM (EET) Cairo, Egypt

The demonstrators continue to chant in Liberation Square, with the atmosphere growing immensely as the already built tension turns quickly into anger. Many of the hundreds of thousands of protesters remaining within Liberation square are all now heated up as if the kettle has already boiled over and spilt on the stove. CROWD CHANTING continues as the weather conditions seem different than the normal January heat.

[MEANWHILE IN A DIFFERENT LOCATION]

INSIDE OF LOCATION; UK SHOP/SUPERMARKET LONDON, ENGLAND—
DAY 1: TIME: 8:54 AM (GMT) London, England

MN80M-THE AMAZING ONE/MALE walks north along the isles past several other shoppers on route towards the check out as he continues pushing his shopping trolley containing a few items. MN80M is trying to recall his shopping list in mind.
"Anything else M. anything else . . . Let me think . . . OK, got the milk, bread, sugar, soft drinks, coffee, tea, cakes." he said to himself.
MN80M smiles and continues to walk pushing his trolley as he points towards his list confirming everything written to those now in the trolley. As he nears the check out, he notices some honey, and walks over to pick up a jar.

[MEANWHILE AT THE SAME TIME
IN A DIFFERENT LOCATION]

INSIDE OF LOCATION; MN80M SISTER F APARTMENT / HELIOPOLIS,
CAIRO, EGYPT:
DAY 1: 25th January 2011—TIIME: 10:55 AM (EET)
Cairo, Egypt

Holding in her right hand a jar of MN80M-SPECIAL-MUMS-JAM, and in her left hand the exact same jar of Honey, MN80M SISTER F (35 Years old) stares at the jar for a moment while standing in the kitchen. She then walks a few steps over towards the refrigerator as she holds the jars firmly in hand.

[MEANWHILE AT THE SAME TIME
IN A DIFFERENT LOCATION]

INSIDE LOCATION: UK SHOP/SUPERMARKET
LONDON, ENGLAND;
DAY 1: TIME: 8:55 AM (GMT) London, England

MN80M-THE AMAZING ONE/MALE is standing in front of the jars of honey that remain placed neatly together on the shelf in-front of him, still looking at the exact same jar as MN80M SISTER F is looking at, yet in different country. MN80M holds the jar of honey in his right hand for a brief moment, and then places it into the trolley and continues on towards the checkout.

"I like this honey. My sisters both do too. Especially MN80M SISTER F, she loves this honey." he said as if in an emotional remembrance mode of past times.

MN80M. THE AMAZING ONE/MALE then smiles and moves on forward pushing the trolley until he reaches the young lady working at the checkout. The sounds of the UK SUPERMARKET is the normal morning sounds of those early birds, especially mothers wanting to get the freshest fruit and vegetables as soon as they are placed out, and also the freshly baked morning bread. MN80M now at the check-out section speaks out to the young lady In Turkish,

"Good morning, how are you?" he said with a smile to the female as he places his items on the counter for her to then push through the scanner, as he briefly watches before moving along to open a plastic bag to place inside his shop—ping items. GIRL ON COUNTER smiles and says back in Turkish,

"Good morning. I am good thanking you." she said as if not been asked already that day.

MN80M THE AMAZING ONE/MALE smiles with an easy response in his gentle tone of,

"Good is good." he said in a suave way while maintaining his smile and eye contact with her.

The female on the counter smiles back as she continues to scan through the items slowly until the end. MN80M-starts to organize and pack his items into the white plastic bags while trying to keep eye contact with the GIRL ON COUNTER,

"That would be twenty seven pounds and forty eight pence please." she said in English.

MN80M pulls out his wallet and takes out £30 GBP and hands over to the female. She then hands him back his change, MN80M does not even look at the amount as he places this straight into his pockets with full trust that the girl on the counter is honest.

"Thank you!" he said In Turkish.

"You are welcome. Thanks for coming and please do come again to visit us." responds the GIRL ON COUNTER as she smiles at MN80M-THE AMAZING ONE/MALE as he instantly repeats twice,

"God willing I shall. God willing I shall."

MN80-M picks up his shopping bags containing all of his items with both hands, and starts to walk towards the exit of the supermarket.

[MEANWHILE IN A DIFFERENT LOCATION]

INSIDE OF LOCATION: MN80M-SISTER F APARTMENT
DAY 1: 11:15 AM (EET) Heliopolis, Cairo, Egypt

Dressed in her grey suit, MN80M SISTER F is about to leave out of her apartment, her dog is jumping around in excitement as she know she is about to leave to go to work and can hear the mobile phone ringing constantly so the dog is barking as MN80M SISTER F shouts out in English, "OK, OK, Calm down, be good. I will be back soon OK. I just have to go to work quickly. Love you!" she said as she quickly goes to open the door and simultaneously answer the ringing phone. She presses a button before placing the phone to her ear saying in Arabic,
"Hello there MN80M SISTER F 1 FRIEND, how are you? I am just about to leave from the door now to go over to the ministry, and then will pass through to you at AN EG MINISTRY 2 office. Can I call you in a minute, the taxi is outside?" A quick silent pause as the dog has gone silent all of a sudden.
"Thank you. Talk to you soon." MN80M SISTER F said as she places the phone into her handbag, picks up the bunch of keys from the side table, opens the door and departs.

[MEANWHILE IN A DIFFERENT LOCATION]

INSIDE OF LOCATION: MN80M-THE AMAZING ONE/MALE APARTMENT
DAY 1: 9:32 AM (GMT)
London, England

MN80M is standing in the kitchen taking out the shop—ping from the plastic bags and placing them into the fridge, freezer and cupboards before he then fills up the kettle quickly with the water from the pouring tap and presses the button on the kettle to boil the water. He opens another bag and takes out the MN80M-SPECIAL OLIVE OIL, and smiles.

[MEANWHILE AT THE SAME TIME
IN A DIFFERENT LOCATION]

EXTERIOR OF LOCATION; TAHRIR SQUARE,
CAIRO, EGYPT—
DAY 1: 11:32 AM (EET) Cairo, Egypt

The demonstrators continue to chant in Liberation Square. Millions of people have now gathered together among thou-sands of army soldiers that are trying best to keep peace with each individual as the heat of the Egyptian sun intensifies more than the already heated crowd.
"Down with the Regime. Down with the Regime."
The CROWD CHANTING is heard continue as the atmo-sphere is more alive than it previously had been moments ago. This now being as if a sudden breeze of air made every-one switch into an aggressive mode with a few rocks and shoes being thrown in the direction of the EG Army Tanks that are among a couple hundred armed riot police standing on the side waiting as if about to charge onto the demonstrators.

[MEANWHILE IN A DIFFERENT LOCATION]

INSIDE OF LOCATION: MN80M-THE AMAZING
ONE/MALE APARTMENT
DAY 1: 9:53 AM (GMT)
London, England

MN80M is in the living room area sitting down on the black leather sofas with a cup of tea in his hand while looking out towards the floor to ceiling Victorian Windows onto the street outside. He picks up the remote control and presses a button to switch on the television, and then takes out from his leather pouch tobacco and rolling papers and starts to roll a cigarette while listening to the TV sounds, changing channels until reaching the news to then catch the end of a live broadcast. The TV NEWS BROADCASTER is speaking in English as the visuals on the television are showing live coverage.

"The current unrest in Egypt has started to escalate. Demonstrators have taken to the streets in protest to the present day regime that has been in power for nearly three decades." The TV NEWS BROADCASTER said as if needing to shout. The TV NEWS REPORTER continues as if attempting to assure the viewers watching and listening of what she speaks of is entirely true, as an angle of hundreds of thousands of Egyptian young men and women continues to play on the television screen in the background in support of her reports. MN80M continues to roll a cigarette while sipping his tea and munching on some MN80M-SPECIAL COLA BOTTLES, and listening to the news reports. The TV NEWS BROADCASTER Continues,

"MN-80—THE EG PRESIDENT 1 is now under pressure as the Egyptian people have already started to come to the streets in protest of the regime. We wait to hear from our correspondent in Cairo in a few moments with an update." The

TV NEWS BROADCASTER said as if needing to quickly hurry off of live air communication.

MN80M presses some buttons on the remote control and puts the volume on the television down, and then lights his cigarette while looking out the window asking politely, "God, please make things peaceful." he said as he makes a sigh while he continues smoking and watching the television news broadcast.

[MEANWHILE IN A DIFFERENT LOCATION]

INSIDE OF LOCATION; MN-80—THE EG PRESIDENT 1 PALACE, SHARM EL SHEIKH, EGYPT; DAY 1: TIME: 11:55 AM (EET) 25th January 2011

MN-80—THE EG PRESIDENT 1 (In the 80's age range) in healthy condition, dressed in a dapper brand new tailored MN80-M-1950's-CLASSY-SUIT, is safely guarded in the Grand Library, sitting down on a golden leather chair, looking out through one of the palatial windows overlooking a superbly kept garden, with many workers keeping busy trimming and pruning plants. A man dressed in a black suit takes one step into the room and speaks silently in a low tone asking In Arabic, "Excuse me Sir . . . Mr. MN-80—THE EG PRESIDENT 1. Sir, May I have your permission to enter, and speak?" THE MAN IN SUIT said.

MN-80—THE EG PRESIDENT 1, with his back towards the man in the suit is still looking out of the window as he raises his right hand and signals for the man to come for— ward. The man in the suit approaches MN-80—THE EG PRESIDENT 1 slowly, and comes to a halt a few feet away

from him. MN-80—THE EG PRESIDENT 1 speaks out
In Arabic,
"Peace and blessings onto you my son. Come closer. Speak to
me." said the President.
The man in the suit takes a couple of short steps towards
MN-80—THE EG PRESIDENT 1 and whispers just
above his shoulder and into his ear.
"Sir . . . MN-80—THE EG PRESIDENT 1, It has begun."
THE MAN IN SUIT said nervously, awaiting the President
response as a silent pause in the room is daunting as the man
in the suit looks around nervously and takes one step back
holding his breath while he continues to await a response.

[MEANWHILE AT THE SAME TIME
IN A DIFFERENT LOCATION]

INSIDE OF LOCATION; MN80M-THE AMAZING
ONE/MALE's APARTMENT,
LONDON, ENGLAND; DAY 1: 9:58 AM (GMT)
London, England

MN80M-THE AMAZING ONE/MALE is in the living
room area sitting down smoking while looking out of his windows onto the trees on the street. MN80M picks up his tea
and drinks slowly as he contemplates what he has just heard
on the news broadcast., thinking out loud in his mind saying
in English,
"Look at how peaceful the leaves can be together on that
tree. Always the same . . . Throughout history, always the
same." he said as he continues to smoke and drink some of
his tea as he turns his head slowly and watches scenes on the
television of the Hundreds of Thousands of young Egyptian

demonstrators in Egypt marching and chanting together as one.

MN80M THE AMAZING ONE/MALE continues,

"You know what!!??!! It's not my fight any more." He said while the TV NEWS BROADCASTER suddenly starts to be heard from the Television speaking.

"Skirmishes have broken out in some parts of Egypt. In the city of Cairo, Liberation Square, also known as the Landmark Tahrir Square, clashes between protesters and the police have commenced. Riots have more or less begun, and other cities like Alexandria, Taba, Qena near Luxor and even Suez, Tanta and Mansoura have all started to hear the news with some protesters there already beginning to clash with police." The TV NEWS BROADCASTER said.

MN80M shakes his head side to side in disbelief in what he is watching on the television.

"It's not my fight. It's not my fight any more." he said to himself as if in disbelief.

[MEANWHILE AT THE SAME TIME
IN A DIFFERENT LOCATION

INSIDE OF LOCATION; MN-80—THE EG
PRESIDENT 1 PALACE, SHARM EL SHEIKH, EGYPT;
DAY 1: 11:59 AM (EET) Sharm El Sheikh, Egypt

MN-80—THE EG PRESIDENT 1 continues to look out through the window as he sits in his chair listening to what the MAN IN SUIT (40/50's) has come to say to him in private. The man in the suit awaits a response from MN-80—THE EG PRESIDENT 1 impatiently and nervously, asking,

"Sir. Would you like me to make the call to the special one. I mean specials ones?" The man in the suit said as he awaits a response, hearing MN-80—THE EG PRESIDENT 1 say, "No. Not now . . . As you mentioned, it has only begun." said the President.

A silent pause in the fully air conditioned palace as MN-80—THE EG PRESIDENT 1 continues with, "Leave me alone now."

The MAN IN SUIT nervously yet boldly responds,

"Sir yes sir. Would there be anything else I can be of services with?" said the man in the suit.

MN-80—THE EG PRESIDENT 1 looks towards the window leading out to the open area palatial garden, takes in a slow but deep breath, and says,

"I request my Military council. The entire team, and every head of each city in Egypt here within the coming 2 hours, each and everyone." said the President out boldly.

"Sir yes sir." said the man in suit instantly.

"Also, make sure the Prime Minister and all the ministers are here within the next 6 hours. But summons me Egypt's' military council first." added the President.

The MAN IN SUIT once again instantly responds with,

"Sir yes sir, Immediate. Thank you for your time my MN-80—THE EG PRESIDENT 1." he said in Arabic as he then steps back slowly, and continues walking until he exits the main door of the special room.

The MN-80—EG PRESIDENT 1, with his back still to the door, continues to look out peacefully onto the gardens outside. Several birds are noticeable flying high and low from the light blue sky, as many of the Japanese garden professionals are working pruning a few very well kept dark and light green old Japanese Banzai trees situated on the right hand side of the palace garden area in a semi-secluded area from the other dark green massive fruit trees that also have Egyptian workers coming and going like moths to a light bulb.

"All praise is due to Allah (God) Blessings be upon thee. Look at how peaceful the leaves can be." MN-80—THE EG PRESIDENT 1 said to himself.

[MEANWHILE IN A DIFFERENT LOCATION]

EXTERIOR OF LOCATION: TAHRIR SQUARE
DAY 1: 25th January 2011—TIME: 12:07 PM (EET)
Cairo, Egypt

The demonstrations continue and some individuals can be seen to commence clashes with the Egyptian police force that are out on the streets separate to the army. Hundreds of thousands of people are running in several directions as the sounds of weapons being fired and gas tanks are heard exploding from a far. The CROWD CHANTING In Arabic continues as the armed riot police move in towards the demonstrators.

[MEANWHILE AT THE SAME TIME
IN A DIFFERENT LOCATION]

INSIDE OF LOCATION; MN80M-THE AMAZING
ONE/MALE's APARTMENT,
LONDON, ENGLAND; DAY 1: TIME: 10:08 AM
(GMT) London, England

MN80M-THE AMAZING ONE/MALE is in the living room area sitting down on the black leather sofa's smoking while looking out of his windows onto the trees on the street. Cars continue to pass from left and right as he focuses on the tree and the silence apart from a swooshing sound each time a car/vehicle goes past each direction. "Look at how peaceful the leaves can be on that tree." MN80M. said to himself in English as he smiles.

MN80Mcontinues to look towards the tree outside his apartment on the street as the cars come and go from left and right. MN80M. THE AMAZING ONE/MALE slowly says to himself,

"God; You know what!!??!! Forgive me for saying, but. I am not even going to bother. They don't really love me anymore, so why show love back more than I already have for all these years, especially after what they took from me. It's not my fight any more. It's not my fight." he said.

[MEANWHILE AT THE SAME TIME
IN A DIFFERENT LOCATION]

INSIDE OF LOCATION; AN EG MINISTRY 1 HEAD
OFFICE, CAIRO, EGYPT;
DAY 1: 25th January 2011—TIME: 12:12 (EET)
Cairo, Egypt—Day 1

A group of (47) high ranking specialists/individuals are conversing around a table with the present day MN-80 EG MINISTER OF SUPER INCOME the MINISTER OF AN EG MINISTRY 1 about the current happenings in Egypt, North Africa and Middle East region. MN80M SISTER F is sitting among the individuals listening attentively as the MINISTER OF AN EG MINISTRY 1 speaks out boldly In English with a stern look on his face,

"Dear team. Thank you all for attending this very important meeting today. As you all know, the recent Tunisia incidents with their president fleeing the country after protests broke out, has some-how managed to stir a lot of feelings amongst many in the region and beyond to possibly act the same. We do not know of the outcome as of yet, but what we do know is that today in Egypt, demonstrations have started to take place." said the Minister in a manly tone of voice. Everybody in the room by now is practically focused across the table as each individual continues to listen as the MIN—ISTER OF AN EG MINISTRY 1 continues his speech in Arabic,

"I suggest we must now focus on our emergency plan for Egypt."

Some eye-brows have now raised as more than thirty of the specialists look at one another in silence, yet mouths looking as if each wants to mumble out something, but his holding back his or her tongue. The MINISTER OF AN EG MINISTRY 1 continues in English,

"I have just got off the phone personally with the MIN—ISTER OF EG INTERIOR that assures me policing and national security of Egypt, all Egyptians as well as our guest tourists is paramount and under good management. Emergency procedures are already in place, and I await updates shortly. I expect updated reports every 30 minutes on my desk from all heads of each department sitting on this table right now. Any and all other consultants here now, feel free to continue as you have done, and also be available to assist with any other emergencies that may arise later today and/or in the future. Thank you all once again for coming on such short notice to this meeting, and I expect the highest and most strictest confidentiality with what has now been mentioned, as well as any and all our operations from this moment onwards, especially to family members or friends. Anyone found to have mentioned anything shall receive an immediate notice for him or her to resign. National security is at risk here, and the politics involved is much higher than I or anyone else here sitting on this table. Please remain wise, and converse among yourselves while alone only. Is this fully understood by each individual on this table?"

The Minister says with a calm face as he looks at the same across the table on practically each individual face, all in agreement nodding heads up and down. The room is silent as both of the Ministers stand up from seated position, MINISTER OF AN EG MINISTRY 1 closes the button on his Grey 60's style suit jacket, smiles, and then walks towards the door, opens it himself, allowing the MINISTER OF SUPER INCOME to exit first and holds out his arm in respect for him to lead, and just as he does, then he exits with his secret service team following behind. MN80M-SISTER F, seated in her seat, face is still in motion, yet her eyes are looking at all the other specialists around the table. She then takes in a silent semi-deep breath as she assesses the situation herself.

[MEANWHILE IN A DIFFERENT LOCATION]

INSIDE OF LOCATION; MN80M-THE AMAZING ONE/MALE's APARTMENT, LONDON, ENGLAND; DAY 1: 10:20 AM (GMT) London, England

MN80M-THE AMAZING ONE/MALE has finished washing for a prayer and walks out of the toilet/ wash room area, into the hallway and into the bedroom to then lay the praying mat on the floor in the bedroom and commence prayers.

[MEANWHILE IN A DIFFERENT LOCATION]

INSIDE OF LCOATION: AN EG MINISTRY 1 HEAD OFFICE

DAY 1: 12:22 PM (EET) Cairo, Egypt—Day 1

MN80M SISTER F sits calm in her chair as others around her start to converse while some stand and depart from the room to attend his or her usual daily duty. The room is filled with quick small chitter-chatter now that both ministers have departed. There is a sense of fear and uncertainty of the outcome of the unknown events. MN80M-SISTER F, and others next to her start completing some notes that they were writing down while the Minister was speaking.

[MEANWHILE IN A DIFFERENT LOCATION]

INSIDE OF LOCATION; MN80M-THE AMAZING ONE/MALE's APARTMENT, LONDON, ENGLAND; DAY 1: 10:27 AM (GMT) London, England

MN80M has completed his prayer, and remains on his knees to express some more words to add after his prayers. MN80M holds his hands together next to his face as he speaks out in a low tone softly In English,

"God, I thank you for my blessings of life, for my mother and my father's life, my sister's lives, and the entire family's life, for each and every life. Allah, please forgive me when I say what I am about to If what I say is of a wrong nature." A long silent pause as MN80M-THE AMAZING ONE /MALE then continues with prayers,

"Yet I feel deep inside that I must focus on me only now, as no one cared for me for the past 9 months really since I left Egypt and came home to London. Or all of those years I dedicated with establishing Equilibrium, then all the other major incidents and situations I have had to live through while living out there, in this day and age. It's too much walahy. Too much, I should have just stayed in my Culver City apartment in Los Angeles with my black cat called Patrickless when I had the chance after that divorce. Even my opportunity to re-locate to Boston or New York would have been fantastic. Would probably been a millionaire by now. But Noooooo! I decide to help and save the World. Look at what I have lost until now ya Allah. Forgive me, and I say Alhamdulillah yes praise to God for all, good and bad, as this all only a test, always a test. As everything is written by your gracious hands, and all that you will to be, shall be. I am only a servant to thee. Forgive me . . . Have mercy on me my lord."

A tear falls from MN80M's eye as the News broadcast can be heard come on a low tone in the background all of a sudden as if the channel on the television was silent for a few moments prior. MN80M-THE AMAZING ONE /MALE smiles, takes in two deep breaths and says, "Hollywood life was much better than London life in many ways, and sure was better than many of those moments I lived in Egypt after that too. No offence, I love Egypt with all my heart and more as you know. But look what happened to me. And why, I am not sure God why? And I have apologized to you a thousand times, and yet still do not know why they did that to me. And why you continue to punish me as if taking away my empathy blessings. This is not my fight. And to even continue to try as much as I have done, especially all that has happened since I have returned and they chose to do that behind my back last August, would be folly in my mind to fight with a certain type mind and ancient way of life, even if that be my own. Please God do not take what I express here as negative apart from the truth you already know, and I speak freely, as I know your creations listen and pass on the messages like Angels and those possibly ahead in time. My heart and gut feelings from yesterday and before any broadcast news on radio and television came to my attention was telling me to go home to Egypt. Yet you alone know Allah (God) why I choose to not go. Forgive me if I am wrong for choosing so. And I know something inside of me regardless of anyone or any creations to say or inspire me to do so, I naturally alone; will go . . . I know this. But I do not want to . . . So please God, if you will for me to go then please facilitate this for me. If not, then this is your will, as that is best for me to serve you, and for my religion Islam, my beginning, and my end. Thank you for listening to my heart and words. Thank you for life."

A silent pause as MN80M slowly manages to get up from his knees and picks up the mat to fold it and place it back inside the drawer.

[MEANWHILE AT THE SAME TIME
IN A DIFFERENT LOCATION]

LOCATION; TAHRIR SQUARE
DAY 1: 25th January 2011—12:32 PM (EET)
Cairo, Egypt

The demonstrations continue and thousands of individuals commence clashes with the Egyptian police force that is now heavily armed with weapons along with riot protective gear and some holding semi-automatic gas tank shot guns. The CROWD CHANTING loud in Arabic, "(???????Must fill it in????????????) Continues as several groups chanting different things n-sync can be heard.

[MEANWHILE IN A DIFFERENT LOCATION]

LOCATION: MN80M's APARTMENT
LONDON, ENGLAND; DAY 1: 10:37 AM (GMT)
London, England

MN80M-THE AMAZING ONE/MALE is in the living room sitting down smoking looking calmly towards the television screen as the news broadcast continues in the background. The TV NEWS BROADCASTER speaking live from Cairo,

"Skirmishes have begun all over Egypt in several cities. Reports coming in show that the city of Cairo is showing the most outrage at this moment in time. Suez protests remain the same, and slightly more peaceful looking than other locations in Egypt as what now looks like an uprising in this Egyptian revolution. We hope to have an update for you all soon, back to you in the studios." said the TV NEWS BROADCASTER in English.

MN80M-THE AMAZING ONE/MALE starts to roll another cigarette, and looks up at the TV every few seconds eagerly awaiting as the TV NEWS BROAD—CASTER continues,

"Thank you. We await that update in the coming hours and days."

MN80M-THE AMAZING ONE/MALE picks up the remote control and presses a button to change the channel to a music channel. The television sounds as each channel flicks through onto the next, MN80M says to himself in mind,

"Yeah right . . . Skirmishes. The whole country is a boiling pot that has been brewing for decades . . . What he should have said is that Nelson Mandela quote, how does it go again?? "When the water starts boiling it is foolish to turn off the heat." (semi-laugh under his breath) I swear to God. I think if this is truly what everyone wants, then the people just need to all get out there and be peaceful. Brave Egyptians, I wish I was with you all right now. God is with you all."

MN80M uses his lighter to light his cigarette, then picks up a mug on the wooden coffee table in front of him, stands up and walks towards the door saying.

"I think I need a cup of tea."

[MEANWHILE AT THE SAME TIME
IN A DIFFERENT LOCATION]

INSIDE LOCATION: AN EG MINISTRY 1
CONSULTANT OFFICE; DAY 1:
12:45 PM (EET) Cairo, Egypt

MN80M SISTER F is involved in a conversation with seventeen other consultants about the present day situation. MN80M SISTER F, as well as others sitting next to her are listening attentively as a MALE (40's) AN EG MINISTRY 1 CONSULTANT 1 speaks out In Arabic,

"War has begun . . . This is a revolution of the people. First Tunisia think they better than us, so we will show them what the Egyptians can do."

The man said with a smirk on his face before taking it off as he looks at what the response from the FEMALE (50's) SENIOR EG MINISTRY 1 CONSULTANT 1 saying back to him,

"My son, forget about a revolution and focus on how to manage our country for now."

She said in Arabic as she lifts her chin up slightly. The Male in his forty's' laughs as if the response he heard was a surprisingly sarcastic one as the MALE (40's) AN EG MINISTRY 1 CONSULTANT 1 responds with,

"How can we focus on work when all of this is happening?" He then moves one step closer as if to continue the conversation irrelevantly just to waste time.

"Please do not be childish?" responds the FEMALE (50's) SENIOR EG MINISTRY 1 CONSULTANT in English and then raising her hand as she points to the door and says in Arabic,

"Go outside now and get some fresh air to start thinking straight. You obviously love Egypt so much you want to be outside with everyone, so go, go out." she said with her serious face now looking even more serious.

The Male (40's) stops laughing and now looks ashamed as he departs from the room slowly dragging his leg and lower lip as the FEMALE (50's) Continues in speaking in English to all others listening curiously,

"Is there anyone else that has an issue with focusing on our jobs at hand?" she asked out loud with her chest held slightly out and her chin up high while looking into the eyes of everyone in the room.

The room is silent as the look on all of the consultant's faces including MN80M-SISTER F remains silent. The FEMALE (50's) SENIOR EG MINISTRY 1 CON—SULTANT continues again In English,

"OK. Where shall we begin!?! First of all, from this moment onwards, this is our team. The seventeen of us, well, sixteen for the moment until he comes back from getting some fresh air, Us seventeen have been assigned a task from within the EG Emergency plan the kind Minister had mentioned to us all in the meeting. The remaining thirty others have been split into similar teams. Three teams, one Mission. Save Egypt."

The air-conditioned room remains silent, all are now fully focused listening with a serious look on his and her faces to what the FEMALE (50's) SENIOR EG MINISTRY 1 CONSULTANT continues to say,

"The vacuum affect this is already having, as well as about to have on our national security, not just for Egypt, but for Africa in general, is frightening. We need to acquire our own intelligence from any way we can to super-seed our knowledge without having to rely only on hourly updates from all ministries. We too want to gather intelligence from this second onwards. Any one has any friends and family abroad, as well as here in Egypt taking part or acknowledging what is happening, then we require you all to know what is happening too. We shall place all reports on our reports board to compare with the other ministries ministries information. Once we feel we have solid leads, we shall focus on positive methods for all within Egypt as well as those departing Egypt in an emergency, and those arriving from abroad into Egypt in the possible coming days."

The FEMALE (50's) SENIOR EG MINISTRY 1 CON—SULTANT takes a pause to drink a glass of water placed on the table in front of her. Just as she does so, the MALE (40's) AN EG MINISTRY 1 CONSULTANT 1 enters the room. The FEMALE (50's) SENIOR EG MINISTRY 1 CONSULTANT stops drinking from her glass of water and continues In Arabic towards MALE 40's that has just walked into the room,

"Thank you for remembering us all."

Many of the consultants in the room laugh together as the MALE (40's) EG MINISTRY 1 CONSULTANT 1 says shyly.

"Forgive my absence and youthful ways."

The man quickly takes his seat among the other consultants waiting patiently. The FEMALE (50's) SENIOR EG MINISTRY 1 CONSULTANT takes another sip from the glass of water and continues In Arabic,

"Failure is not an option for us Egyptians. Everyone in this room is an Egyptian. We love Egypt. Some have been here for one year and some of us for five to ten years and some of us even for nearly twenty years, with some thirty and more. We must maintain our strength within this office for the best results for Egypt and the Egyptian people God willing. I have faith in each and every one of us to do our best. Thank you for all coming in today. Are there any questions?" she said.

Everyone in the room looks shocked as some start to also drink from the glasses of water in-front of them all on the board room large desk. The FEMALE (30's) EG MINISTRY 1 CONSULTANT 1 sitting near the head of the table then asks In Arabic,

"So what happens if what happened in Tunisia happens here will we all still have our jobs?" and then takes a sip of the water from the her glass awaiting a response as the FEMALE (50's) SENIOR EG MINISTRY 1 CONSUL—TANT replies with,

"I think we should focus on the day at hand. You are working today right?"

The FEMALE (30's) EG MINISTRY 1 CONSULTANT 1 agrees nodding her head and then saying In Arabic, "Yes" and continues to shake head in agreement twice. The FEMALE (50's) SENIOR EG MINISTRY 1 CONSULTANT looks around at everyone on the table,

"Well then. Good. Let's focus on today then . . . Any more questions?" said the FEMALE SENIOR CONSULTANT. MN80M SISTER F quickly asks eagerly in English,

"When can we view reports on how many tourists have departed from Egypt already, as well as any updates? Also, what is our status with tourism police services?"

The FEMALE (50's) SENIOR CONSULTANT reply is, "Good question. OK, basically, the report you all have in front of you is our emergency plan each sector. Reports such as you just requested we aim to have for you all each hour, on the hour, once we receive confirmation the information is credible. In regards to the police matters for those tourist within, as well as coming into Egypt, I would suggest we await updates from the minister himself in regards to homeland security. Are there any more questions any one has before I head off into an important meeting?"

The table remains silent all of a sudden, until a MALE (70's) SENIOR EG MINISTRY 1 CONSULTANT speaks out in Arabic in the lowest of tones, barely able to hear, "What do we have for lunch today?"

Everyone in the room laughs out loud together. The MALE (40's) EG MINISTRY 1 CONSULTANT 2 mentions a food chain name saying.

"Would be best today",

Everyone in the room continues to laugh. The MALE (70's) SENIOR EG MINISTRY 1 CONSULTANT responds in a slightly louder tone to over-come the laughter in the room, "Laugh all you like. At the end of the day, we must all eat." They all continue to laugh and some of those near the elderly gentleman place their arms around his shoulder in a show of affection. The FEMALE (50's) SENIOR CON—SULTANT says out loud in English,

"I am glad we can all keep our sense of humor, as well as our hunger."

Everyone in the room laughs on as the FEMALE (50's) Continues now speaking in Arabic,

"Failure is not an option for us Egyptians."

The senior consultant stands slowly, and walks towards the door before stopping and turning around to say,

"Enjoy this day people. Today we make history."

She then opens the door and exits the room with her assistants following. The remaining face of everyone in the room is a surprised and shock look combined with the contagious laughter from moments ago. The MALE (60's) EG MINISTRY 1 CONSULTANT sitting next to MN-80 M. SISTER F speaks to her in English as others are in conversation already with one another,

"You know something; things were never like this in life twenty years ago. I hope everything manages to work out OK for us all. I am very tired of all of this non-sense with life and struggles. My son wants to get married to his second wife, and he cannot even afford his first wife. I don't know what this world is coming to these days."

MN80M SISTER F looks at him and smiles, "I am sure everything will work out to the best in the end." MN80M— SISTER F phone rings and she answers quickly by pressing the button yet holds the phone down next to her leg on the side of her thigh.

"Excuse me one moment OK. Let me answer this call, very important."

MN80M SISTER F stands and places the phone to her ear as if she just now answers phone,

"Hello MN80M SISTER F speaking . . . Yes,,, OK. Yes. OK. Yes. No problem, will call you back once able to. Thank you!"

MN80M SISTER F looks back at her seat and picks up her hand bag and laptop bag before departing the room,

"Please excuse me; I too have to leave the office for a while. I hope to see you at the next meeting again yeah!??!"
She says to the MALE (60's) EG MINISTRY 1 CONSUL—TANT In Arabic as he then responds with,
"God willing I shall be. I see you then."
MN80M SISTER F shakes hands with a couple more consultants before making a sharp exit.

[MEANWHILE IN A DIFFERENT LOCATION]

INSIDE OF LOCATION; MN-80—THE EG
PRESIDENT 1 PALACE,
SHARM EL SHEIKH, EGYPT;
DAY 1: TIME: 13:29 AM (EET)

MN-80—THE EG PRESIDENT 1 (80's) continues to look out through the window while sitting in his chair, the man in the suit comes back to update with news reports. The man in the suit now awaiting a response from MN-80-—THE EG PRESIDENT 1 as he stands at the door and awaits the hand signal for him to enter as he knows he can see his reflection from the super clean bullet proof floor to ceiling windows.
"Sir. MN-80—THE EG PRESIDENT 1. The Military Council has arrived here now and are all awaiting your further instructions. Nearly all of the ministers have arrived also in Sharm El Sheikh and they await at the conference halls in the secure hotel. Within the coming 90 minutes, the remainder shall arrive." The MAN IN SUIT spoke out softly in Arabic as MN80—THE EG PRESIDENT 1 continues to look out of the window, and signals with his hand for the man in the suit to leave him alone, and so he does vanish from the window reflection. MN80M THE EG

PRESIDENT 1 smiles for a second before his face returning back to normal neutral mode and him saying to himself in Arabic,
"God help us all . . . We need true specialists. We need the special one I think. And may be one more, but how? And who?"

[MEANWHILE AT THE SAME TIME
IN A DIFFERENT LOCATION]

EXTERIOR OF LOCATION; TAHRIR SQUARE,
CAIRO, EGYPT—
DAY 1: 25th January 2011—13:31 AM (EET)

The demonstrations continue as the CROWD CHANT-ING out loud echo's from location to location within Liberation Square. A group of police armed with batons and dressed in riot gear come storming around one of the side roads near the nearly placed up construction works and a few metal huts, running fast straight towards the direction of some of the activists chanting together among a separate crowd of thousands of Egyptians. Some of the crowd starts to run backwards while others stand still to defend against the on-coming thousands of police men. Some wearing ordinary clothing like many of the civilians, yet holding large wooden sticks, some sticks with many big nails at one end. The CROWD CHANTING continues as many brave young Egyptian men continue to stand firm as the police reach within a short distance from them raising batons as if to harm them. The CROWD CHANTING in a fearless tone continues as hundreds flee the scene.

[MEANWHILE AT THE SAME TIME
IN A DIFFERENT LOCATION]

INSIDE OF LOCATION; MN80M-
THE AMAZING ONE/MALE's APARTMENT,
LONDON, ENGLAND;
DAY 1: 11:32 AM (GMT)

MN80M is laying on his very large double queen size bed in contemplation mode while taking in deep breaths and speaking in mind what his heart feels and his mind combined about this present day situation. MN80M-THE AMAZING ONE/MALE smiles and then says,

"I can just sense it right now. Everything has started wrong, and if no one properly gets involved, then this will all end wrong for too many people in Egypt before the next country. Where the hell is he? I would have thought someone special got involved by now. Many can die. And Egypt will not prosper for the best. I pray that good over comes evil overall, but I do not think I can get involved."

MN80M said as he turns onto his side from laying on his back, and now has a smile on his face as he takes in another deep breath. MN80M-THE AMAZING ONE /MALE continues in English,

"I need to make a plan to help strengthen Egypt . . ." he said with a big smile on his face.

MN80M takes two deep breaths, his smile is no longer visible as he then lets out a breath saying,

"No, wait a minute! what am I talking about!?!?! Leave them to do what they want ahsan . . . This is why I am in this position now. If it was not for all the red tape I had to go through for Equilibrium to be established and recognized legally in Egypt, (with thanks to Mr. Mystery 2 and his honorable travel company "e" established and based in Cairo in Egypt and for all the assistance he and they did) then I would have thought the legal process of things just took ten times longer than what I am used to here in England. But that is not what killed me. What killed me was trying best to get married again, as well as all the hassle I went through from certain situations until I had to leave. They don't really care for me anyway. Why should I continue to show more love than I already have done?? Please God, show me why. Show me a sign. Especially how they stopped me from doing what I was supposed to, and what they did behind my back last year and before is unforgivable"

MN80M turns onto his back again and places his hands on his head, and then taking in a deep breath and letting it out slowly.

[MEANWHILE AT THE SAME TIME IN A DIFFERENT LOCATION]

EXTERIOR OF LOCATION; TAHRIR SQUARE, CAIRO, EGYPT— DAY 1: 25th January 2011—13:34 AM (EET)

Helicopters continue above in the sky as the crowd and riot police continue clashing with one another in serious battle mode. The CROWD CHANTING continues as some civilians are already wounded. A group of police armed with batons start to strike the protesters that are closest to them. Sounds of screaming can be heard as rocks have started to be thrown onto people and police in riot gear all now in a ferocious battle. The CROWD CHANTING,

"Down with the regime. Down with the Regime." continues. The face of THREE YOUNG MEN that are trying to push back the riot police is highlighted at this moment as they are being attacked by batons, pouring with blood from faces. They too also start to physically attack back at the police in a defense mode. A young man picks up a rock and throws in the direction of the riot police ahead of him and stands to watch as the rock is in-motion fast in the air, leading towards the head of a policeman in riot gear. Just as the rock reaches his face and connects hard, the blood slowly, then in a rapid pace, burst out of the police man face. The majority of men and few women start to run for his or her lives as thousands of other armed police in riot gear approach with some EG ARMY TANKS.

MN80-M. THE SPECIAL ONE/*FEMALE* is noticeable from a distance in battle utilizing Judo techniques to disarm several armed police men in battle with the other THREE YOUNG MEN.

[MEANWHILE AT THE SAME TIME
IN A DIFFERENT LOCATION]

EXTERIOR OF LOCATION: AN EG
MINISTRY 1 HEAD OFFICE;
CAIRO, EGYPT.
DAY 1: 25th January 2011

MN80M SISTER F is standing outside the EG MINIS-TRY 1 office in central Cairo, Egypt, speaking on her mobile phone In Arabic,
"Yes. I am outside the Ministry at this minute. I am going to get something sweet to drink, Would you like anything before I come up to you all? OK then, I will see you soon." she said.

A silent pause for a moment as the response from MN80M-SISTER F 1 FRIEND in Arabic on the other end of the phone call can be heard over the loud—speaker,

"Please hurry up, I am worried about my mum, and want to get to her as quickly as possible, I have to go and pick up my girl first, she has orders to stay at home inside but she is being naughty and does not listen to me. I have to make sure they are ok . . . OK, see you soon then." she said hurriedly.

"I will be with you in two minutes Insha Allah." MN80M SISTER F said in English with a smile as she continues to walk.

[MEANWHILE AT THE SAME TIME
IN A DIFFERENT LOCATION]

INSIDE OF LOCATION; MN80M's APARTMENT,
LONDON, ENGLAND;
DAY 1: 25th January 2011—London England

MN80M-THE AMAZING ONE/MALE is still laying on his bed in contemplation mode, looking up towards the ceiling. The sound of two birds tweeting outside the window is heard.

[MEANWHILE AT THE SAME TIME
IN A DIFFERENT LOCATION]

INSIDE OF LOCATION; MN-80—THE EG
PRESIDENT 1 PALACE,
SHARM EL SHEIKH, EGYPT;
DAY 1: 25th January 2011

MN-80—THE EG PRESIDENT 1 (80's) continues to look out through the window while sitting in his golden chair. The sound of one bird tweeting outside the window is heard.

[MEANWHILE AT THE SAME TIME
IN A DIFFERENT LOCATION]

EXTERIOR OF LOCATION; TAHRIR SQUARE,
CAIRO, EGYPT—
DAY 1: 25th January 2011

The crowd and riot police are now clashing with one another in serious battle. MN80M-THE SPECIAL ONE/FEMALE is noticeable alone at a far utilizing a sling—shot to disarm some of the riot police men with her special marbles from the pouch attached to her side hip.

[MEANWHILE AT THE SAME TIME
IN A DIFFERENT LOCATION]

INSIDE OF LOCATION; MN-80—THE EG
PRESIDENT 1 PALACE OFFICES,
SHARM EL SHEIKH, EGYPT;
DAY 1: 25th January 2011—Sharm El Sheikh Egypt
13:39 AM (EET)

The General and fourteen Supreme Military Council members are all waiting for MN-80—THE EG PRESIDENT 1 in the grand private meeting chambers. The faces of the Military Council members are as if in awe and shock, yet standing firm next to the General, yet it is if as they themselves, not know, what is going on exactly, and all eagerly

await higher approval and information access from the EG PRESIDENT 1 himself. The door opens, and as MN-80-
—THE EG PRESIDENT
1 is about to walk into the room. The General and all (14) Military Council members in the room proceed with usual protocol and stand to salute MN-80—THE EG PRESIDENT 1 as he enters the room and continue to stand in the same position until given the order to do otherwise by MN-80—THE EG PRESIDENT 1 himself only. The MAN IN SUIT walks into the room first, and takes a serious look around from left to right boldly before looking at the General in command of the Egyptian Army.

CHAPTER SIX

104: Manhood . . . MONTHS AGO . . . .

INSIDE OF LOCATION; MN80M's
APARTMENT, LONDON, ENGLAND;
DAY 2: 26th January 2011—12:32 PM—
London England

MN80M-THE AMAZING ONE/MALE has just finished praying and stands to place his praying mat on the side of the bed and then walks over to his bed and picks up the duvet to shake and place back onto the bed neatly. Once finished, MN80M sits down on the bed and switches on the TV, as well as his laptop to check his email. The TV audio sounds with the TV NEWS BROADCASTER speaking, "Current unrest in Egypt has seen tension rise overnight as Egyptians have taken to the streets to demonstrate against the present day MN-80—THE EG PRESIDENT 1". Said the news broadcaster just as MN80M-THE AMAZING ONE/ MALE stands up from his seated position on the bed and walks out of the room as the TV sounds continue in the background with the TV NEWS BROADCASTER continuing,

"The situation as it is has proven to be that similar of recent events in Tunisia, and we have news reports in a minute ago that the city of Cairo has shown the most violence with many people seriously injured," she said.

MN80M-THE AMAZING ONE/MALE walks back into the room holding a cup of tea still listening attentively yet face not showing much interest as the TV NEWS BROAD-CASTER continues,

"Cairo on the other hand seems to have just gotten started. One of the next leading MN80-EG PRESIDENTIAL candidates has departed from his location in Europe on route to Egypt. I hope to have more updates for you all in the studio shortly."

MN80M. THE AMAZING ONE/MALE smiles and says out loud, "Yeah, good day to you too with your news-trouble making. None of you news reporters really love Masr. OK, we need change, I agree, but not like this. Not like this." he said out loud.

MN80M's phone rings on the table next to him. He turns down the sound of the television as he answers the ringing phone.

"Hello MN80M Speaking . . . yes. yes . . . yes. I can see on the news everything. So where are you now? Home? and why private number for? OK, I am coming to see you for a minute, but I just got an email and have to go see some one first down central London OK. see you soon then. Bye."

MN80M-THE AMAZING ONE/MALE presses a button as he puts down the phone, and stands up on his feet. Takes in a deep breath, and walks over towards the cupboard to take out his special black suit jacket. Places it on, and then his shoes before he walks out of the door dressed in his dapper suit holding a EG light brown promotional leather briefcase.

[LATER IN A DIFFERENT LOCATION]

EXTERIOR OF LOCATION; TRAIN STATION, LONDON, ENGLAND:
DAY 2:

MN80M waits on the platform as the train approaches slowly and comes to a halt before he enters as the automatic doors open making a beeping sound. MN80M walks towards a seat and sits down. He then takes out his mobile phone from his pocket to send a sms/text message just as the automatic doors closing sound is heard. MN80M-THE AMAZING ONE/MALE looks at his phone.

[MEANWHILE AT THE SAME TIME IN A DIFFERENT LOCATION]

INSIDE OF LOCATION: AN EG MINISTRY HEAD OFFICE, CAIRO, EGYPT;
DAY 2:

A group of seventeen high ranking specialists/individuals are conversing around a table, while some are standing in conversation at the other side of the room. MN80M SISTER F phone vibrates from an sms message, and she presses the button to read the message. MN80M SISTER F looks at the message for a moment, then looks away for a moment, and decides to send a reply message.

[MEANWHILE AT THE SAME TIME IN A DIFFERENT LOCATION]

INSIDE OF LOCATION;
TRAIN, LONDON, ENGLAND:
DAY 2:

Travelling at high speeds, the train continues towards the destination of London, Liverpool Street. MN80M-THE AMAZING ONE/MALE remains sitting on his seat as the train is in motion. The phone makes a loud sound from the incoming sms/text message, and he presses the button to read the message. MN80M reads the message, he replies to the message, and then stands up to walk to the train doors as the train is about to reach his destination.

[MEANWHILE AT THE SAME TIME
IN A DIFFERENT LOCATION]

INSIDE OF LOCATION; AN EG MINISTRY HEAD
OFFICE, CAIRO, EGYPT;
DAY 2:

The atmosphere is lively with specialists moving around the room in different directions while continuing with his or her assignments. MN80M-SISTER F is sitting awaiting a reply from MN80M-THE AMAZING ONE/MALE to her message. The message comes, and she reads it, and then stands to walk out of the room. "Excuse me for a moment; I have to make a call."

She says in a request as she stands from the table to be excused from the other consultants sitting around her in conversation. Just as she takes a few steps nearer the door, she presses a button on the phone to call MN80M-THE AMAZING ONE/MALE.

[MEANWHILE AT THE SAME TIME
IN A DIFFERENT LOCATION]

INSIDE OF LOCATION;
TRAIN, LONDON, ENGLAND:
DAY 2:

MN80M-THE AMAZING ONE/MALE is standing at the doors waiting to get off the train once the train comes to a halt. While holding his phone in his right hand, MN80M presses the button to switch off his phone. The train stops, doors open and MN80M exits, and enters a stair case heading down underground to connect to another train. MN80M-reaches underground and onto a new platform, and boards a London underground train heading south.

[MEANWHILE AT THE SAME TIME
IN A DIFFERENT LOCATION]

INSIDE OF LOCATION; AN EG MINISTRY HEAD
OFFICE, CAIRO, EGYPT;

In a less vibrant corridor adjacent to the meeting room, MN80M-SISTER F is standing while speaking on her phone as other consultants enter and exit the area towards the main meeting room. She is moving around in small steps speaking in her mind,
"Off! What is your phone off for now? You just sent me a message."
MN80M SISTER F said as she decides to send a message and puts the phone back into her pocket and walks back into the room.

[MEANWHILE AT THE SAME TIME
IN A DIFFERENT LOCATION]

INSIDE OF LOCATION; LONDON
UNDERGROUND, ENGLAND:
DAY 2:

Underground and moving over 80mph the train has nearly each carriage half full. MN80M-THE AMAZING ONE/ MALE is sitting on a seat on the train watching other people's faces that are around him as the train comes to a halt at each stop. The sounds of the underground continue loud as passengers come and go past MN-80 M.

[MEANWHILE AT THE SAME TIME
IN A DIFFERENT LOCATION]

INSIDE LOCATION: AN EG MINISTRY
AUTHORITY, HEAD OFFICE,
CAIRO, EGYPT:
DAY 2:

The consultants are in another serious conversation together about the present day situation. The FEMALE (50's) SENIOR EG MINISTRY CONSULTANT 1 speaks out in Arabic in a hurriedly tone,
"Ok everyone. We have all read the emergency reports." she said.
The room is silent for a moment as she continues in English, ". . . has anyone anything to add to this or ask about this?" she said in her bold manly tone of voice.
The room is silent again as the consultants faces remain still; MN80M SISTER F's face remains the same with a

small smile. The FEMALE (50's) SENIOR EG MINISTRY CONSULTANT 1 continues in English,
"Ok. Good. In one hour I want us all to gather again to go over what we have been assigned to accomplish today as well as the coming days." she said as she closes the note pad in her hands.

[MEANWHILE AT THE SAME TIME
IN A DIFFERENT LOCATION]

EXTERIOR OF LOCATION;
LONDON UNDERGROUND,
CENTRAL LONDON, ENGLAND:
DAY 2:

MN80M-THE AMAZING ONE/MALE is outside the train station walking towards a coffee shop located at the corner of the street. As he walks, he takes his phone out of his pocket to make a call.
"Ok now, let's see what this company wants from me." he said to himself.
MN80Mcontinues to walk and crosses the street while holding the phone awaiting an answer from the call. MN80M-THE AMAZING ONE/MALE smiles while looking up at the grey sky,
"Good afternoon, yes, hello, I am in central London now, and was wondering where your offices were exactly for this meeting?" he asked.
MN80M continues to walk and cross the street while holding the phone in conversation,
"Ok. Yes I know the way now. Thank you." he said, now with a big smile.

MN80M continues to walk and cross the street while holding the phone, and then places it into his pocket before he enters the coffee shop to buy a hot drink. The phone receives a message, no tone heard. MN80-M continues into the shop.

[MEANWHILE AT THE SAME TIME
IN A DIFFERENT LOCATION]

INSIDE OF LOCATION; AN EG MINISTRY
AUTHORITY HEAD OFFICE,
CAIRO, EGYPT:
DAY 2:

The consultants continue in serious conversation together about the present day situation. MN80M-SISTER F phone vibrates silently from a delivery report for the message she had sent MN80M the other consultants sitting on the table are listening attentively as they all take notes and share notes silently. The FEMALE (50's) SENIOR EG MIN-ISTRYCONSULTANT 1 starts to speak in English to the consultants,
"At this moment, right now, many demonstrations continue, and yes, this has affected our tourism into a vaccine mode along with nearly everything else we are managing. The embassies have all been alerted of our change in security status from amber-green to amber-red. This meaning, as you all should already know, all and any tourists have been alerted to depart, and the embassies now have to take procedures into their own hands to assist those departing."
said the FEMALE (50's) SENIOR EG MINISTRYCON—SULTANT 1.

The FEMALE (50's) picks up a glass of water on the table and drinks slowly before continuing in the Arabic language,

"I expect us all to continue as we have been and further updates shall follow shortly. We must focus on that in front of us." she said in a bolder manner. Possibly because of the two gulps of water she just had.

A long silent pause and somewhat calmness is now sensed around the room of consultants. MALE (40's) EG MINIS—TRY CONSULTANT 1 smiles, and asks in Arabic,

"How can we focus on what is in front of us when there are people fighting outside? Everything is madness. Especially when many feel same or similar ways to those outside pro—testing? This is all very emotional to me." he said as he then puts one of his hands on to the top of his head.

The FEMALE (50's) SENIOR EG MINISTRYCONSUL—TANT 1 responds back to his questions in English with,

"Emotional to us all I am sure. Thank you for your questions. I think you know as well as I do, we all have a job to do, and considering we all still have a job, I suggest we focus on the job at hand now." she said in a firm yet dark tone of seriousness.

Another one of those long silent pause moments is sensed as the FEMALE continues in Arabic to eliminate the awkward atmosphere,

"Does anyone else have any questions?"

A silent pause as the face of everyone around the table is in awe combined with excitement and passion to get what is required accomplished.

[MEANWHILE AT THE SAME TIME
IN A DIFFERENT LOCATION]

EXTERIOR OF LOCATION: TAHRIR SQUARE, CAIRO, EGYPT—
DAY 2:

Tens of thousands of demonstrators continue to chant in Liberation Square. Matters have now escalated, and triple the amount of people are now together chanting anti-regime slogans. Thousands of police men attempt to maintain marshal law and order.

[MEANWHILE AT THE SAME TIME IN A DIFFERENT LOCATION]

EXTERIOR OF LOCATION; CENTRAL LONDON, ENGLAND: DAY 2:

MN80M-THE AMAZING ONE/MALE is walking along the pavement with his coffee in hand smoking a cigarette as he looks up at each road sign to see which one and locate the road he needs to go into for his meeting. The regular London traffic and hustle and bustle of central London is lively and upbeat together with the blue and bright white cloudy sky. MN80M-THE AMAZING ONE/MALE starts to figure out what is the best route to take as he crosses over another road,

"OK, where is this place M? Where is this place?" he said to himself.

"Not this street, the next one maybe, or next one." MN80M said again.

MN80M-THE AMAZING ONE/MALE continues to walk and his phone starts to ring. MN80Manswers his mobile phone,
"Hello there MN80M SISTER F how are you? is everything ok!?! I see the news; it seems things are getting a little hectic over in Africa ha! Looks like we need a new Hero, what do you think?" he said while holding back a laugh.

[MEANWHILE AT THE SAME TIME
IN A DIFFERENT LOCATION]

INSIDE OF LOCATION; AN EG MINISTRY
AUTHORITY HEAD OFFICE,
CAIRO, EGYPT:
DAY 2:

MN80M SISTER F is on her mobile phone speaking to MN80-M, while she is now sitting among a few other consultants around the office table.
"Hi M, yes I am ok thanks. Everything is ok with me thank God. And yes as you see on the news things are not the usual obviously. Anyway. What is this job offer you are talking about in your sms message to me earlier?"

[MEANWHILE AT THE SAME TIME
IN A DIFFERENT LOCATION]

EXTERIOR OF LOCATION;
CENTRAL LONDON, ENGLAND:
DAY 2:

MN80M THE AMAZING ONE/MALE continues walking on the road and decides to stand still on the side-street to

speak to MN80M SISTER F. MN80M-THE AMAZING ONE/MALE takes in a slow deep breath,
"Basically, what happened was . . . Do you remember my first Equilibrium project in Egypt I managed to secure? He put my name forward to one of his associates here in the UK that are linked with Los Angeles office, and apparently they seeking individuals in Egypt to work today or tomorrow and so on, as journalists and correspondents for the media." he said as if in one breath.

[MEANWHILE AT THE SAME TIME
IN A DIFFERENT LOCATION]

INSIDE OF LOCATION; AN EG MINISTRY
AUTHORITY HEAD OFFICE,
CAIRO, EGYPT:
DAY 2:

MN80M SISTER F is on her mobile phone speaking to MN80-M, this time with a serious look on her face as she listens attentively.
"Yeah but you are not a journalist, and you don't do that type of work, so why bother for anyway, It's just a waste of time." she said discouragingly.

[MEANWHILE AT THE SAME TIME
IN A DIFFERENT LOCATION]

EXTERIOR OF LOCATION;
CENTRAL LONDON, ENGLAND:
DAY 2:

MN80M-THE AMAZING ONE/MALE is standing speaking on the phone.
"What do you mean waste of time? I have my own film production company in Egypt; I can do as I please. Plus, if they want to pay good, then why not!??! Especially if I can report the truth, instead of them selecting others to do as they please all the time."

[MEANWHILE AT THE SAME TIME
IN A DIFFERENT LOCATION]

INSIDE OF LOCATION; AN EG MINISTRY
AUTHORITY HEAD OFFICE,
CAIRO, EGYPT:
DAY 2:

MN80M SISTER F is on her mobile phone speaking to MN80-M, still with a serious look on her face as she listens attentively, and moves around slightly.
"I know you can, but I am just saying, they not worth it. Focus on you and what you are doing there. Everything here will be over soon hopefully, and if you want to come out next month may be to write your own stories or articles, then great."

[MEANWHILE AT THE SAME TIME
IN A DIFFERENT LOCATION]

EXTERIOR OF LOCATION;
CENTRAL LONDON, ENGLAND:
DAY 2:

MN80M-THE AMAZING ONE/MALE is standing speaking on the phone.

"What are you talking about!?? Next month for what!? Why is it you are all forever holding me back from doing that which I choose to do . . . ?" he said as if ending a possible argument.

MN80M-THE AMAZING ONE/MALE starts to walk and continues speaking on the phone,

"I am practically at the offices now about to walk in and see what they will offer me. So once I am done, I can let you know if I will be coming to Egypt or not, ok."

[MEANWHILE AT THE SAME TIME
IN A DIFFERENT LOCATION]

INSIDE OF LOCATION; AN EG MINISTRY
AUTHORITY HEAD OFFICE,
CAIRO, EGYPT:
DAY 2:

MN80M SISTER F is speaking to MN80M-THE AMAZING ONE/MALE on the phone. She seems slightly agitated more than usual,

"No, I don't mean it like that. Of course you can come any-time you want to. Our home is here too, and you have your company, you can do as you wish to. Just be careful with them ok, and try not to speak too much."

[MEANWHILE AT THE SAME TIME
IN A DIFFERENT LOCATION]

EXTERIOR OF LOCATION;
CENTRAL LONDON, ENGLAND:
DAY 2:

MN80M-THE AMAZING ONE/MALE is walking speaking on the phone.

"And what do I have to speak about anyway.!??! look, I think I have arrived on the street now, I will message you after the meeting ok. I am happy you are ok and all is well. Salam for now sis." he said in a more reassuring way. MN80M-THE AMAZING ONE/MALE presses the button on his phone, and continues as he turns right onto a new road for a few yards before entering a building.

[MEANWHILE AT THE SAME TIME
IN A DIFFERENT LOCATION]

INSIDE OF LOCATION; AN EG MINISTRY
AUTHORITY HEAD OFFICE,
CAIRO, EGYPT:
DAY 2:

MN80M-SISTER F places her phone into her pocket and rises from her seat on the table and walks towards FEMALE (50's) SENIOR EG MINISTRY CONSULTANT 1 and then speaks out in Arabic saying in a low whispering tone,
"Excuse me every one for a moment." she said.

MN80M SISTER F walks over towards the corner of the room until she reaches the side of FEMALE (50's) The SENIOR EG MINISTRY CONSULTANT that notices her coming and asks in Arabic,
"Yes MN80M SISTER F, how can I help you?" she said with a semi smile.

"I Just heard news from my brother in London that news agencies are trying to recruit new journalists to take part in reporting events back to them." said MN80M SISTER F in Arabic.

"Seriously, since when?" said the SENIOR CONSULTANT in Arabic instantly.

"As far as I know, for him, he heard this morning. He is about to head into a meeting now to see what they are offering. Once he has finished, he said he will let me know." "Very good MN80M SISTER F, make sure you update this on our special board. I know he is your brother and all. But we need to know as much as we can from as many places and people as we can to help Egypt's' emergency."

MN80M SISTER F agrees by nodding her head. The FEMALE (50's) SENIOR EG MINISTRY CONSULTANT picks up some papers next to her on a desk and a couple of folders before looking back and saying, "Thank you MN80M SISTER F. I await to hear updates about this all." she said, and walks away towards the doors.

[MEANWHILE AT THE SAME TIME
IN A DIFFERENT LOCATION]

INSIDE OF LOCATION;
CENTRAL LONDON, ENGLAND:
DAY 2:

MN80M-THE AMAZING ONE/MALE is waiting in the reception area to be in a meeting with a female journalist (30's) from the news company. The JOURNALIST also known as EMPATHY TARGET 2 or 12 arrives and greets MN80M-THE AMAZING ONE/MALE with a smile on her dark olive complexioned face. "Hello. Thank you for coming on such short notice. Would you mind if we had our meeting across the road in the cafe? It's just that our office is fully booked right now, and apparently all the tables in the restaurant are full." said MN-80M. EMPATHY TARGET 12.

"Hello. Sure, not a problem at all. Lead the way." MN80M-THE AMAZING ONE/MALE said as he now smiles back while watching EMPATHY TARGET 12 walk ahead of him and out of the building doors continuing after her to the exit saying while now standing nearer to her,

"I have done my research on you. Congratulations on your career thus far. Your work in Iraq proved fruitful for many, especially yourself."

MN80M smiles, and continues after her towards the exit. The Female looks back at MN80M and into his bold green eyes before she smiles twice.

[MEANWHILE IN A DIFFERENT LOCATION]

INSIDE OF LOCATION; CENTRAL LONDON, ENGLAND:

DAY 2:

MN80M-THE AMAZING ONE/MALE is sitting across from MN-80 M. EMPATHY TARGET 12 along one of those rounded semi-small coffee tables in conversation mode with her while both drinking a hot beverage. MN-80 M. EMPATHY TARGET 12 smiles before she says,

"So you see, what we are looking for and interested in is, what is happening now in Egypt. As you already know from the email, our CEO received your information from an associate of his. We thought you were in Egypt MN80M" MN80M-THE AMAZING ONE/MALE takes a sip of his coffee before responding with,

"Yes, my company is in Egypt, registered just on Tahrir Square actually several years ago." MN80M said and then continues to drink.

"Oh, OK." MN-80 M. EMPATHY TARGET 12 said as she smiles awaiting MN80M

"Also, what I see on the news right now, and what it is your services and any services require, is a journalist and/or correspondent on the ground, someone to report live what is happening right!?!" said MN80M

"Yes," The journalist eagerly waiting said quickly.

"Well, let us get one thing straight. From what I have heard today, I must tell you now, I am not an activist. I am a opportunist if anything, but not one to stir or make trouble." said MN80-M firmly.

MN-80 M. EMPATHY TARGET 12 looks slightly shocked,

"No one said anything about making trouble. And also, I have to say, we do not guarantee you any work, and are not affiliated with you or any other individual, especially if any—thing may go wrong. We have individuals in Egypt ready and able to deal with things if needed, as well as our links contributing in New York, here in London, other cities in Europe too, and major links with all the networks, and even our Los Angeles department is headed up by that famous man I mentioned earlier, his brother. Have you heard of him?" she said as she then moves about in her chair.

"First of all, it is I that guarantees work, not you. Secondly, I work alone, much faster that way, even superman cannot catch up with me and not many alive can say that to be true, yet it is when I move alone that I succeed best, as well as select my own team or way to work in this life and day and age, do you understand what I am saying." MN80-M said in a suave way yet slightly frightening.

MN80Mtakes a pause looking her in the eyes directly before continuing with,

"The major links you have are fine, for you, and yes I have heard of the man you mentioned. He produces hit Television Music Shows . . . TV Shows like talent ones right!?!" he said in a more calm and subtle tone.

MN-80 M. EMPATHY TARGET 12 looks at him with more ease and says to herself in her mind in faith that he does not hear her,

"He has the most amazing eyes. I could just wake up in the morning to those beautiful and stunning green eyes for the rest of my life."

MN-80 M. EMPATHY TARGET 12 then smiles at MN80M-THE AMAZING ONE/MALE and so he smiles back. MN-80 M. EMPATHY TARGET 12 takes in a slow deep breath of the cold air as she says out loud in English,

"So tell me then, if you have researched me, I obviously know minimal to nothing about you. Except that you dress very smart, and have a company in Egypt." she said.

"One here too." responded MN80M-THE AMAZING ONE/MALE quickly allowing MN-80 M. EMPATHY TARGET 12 to continue with,

"Do you think what happened to me in Iraq, and my person is the same as what is happening with the Egyptians?" she asked abruptly.

MN80M THE AMAZING ONE/MALE looks up at her,

"No not at all! But it might happen to one of our brotherly countries next to us, maybe Yemen, or Libya could suffer like you all may be did and still do, but no, not Egyptians. Not Egypt." said MN80M

"Why do you think so?" she asked back.

MN80M-THE AMAZING ONE/MALE now looking at her as if the meeting is turning towards a different direction takes a sip of his hot beverage.

"Because you are talking about apples and oranges, two different things in life, plus the Egyptians are the way we are for different reasons. Adding, no one is going through the treatment in Egypt that you were all going through in Iraq. The Egyptians have internal issues we deal with ourselves." he said. The waitress in the coffee shop comes over and re-fills the mugs of coffee on the table and then walks away as if not hearing any part of the conversation. MN-80 M. EMPATHY TARGET 12 then asks,

"So you think the present day president should stay in power, or his son?? Who do you think should be the next MN-80—THE EG PRESIDENT 2?" she said while loudening her tone of voice on the last few words as if to highlight future matters.

MN80M THE AMAZING ONE/MALE looks at her straight in the eyes saying,

"I do not think it is about who stays and who goes as much as that is best for Egypt over-all." he said quickly.

MN-80 M. EMPATHY TARGET 12 moves her seat in closer.

"What do you mean? So you think (Must fill in name) or (Must fill in name) should stay?"

She says in a low serious tone as MN80M-THE AMAZING ONE/MALE responds with,

"You seem to be asking the same question twice or in different ways. I took notice these things you know . . ." he said back to her quickly.

EMPATHY TARGET 12 blushes as MN8M. continues speaking,

"Basically, if we have a selected few faces on the table, regardless of name, over-all, I would say the one the people select, and mainly because that individual has the peoples interests at heart, as well as Egypt."

MN80M takes a moment to pause and catch his breath. "If the most educated, and experienced at this moment in time is (Must fill in name) and the people themselves elect him peacefully, then so be it. When you think about it, he is the most experienced, and some say, he has no hunger like another may have once a new person and party come to power, and then starts to possibly do things or take things that one who may be already full would not take. if that saying makes any sense to you." MN80-M said as if letting all out in one breathe.

MN-80 M. EMPATHY TARGET 12 looks on seriously, now asking,

"So you think (Must fill in name) should be the next MN80-THE EG PRESIDENT 2?"

A longer moment of silence as if time stood still in the coffee shop came about and had a sense of cold air chill come through as if the open door allowed the busy London street breeze to come in. MN80M-THE AMAZING ONE/MALE still sitting directly in front of her smiles before responding,

"Now you are twisting my words. First I tell you I am not an activist and one who takes part in trouble making. When fact is, I am into film making. Not trouble making . . ." said MN80M.

The Female smiles

MN-80 M. EMPATHY TARGET 12 says to herself in mind,

"How about love making . . ."

{EMPATHY INCREASE}

MN80M THE AMAZING ONE/MALE smiles as he continues to say,

"Look yeah. I read all the company rules and information, and pay rates. Those rates I am not fond of actually,
 especially for a hazardous environment. But feel free to give me an application form just in case when I go out to Egypt I am able to produce some work for your services. Then I shall be in touch with you. Is that OK!??!" said MN80M while MN-80 M. EMPATHY TARGET 12 moves her chair closer,

"Well, as it says, we pay £60 per minute for phone to phone. And £350 per minute for insight-via (Must fill in name) If you are afraid that you may be in need of asylum, we can assist with that too. The company helped me, and may help others that are in need. But yes sure. Is that OK if we get this from the office? and also, just one last question? Is there anyone else you think would be a good candidate for the next presidency?"

MN80M. Smiles.

Moments of silence as both slowly sip their coffees. Twelve of fourteen other individuals are within the seated area of the coffee shop. They both continue to look at one another while MN80M-THE AMAZING ONE/MALE says to himself in mind, "The presidency. Yes. Me. (laughs) only joking with you, they may as well make me King." and then opens his mouth to say out loud,

"Well, the news keeps showing this man I see called (Must fill in name) my research shows he was high up in the (Must fill in name) or something similar. Very intelligent man apparently, so if this is what the people want, then maybe he or she will be the next MN-80—THE EG PRESIDENT 2. God knows. Until then though, those forms from the office would be nice. And I shall be in touch in the near future once landed in Egypt. And for your information, if anything, I am not like you, and I do not need asylum, it would be me trying to claim asylum back into Egypt, not the other way around." MN80-M said trying his best not to sound to rude.

The female stops smiling as she continues to glare into MN80M's eyes.

[MEANWHILE AT THE SAME TIME IN A DIFFERENT LOCATION]

INSIDE OF LOCATION; AN EG MINISTRY AUTHORITY HEAD OFFICE, CAIRO, EGYPT: DAY 2:

MN80M SISTER F is on the phone to her friend that is sit—ting in the offices near, both in conversation about recent events.

"Seriously, impossible, when and how?" says MN80M SISTER F In Arabic as MN80M SISTER F 1 FRIEND responds In Arabic,

"With my own eyes I am telling you. Everything has seriously begun. What shall we do?"

A silent pause from the both of them to catch their breath as MN80M SISTER F then says,

"What are you all doing at the office still?" she said while catching her breath as MN80M SISTER F 1

FRIEND frustrated responds over the loud-speaker,

"I have advised most to go home already, not much work is getting done here anyway." she said as the sounds of each office in the background is the only thing creating noise. "OK. The same situation here with us, they asking us to do the same if we like, and any one that wants to stay at home can. I may go home soon, I am not sure. But call me if you need anything OK."

"You too OK."

[MEANWHILE IN A DIFFERENT LOCATION]

INSIDE OF LOCATION;
CENTRAL LONDON, ENGLAND:
DAY 2:

MN80M-THE AMAZING ONE/MALE is standing in the office foyer filling in the forms that the MN-80 M. EMPATHY TARGET 12 has handed into his hands.

"I think this is about everything for now right!!?" Said MN80M.

"Umm . . . Yes, I think that is everything." responds MN-80 M. EMPATHY TARGET 12 as she looks briefly at the paper work then back to his eyes.

"Ok. Let me just read over things one more time." said MN80M

MN-80 M. EMPATHY TARGET 12 nods her head in agreement, turning around and then continues to send an sms/text message from her mobile phone as MN80M-THE AMAZING ONE/MALE continues to proof read over the documents. MN-80 M. EMPATHY TARGET 12 smiles as she finishes sending the message.

[MEANWHILE AT THE SAME TIME
IN A DIFFERENT LOCATION]

EXTERIOR OF LOCATION;
CAIRO STREETS, EGYPT:
DAY 2:

Demonstrations continue as the sounds of some explosions are now heard among screams and individuals running.

MN80M—EMPATHY TARGET NUMBER 4 (Female/20's to 30 Year Old) is standing on the street among other demonstrators. She takes her phone out of her pocket, and reads the message that just arrived making a vibration sound. The Message Reads,

"Get ready for someone else on your team. I think we may have someone special, he is super hot, super smart, and has the best green eyes I have ever seen. Oh, and he is connected ;)"

MN80M EMPATHY TARGET NUMBER 4 smiles, and places her phone back into her pocket as the

CROWD CHANTING in Arabic,

"Down with the regime." and "(???Must fill in???) Continues.

THE SPECIAL ONE/FEMALE is noticeable a far wearing her EG FLAG bandanna still wrapped around her face watching EMPATHY TARGET NUMBER 4 like a hawk to prey.

[MEANWHILE AT THE SAME TIME
IN A DIFFERENT LOCATION]

INSIDE OF LOCATION;
CENTRAL LONDON, ENGLAND:
DAY 2:

MN80M and MN-80-M-EMPATHY TARGET 12 are in conversation. MN80M seems slightly agitated now from some reason or another,

"ok then. I guess everything is in order."

MN-80 M. EMPATHY TARGET 12 smiles as she says in her mind,

"Ok then you sexy looking thing you I could have you for breakfast, lunch and dinner." She smiles again then speaks out saying to MN80-M,

"Ok then. Thank you for coming to speak to us on such short notice. Good luck with everything with your company and all." she said.

MN80M-THE AMAZING ONE/MALE smiles

"Thank you. Good destiny to you too. You have my number on the forms. Yet pass me yours in case I need to directly make contact about anything." he said.

MN80Mhas an even larger smile than normal on his face as MN-80 M. EMPATHY TARGET 12 takes a piece of paper, and writes her number down, and then hands over to MN80Mand he accepts, and walks out of the door.

[MEANWHILE IN A DIFFERENT LOCATION]

EXTERIOR OF LOCATION;
CENTRAL LONDON,
ENGLAND:
DAY 2:

MN80M-THE AMAZING ONE/MALE is walking on the street towards Hammersmith Train station, passing street to street while thinking in mind,

"What in God's name is happening? They speaking about Individuals involved to take down MN80-THE EG PRESIDENT 1. And even though I want change, I do not want any foreigners or other nations thinking they can get involved with Egypt as if Egypt is his or hers. President or no President, the MN80-EG PRESIDENT 1 is a MN80—EG PRESIDENT. And when Egypt has a MN80—EG PRESI-

DENT, he is our Pharaoh. Until 'WE' choose as the people to change into what we want, not anyone else."

MN80M-THE AMAZING ONE/MALE said as he takes his phone out of his pocket and switches it on while still trying to figure out life as it is.

"God what is happening?"

MN80M-THE AMAZING ONE/MALE looks at his phone, and notices an incoming message,

"MN80M SISTER F is calling." he said again. The phone vibrates and MN80Mpresses the button to make a call back while still walking on the now busy main road. Cars continue to pass from left to right as MN80M-THE AMAZING ONE/MALE continues to walk and speak his mind.

"Come on MN80M SISTER F answer your phone. Answer your phone. Don't press silent."

MN80M-THE AMAZING ONE/MALE continues to walk and puts his phone back into his pocket. "So if they trying to bring down MN-80—THE EG PRESIDENT, they not necessarily are having the interests of the Egyptian people at heart. But God, Why? I know things are bad in Egypt, and my own experiences took me away from Egypt because I hate the way the system works. But that is Egypt. Dad used to say to me, "This is how Egypt has been all her life, and how Egypt will be a for all of her life." So even with change, and a change for what some want to look like Dubai, this will come in time. But not like this God. Not like this."

MN80M-THE AMAZING ONE/MALE nears the London underground Train Station main entry/ exit doors and the phone rings, MN80M answers the phone and speaks in English,

"Hello MN80M-SISTER F thank you for calling back . . ."

[MEANWHILE AT THE SAME TIME
IN A DIFFERENT LOCATION]

INSIDE OF LOCATION; AN EG MINISTRY
AUTHORITY HEAD OFFICE,
CAIRO, EGYPT:
DAY 2:

MN80M SISTER F is on the phone to MN80M-THE
AMAZING ONE/MALE asking questions quickly to him
in English,
"MN80M don't accept the assignment. What happened!?!
What did they say to you!??"

[MEANWHILE AT THE SAME TIME
IN A DIFFERENT LOCATION]

EXTERIOR OF LOCATION;
CENTRAL LONDON, ENGLAND:
DAY 2:

MN80M-THE AMAZING ONE/MALE is standing at
the train station main doors speaking to MN80M SISTER
F on the mobile phone answering back in Arabic,
"I do not know what to tell you MN80M SISTER F." he
said.
MN80Mscratches his head as he looks around at the many
commuters entering and exiting the train station. MN80M-
THE AMAZING ONE/MALE speaks out in English,
"Something very fishy is going on here."
MN80M SISTER F loud tone over from the phone speaker
can be heard saying,
"What do you mean? What happened?" she said.

MN80M THE AMAZING ONE/MALE continues,
"These people seem to be very well organized. And I know I
went into this meeting with accepting an assignment for my
career and company on mind, but not this"
A long silent pause until the voice again from MN80M SIS-
TER F via the phone speaker in a more confident tone says,
"What do you mean?" she asked again.
MN80M looks around his shoulder before saying back, "I
know I want change too yeah, but not like this. They have
news agents coming in from New York, LA, Europe, and
other locations I am sure. And the thing is, I did not get the
feeling they want me to say the truth as it is when I see things
out there. Yet, if anything, I can swing this Egypt's way if you
know what I mean." MN80—M said.
A moment of silence comes from them both as more commuters come and go past MN80M-THE AMAZING
ONE/MALE as if in their own worlds.

[MEANWHILE AT THE SAME TIME
IN A DIFFERENT LOCATION]

INSIDE OF LOCATION; AN EG MINISTRY
AUTHORITY HEAD OFFICE,
CAIRO, EGYPT:
DAY 2:

MN80M SISTER F is on the phone to MN80M-THE
AMAZING ONE/MALE in a more silent environment,
and is drinking from her small tea cup some green tea.
"Why? What did they say?"
MN80M SISTER F says in Arabic, as she sips on her tea and
places the phone on loud-speaker. MN80M-THE AMAZ-
ING ONE/MALE can be heard saying back in English,

"Sensing not much what they said, but how the woman said each word. Basically, they are planning something very BIG in the media." he said as the sounds of the London Underground continue behind his tone of voice.

MN80M SISTER F continues to sip her tea and replies back in English,

"Well, I am sure everything is OK. I heard a big demonstration will go again on Saturday, if you want to come next month to write about something then great." she said as she sips her tea.

The sounds of the London atmosphere can be heard via the loud speaker tones as MN80M-THE AMAZING ONE/MALE says in Arabic,

"Are you crazy." and then he continues in English,

"I have my return ticket from last year anyway. I can come on my own if I want."

MN80M SISTER F quickly responds with, "I know that. I am not saying not to come. I am just saying M, if you want to come to write about this all, may be next month is better. But if you are saying you want a holiday, then by all means, come tomorrow."

"Yeah well. I am just saying. And keep in mind, I did not have to tell you any of this information. Especially since I know Big brother is listening on the airwaves." he said firmly.

MN80M SISTER F agrees nodding her head as she responds with,

"All right MN80M-THE AMAZING ONE/MALE. Whatever. I will speak to you later then."

MN80M-THE AMAZING ONE/MALE responds with, "OK then, safe." and then the line is disconnected.

[MEANWHILE AT THE SAME TIME
IN A DIFFERENT LOCATION]

INSIDE OF LOCATION; AN EG 1 MINISTRY AUTHORITY HEAD OFFICE, CAIRO, EGYPT: DAY 2:

The super air conditioned room has a lively atmosphere. MN80M SISTER F places her phone back into her pocket as she heads in the direction of FEMALE(50's)SENIOR CONSULTANT sitting at the corner of the palatial room. Half a dozen other associates are all walking around in conversation and/or running an errand on one of their assignments.

[MEANWHILE AT THE SAME TIME
IN A DIFFERENT LOCATION]

INSIDE OF LOCATION: LONDON, ENGLAND. UNDERGROUND TRAIN: DAY 2: 26th January 2011— London England

MN80M-THE AMAZING ONE/MALE is sitting on the train, with many passengers beside him as well as in-front on other chairs. The sounds of the usual London underground motions continue as well as the smell in the air of the condensed amounts of human perspiration flying through the air from the wind coming through half open windows at both ends of the carriage. MN80M-THE AMAZING ONE/MALE looks around slowly as he speaks to himself in mind,

"God. Why? and what can I do?? Only me? Who am I? *A nobody.* Especially to the majority of Egyptians in Egypt." he said to himself silently.

MN80Mlooks around at the other passengers on the train as he continues privately in mind,

"Look at every one here. Look at me."

MN80M looks at his reflection on the glass behind the passenger sitting in front of him. MN80M-THE AMAZING ONE/ MALE attempts a smile, yet is unsuccessful, and continues,

"I am from London. I gave my life to Egypt, and more. I am tired too. Enough now." he said again to himself silently as the other passengers remain at a short distant unable to hear.

MN80M looks at the passengers around him before saying,

"What can I do? What can I do God? Please show me. What can I do with no money? How can I get there? And even if I was able to. What would I do for Egypt with this now? Especially after what happened to me, and on top of this all, what happened without me before Ramadan last year with you know what God." said MN80M

MN80Mthen shakes his head slightly, and continues to look at passengers next to him while in contemplation mode of trying to figure out what is best to do. MN80M-THE AMAZING ONE/MALE takes in a few silent deep breaths before continuing,

"How can they want to bring down Egypt like this . . . How is it first Tunisia, then Egypt. And the woman did say in private Yemen is soon too. So what next God?? And why?"

MN80Mshakes his head, and continues to look at passengers next to him and speak silently in mind.

"I know I have my own issues to deal with, and yes, personal. But this is on our whole nation, Egypt. How can I sit back and let them just try to take over Egypt, especially with a secret media campaign taking place."

MN80M continues to slowly from left to right take a good look at the passengers around him in a peaceful looking way only for brief seconds before saying to himself, "God help

Egypt." and then looks at his reflection on the glass behind the passenger sitting in front of him.

[LATER IN A DIFFERENT LOCATION]

EXTERIOR OF LOCATION: LONDON, ENGLAND
TRAIN STATION; NIGHT—
DAY 2

MN80M-THE AMAZING ONE/MALE is standing outside a train station on the phone to a friend.
"So are you home? I can come around now, or later tonight. Ok see you then."
MN80M-THE AMAZING ONE/MALE starts walking among other passengers exiting the train station as the rain starts to trickle down from the grey cloudy sky.

[LATER IN A DIFFERENT LOCATION]

INSIDE OF LOCATION; AN EG MINISTRY 1
AUTHORITY HEAD OFFICE,
CAIRO, EGYPT;
NIGHT;

Some consultants are in a serious conversation together about the present day situation. MN80M SISTER F is taking notes as the FEMALE (50's) SENIOR CONSULTANT is speaking in English,
"OK everyone. We all have our updates with the situations at hand. Our report board has been updated. We have com—pared our information with others coming in from minis—tries. We have some strong links within our team apparently. I noticed over five of our own data co-relate with that of the

ministry of information, and secret service." she said out loud making sure the entire room could hear every word. Everyone in the room is silent as they are part in shock and part ready for the news to come next out of the Senior Consultants mouth. The FEMALE (50's) SENIOR CON—SULTANT continues in Arabic,

"Keep the information coming people. We need everything we can, as soon as we can." she concluded as she closed her note pad book and smiles.

[MEANWHILE AT THE SAME TIME
IN A DIFFERENT LOCATION]

INSIDE OF LOCATION:
MN80M-UK-TEDDYBEAR-HOME
LONDON, ENGLAND,
NIGHT;

MN80M-THE AMAZING ONE/MALE is sitting drinking his hot beverage in conversation with MN80M-UK-TEDDY-BEAR. The TV sound in background is louder than a moment ago and MN80M-UK-TEDDY-BEAR. looks up saying,

"So basically M. They will pay you for doing this right!?!" he said as he picks up the remote control to lower the television. MN80M—THE AMAZING ONE/MALE responds,

"Yeah, but for what!?? £30-£60 per minute. Is it worth it? plus, did you not hear what I said these past few minutes.??" said MN80M

MN80M-UK-TEDDY-BEAR. looks at him with his eye brows now slightly curled in a frustrated manner, "Yes M, but do you have any money? No! Is anyone helping you? No! All those years you spent in Egypt and what did you get!?! more

Grey hair, stress, and back to square one like when you came back from Los Angeles six years ago right!" he asked.

MN80M THE AMAZING ONE/MALE now has his eyebrows the same,

"I know. I know" MN80—M said as MN80M-UK-TEDDY-BEAR. quickly responds with, "So if any—thing. You need to do this for you." said his friend.

Moments of silence as they both seem to need to catch their breath back. MN80M-THE AMAZING ONE/MALE speaks,

"To be honest, I am not really bothered any more. I don't mind doing this, but like I said. They want to pay peanuts, while they get all. Plus on top of this all, from what I just heard over at that office, this is bigger than this seems. And I have my own issues to deal with too." said MN80—M while allowing a moment for his friend to then say,

"You are stubborn M. All you are doing is closing doors on yourself."

"Not really, especially when they already closed the doors on me several times, and what, now I am supposed to go and help them . . ." said MN80-M in a selfish way.

"Why not then??" asked his friend.

"From the eighty plus million humans living there yeah, how many do you think know of me? Near enough none. So how many cares. Same, near enough none of them. And even if there is, those too have already practically turned backs on me." MN80-M said as he looks the other way and then back again.

MN80M-UK-TEDDY-BEAR. Sits back slightly saying, "Yeah but why not?" to MN80M—THE AMAZING ONE/MALE's response,

"How many millions do you think live outside of Egypt.? many. and how many of those do you think is running to Egypt now?" said MN80M

He then lights a cigarette as the news broadcast on the television now seems to be filling the sounds within the smoke filled room. The outside atmosphere continues as MN80M-UK-TEDDY-BEAR. says,

"Probably none."

MN80M-THE AMAZING ONE/MALE has a smile and response of,.

"Exactly."

MN80M then picks up his tea and continues to drink. The TV News broadcasts comes live and MN80M and MN80M-UK-TEDDY-BEAR. look at each other as MN80M-THE AMAZING ONE/MALE says.

"Think I should go, and plus I need to get home and change out of this suit."

MN80M stands up, places on his suit jacket. He takes a look around,

"Ok safe." said MN80M

MN80M puts his fist out and MN80M-UK-TEDDY-BEAR. Puts his fist to MN80M fist, both smile as connecting fists.

"Safe M. Just think about what a real man would do." said MN80M-UK-TEDDY-BEAR. "What are you trying to say, I am not a man??" responded

MN80-M quickly.

Both laugh as MN80M MN80M-UK-TEDDY-BEAR. says back in English,

"You know exactly what I mean M . . . Just be safe ok." he said.

MN80M THE AMAZING ONE/MALE nods his head in agreement,

"Safe." said MN80-M as he smiles removing fist and turning around to exit the door.

{EMPATHY INCREASE}

[MEANWHILE AT THE SAME TIME
IN A DIFFERENT LOCATION]

INSIDE OF LOCATION;
MN80M SISTER F's APARTMENT,
CAIRO, EGYPT; NIGHT:

MN80M SISTER F has just walked into the apartment and rushes into the bathroom. The dog is barking and jumping in excitement around her as she comes in and walks through the hallway fast.

"Ok. Ok. Ok. I missed you all too. Let me just get into the toilet first."

MN80M SISTER F shouts out while laughing, and then she continues to walk through the hallway in a rush into the bathroom/toilet as the dogs continue barking and following her feet.

[MEANWHILE IN A DIFFERENT LOCATION]

INSIDE OF LOCATION; MN80M's APARTMENT,
LONDON, ENGLAND; NIGHT:
DAY 2: The 26th January 2011.

MN80M is sitting down smoking while watching television in his living room area.

"What's the time now anyway?" he said in mind as he looks at his watch and continues speaking his mind.

"I think it is time to pray. I need to wash and pray Insha Allah. Then maybe write another poem or two."
MN80M finishes smoking, sips his can drink and stands to go into the other room to pray.

[MEANWHILE IN A DIFFERENT LOCATION]

INSIDE OF LOCATION; MN80M-
SISTER F's APARTMENT,
CAIRO, EGYPT;
NIGHT:

MN80M SISTER F is sitting down on the sofa with her laptop on her lap, and phone in hand while the dogs calmly sit next to her. The television sounds are heard as MN80M SISTER F says in her mind, "Ok, I better call M. Or at least send him a message first." MN80M SISTER F starts to send an sms / text message.

[MEANWHILE AT THE SAME TIME
IN A DIFFERENT LOCATION]

INSIDE OF LOCATION; MN80M APARTMENT,
LONDON, ENGLAND;
NIGHT:

MN80M-THE AMAZING ONE/MALE is on his knees and has just finished praying in the bedroom. MN80M holds his hands near his face in a prayer motion.
"Dear God. Please forgive me for any sins. Show mercy on me, my family, and all of Adams' children. I pray you show me a sign in order for me to know what is best to do. Shall I try my best to help stop the media propaganda against Egypt

that could potentially turn into a war? or shall I just be like tens of millions of other Egyptians outside of Egypt that may do minimal to nothing." MN80-M said while now taking in a deep breath.

MN80M puts his head closer to his hands and exhales a gentle breath of warm air from his mouth as he continues. "And why me? Why me God? What can I do on my own?" The phone message comes through making a sound. MN-80—M. looks at his phone to read the message. He then stands up, picks up the prayer mat, and folds the mat, then places mat on the bed. MN80Mlooks at his phone again, with a smile on his face this time.

"MN80M-SISTER F. So why does she not call then. Call me." he said.

MN80M starts to write a message on his phone as he walks out of the bedroom and into the living room area.

[MEANWHILE AT THE SAME TIME
IN A DIFFERENT LOCATION]

INSIDE OF LOCATION;
MN80M SISTER F's APARTMENT,
CAIRO, EGYPT;
NIGHT:

MN80M SISTER F is working on her lap—top watching TV as a message comes through on her phone and she then reads the message.

"Ok, MN80M-THE AMAZING ONE/ MALE replied to my message. Good. "Hi, Call me."

MN80M SISTER F presses a button to make a call back.

[MEANWHILE AT THE SAME TIME
IN A DIFFERENT LOCATION]

INSIDE OF LOCATION: MN80M.'s APARTMENT,
LONDON, ENGLAND;
NIGHT:

MN80M-THE AMAZING ONE/MALE is in his living room watching TV and still smoking as the TV news broadcasts continue as he says to himself, "News! News! News! Fucking news is doing my head in . . . All this Bullshit. What the fuck is going on in Egypt?" said MN80M

The TV NEWS BROADCASTER surprisingly and suddenly as if in a covert operation leaps into the picture on the Television screen screaming out,

"The Egyptians have now clashed with police and eye wit— nesses as well as video footage via (Social Network Number 1) has proven that one casualty is already mentioned. A young man, shot in the head as he was amongst the demonstrators throwing rocks at the police." she said out loud while gasping for air to breathe.

The phone rings.

"Hello MN80M SISTER F. How are you? Is everything ok?" said MN80-M as he lowers the sounds on the Television as MN80M SISTER F continues speaking on the loudspeaker.

"Yes I am good thank you. But as you know, things are kicking off." she said.

MN80M THE AMAZING ONE/MALE responds

"Yes I can see on the news. What's this about someone getting shot in the head? and another boy apparently was walking towards the police and after like 400 meters, he too was shot. What the fuck is going on?" MN80-M said.

MN80M SISTER F says back in English, "MN80M I have not even been watching the news properly. But yes it is getting worse. And tourism is being hit the most, anyway. Are you coming or what?" she said as if having a thousand things on her mind.

MN80M-THE AMAZING ONE/MALE eyes and eyebrow move inwards as he says,

"Coming how right now with no money?"

MN80M SISTER F responds with, "I thought you said you have your ticket?"

A moment of silence for a second as MN80M THE AMAZING ONE/MALE says,

"I do. But I may have to pay a fee at the airport to change it, unless there is another way." he said.

MN80M SISTER F quickly says, "How much?",

"I am not sure. I don't know yet, but last time I asked in August when things happened it was £400. And that's the price or a new ticket." MN-80 M says awaiting MN80M SISTER F to speak,

"So what are you going to do?" she said.

Another moment of silence can be heard as MN80M-THE AMAZING ONE/MALE then takes in another deep breath.

"I do not know yet, what about you? I heard on the news that the MN-80—THE EG PRESIDENT 1 wants the prime minister and his ministers to resign. Does that mean you have to lose your job as a consultant?"

"I do not know M. I do not know. Everything is mayhem now."

"Yes I will let you know. But hay! that's not fair if you will lose your job. You just started like twelve months ago, and it took you practically ten years to get the job struggling working your arse off, for in the end, what!??"

The sounds of the television and news broadcast now feeling like a million miles away for them both as the silence is only one part of the emotions felt by brother and sister. MN80M SISTER F continues speaking,

"I don't know yet M. No one does. Just let me know if you are coming home or not OK." she said.

MN80M THE AMAZING ONE/MALE responds,

"God willing I shall let you know OK. Just stay safe, and thank you for calling."

"That is OK M. Take care OK."

MN80M-THE AMAZING ONE/MALE continues to smile, yet a feeling of sadness and anger coming over in regards to the matter at hand.

"You too my sister. Salam."

MN80M SISTER F responds with the same, "Salam." she said.

[MEANWHILE AT THE SAME TIME
IN A DIFFERENT LOCATION]

INSIDE OF LOCATION; MN80M SISTER F's
APARTMENT,
CAIRO, EGYPT; NIGHT:

The floor to ceiling balcony windows is wide open yet the metal gates remain closed as a gush of wind comes through into the apartment. MN80M-SISTER F has just finished the phone call and continues working on her laptop as the TV news broadcasts with the NEWS BROADCASTER saying in Arabic,

"The day's events have unfolded. And many more have come to the street of Egypt to demonstrate. Some rioting has broken out in nearby town of Suez, with some casualties. But the police maintain control." The NEWS BROADCASTER said.

MN80M SISTER F looks up at the TV screen before saying out loud,
"Oh M. You sure would love to be here I know." she said with a smile on her face.

[MEANWHILE AT THE SAME TIME
IN A DIFFERENT LOCATION]

EXTERIOR OF LOCATION: TAHRIR SQUARE,
CAIRO, EGYPT—NIGHT:
DAY 2: TIME: 23:23 PM (EET) 26th January 2011

The night has come swiftly and Tens of Thousands of demonstrators continue to chant in Liberation Square. The CROWD CHANTING continues.
"Down with the regime." combined with, "(???Must fill in???)
And then continues. "Down with the Regime. Down with the Regime." is all that is said and heard by the defiant brave young Egyptian men and women.
MN-80 M. THE SPECIAL ONE/FEMALE is noticeable a far with her 12 ASSOCIATES all wearing EG bandanna's to cover their faces and true identity as they watch. The extreme heat in the somehow humidified air has many thousands still grasping for air as the demands of the Egyptian people continue.

[MEANWHILE AT THE SAME TIME
IN A DIFFERENT LOCATION]

EXTERIOR OF LOCATION: CITY OF SUEZ,
EGYPT—NIGHT:
DAY 2: TIME: 23:24 PM (EET) 26th January 2011

Two helicopters hover above the main market area of the city as thousands of Egyptian demonstrators are in battle with riot police that are in both plain clothing and professional riot protective gear fighting some of the civilians within the crowds of tens of thousands of people. The CROWD CHANTING continues,

"Down with the regime. Down with the Regime." as the sounds of the Helicopters coming lower becomes felt by the air pressure now blowing away the dust on the streets as the battles continue.

[MEANWHILE AT THE SAME TIME
IN A DIFFERENT LOCATION]

EXTERIOR OF LOCATION: SINAI PENINSULA,
EGYPT—NIGHT:
DAY 2: TIME: 23:24 PM (EET) Sinai Peninsula, Egypt—
26th January 2011

A hundred thousand stars and more are noticeable high up within the clear dark blue sky of the Sinai Peninsula. The Egyptian demonstrators are gathering together, mainly Bedouin tribal men. A quick glance up into the sky above by any eye would catch a glimpse of one thousand stars and more. One or two night fires ablaze from afar as well as the motorway lights across the borders of Israel, Jordan and the Kingdom of Saudi Arabia.

[MEANWHILE AT THE SAME TIME
IN A DIFFERENT LOCATION]

EXTERIOR OF LOCATION: TAHRIR SQUARE,
CAIRO, EGYPT—NIGHT:
DAY 2: TIME: 23:25 PM (EET)—26th January 2011

Major skirmishes commence as the demonstrators continue to chant in Liberation Square while some battle on-coming riot police in one-on-one fights. The CROWD CHANTING
"Down with the regime. Down with the Regime." and "(???????Must fill it in????????????)" continues as the sound of the crowd intensifies.

[MEANWHILE AT THE SAME TIME
IN A DIFFERENT LOCATION]

INSIDE OF LOCATION; MN80M-THE AMAZING
ONE/MALE APARTMENT, LONDON, ENGLAND;
NIGHT:
DAY 2:

MN80M-THE AMAZING ONE/MALE is in his living room watching TV and smoking roll up cigarettes as usual while the TV news is on low in the background.
"News! News! News! Why the hell am I watching this news for . . . My people are fighting, and I am just watching like the rest of the world from outside, what in God's name man, M. Sort it out . . . ." he said to himself.

[MEANWHILE AT THE SAME TIME
IN A DIFFERENT LOCATION]

EXTERIOR OF LOCATION: TAHRIR SQUARE,
CAIRO, EGYPT—
NIGHT: DAY 2: TIME: 23:25 PM (EET)
26th January
2011

Skirmishes commence as the demonstrators continue to chant in Liberation Square while thousands are now in battle with more of the on-coming riot police. MN80M-ALI and his 12 ASSOCIATES are standing chanting war songs as they watch safely from one side of the square anticipating the moment they desire to move in as the CROWD CHANTING

"(???????Must fill it in????????????) In-front of them continues. Many screams are heard as well as the RIOT POLICE in Arabic shouting,

"Move back. Move back. Move back." the police said towards the CROWD CHANTING that now intensifies, "Down with the regime. Down with the regime." and "(???????Must fill it in????????????)" the crowd shouted back. Riot police fire into the crowd using double barrel shot—guns loaded with tear gas while other police start to force back the crowds. The CROWD CHANTING "(???????Must fill it in????????????)" continues as the RIOT POLICE also continue to shout louder in Arabic,

"Move back. Move back. Move back." the RIOT POLICE said.

The defiant youthful Egyptian crowd filled with thousands of Egyptian young men and women remain standing firmly as the CROWD CHANTING

"Down with the regime. Down with the regime . . ." continues louder, and louder, and louder.

MN-80 M. THE SPECIAL ONE/FEMALE is noticeable in a battle mode among her 12 FEMALE ASSOCIATES against riot police from the bridge. MN-80 M. THE SPE—CIAL ONE/FEMALE quickly takes out her sling-shot and the special space pouch from her lower side MN80M-FEMALE-URBAN-COMBAT-TROUSER pocket filled with MN80M-SPECIAL MARBLES, some of these objects look to the human eye like small pebbles or ground rocks, she loads them into her sling-shot, pulls back, then let's go quickly, allowing the marbles to be released rapid out towards the direction of the riot police.

CHAPTER SEVEN

104a: Manhood . . .

INSIDE OF LOCATION; MN80M's APARTMENT
DAY 3: 27th January 2011—
London England

MN80M-THE AMAZING ONE/MALE is just waking up in his double queen sized bed and switches on the television. The TV news continues on low in back—ground as MN80M moves around slowly in the bed and smiles before he says in English,

"In the name of God." he said and then lowers the volume on the television. MN80M's face is still as he continues speaking out in mind,

"I think I need a cup of tea before I wash and pray." he said as the TV NEWS BROADCASTER from TV can be heard saying,

"Current unrest continues in Egypt. The presidential candidate has been arrested within 24hrs of arrival into Cairo by the police." said the news broadcaster.

MN80M THE AMAZING ONE/MALE looks up in surprise,

"Whaaaaaaaat! Bully tactics by the government. That isn't right at all. What happened to freedom of speech? I know he could have been considered to be throwing fumes to the already flamed situation by just travelling there in rally of his campaign, but come on now . . ." MN80Msaid as he highers the volume on the TV.

[MEANWHILE AT THE SAME TIME
IN A DIFFERENT LOCATION]

EXTERIOR OF LOCATION: TAHRIR SQUARE,
CAIRO, EGYPT—
DAY 3: 27th January 2011

The morning air filled with anger and continuing rage as more skirmishes commence while the demonstrators continue to chant in Liberation Square. The police continue to fire tear gas into the CHANTING CROWD.
"The people and the army are one hand." The People and the Army are one hand.
The People, and the Army, are one hand. The People and the Army are one hand." is shouted out loud.

[MEANWHILE AT THE SAME TIME
IN A DIFFERENT LOCATION]

INSIDE OF LOCATION; MN80M APARTMENT,
LONDON, ENGLAND;

MN80M continues with what he was doing and looks up to listen and watch the news broadcast on the television.

As the TV NEWS BROADCASTER continues moving around on the screen, now speaking live from Cairo,

"The fighting has truly broken out over night in several locations. Many casualties and some reports of death, this is a day Egypt has not seen in a very long time." said the news correspondent.

The TV shows images of fighting, and unrest as the UK TV NEWS BROADCASTER continues asking questions from the London studios,

"So could you tell us then? How is your situation there in Cairo, are you safe?" said the UK TV NEWS BROADCASTER.

MN80M-THE AMAZING ONE/MALE higher s the volume on the TV eagerly awaiting the next words from the TV NEWS BROADCASTER based now in Cairo.

"For this moment in time, yes I am safe, but we are still unsure what may come. The best of the best in the media are being sent to Cairo daily to report on this uprising, and once we have more information, we will surely delivery this to you all. Back to you in the studio." said the TV NEWS BROADCASTER.

MN80M lowers the volume on the Television to a level that he can hear himself speak more comfortably.

"God, you see what I mean. What chance does anyone have, if the presidential candidate has already been arrested within 24 hours of arrival, plus, like they said, they are sending the best of the best to report on matters." he said while shaking his head from side to side as he continues to express his deepest emotions and thoughts to himself.

"I have my own fights to deal with in regards to Egypt. This is not my fight any more. It is not their fight either with Masr, but still, this is not my fight. They already apparently have enough special ones, especially with nearly Eighty million

Humans alive in that country. This is not my fight." he said again, but this time MN80Mshakes his head from side to side with his lips now tightly together and whispers.

"This is not my fight." he said again whispering twice.

MN80Mswitches off the TV and stands up and then says in mind,

"I . . . I have to pray."

[MEANWHILE AT THE SAME TIME IN A DIFFERENT LOCATION]

EXTERIOR OF LOCATION: TAHRIR SQUARE, CAIRO, EGYPT— DAY 3: 27th January 2011—Cairo, Egypt—Day 3

Dozens of helicopters continue passing above in the sky, many of those remaining in the air as the skirmishes commence while the demonstrators continue to chant in Liberation Square while police continue to fire tear gas into the crowd. The CROWD CHANTING,

"Down with the regime, down with the regime . . ." continues to be said by the Egyptian crowd as the Egyptian riot police commence battle with thousands of the Egyptian demonstrators, both male, and female civilians, and many of those innocent by-standers.

A FEMALE NEWS REPORTER can be noticed within the crowd speaking/corresponding via her phone,

"Yes this is true, right now police are hitting civilians with weapons, and we are not sure what this outcome shall be more than the bloodshed we have seen. The people are now chanting 'Down with the regime, down with the regime.'

also MN-80—THE EG PRESIDENT 1's pictures have been torn down from the streets of Cairo. I hope to be able to get back to you all very soon with an update, back to you in the studios." She said in a broken tone English as the sounds of the CROWD CHANTING behind her intensifies.

[MEANWHILE AT THE SAME TIME
IN A DIFFERENT LOCATION]

EXTERIOR OF LOCATION; STREET,
LONDON, ENGLAND;
DAY 3:

MN80M. THE AMAZING ONE/MALE is walking on route to MN80M-UK-TEDDY-BEAR HOME. As MN80M continues to walk, he is in conversation via the secret MN8E-PAD and passing in and out through/past many commuters that just came out of the train station. Hay! It's MN80-M. Are you home? Ok. I need to speak to you today, so expect me to pass round, is that ok?? Ok, just dealing with few things with MN80M-UK-TEDDY-BEAR for days now. Yeah sure, ok, no!, no!, no!, I don't' touch snow or any heavy drugs, you of all people know that, but even though they got him on lock down, he still gets things into him, I don't know how a Teddy-Bear can smoke, but he has cut down big time, I'm doing best to help him too, as nicotine is my killer, even he keeps telling me I smoke too many cigarettes, and tobacco roll ups, and that's from a legendary smoker. Ha-ha-ha. Have to laugh, anyway, let me sort this out, and then I am on my way to you silently so we can arrange the mission plans, is that ok. Ok then. See you soon Insha Allah." MN80M. said as he places the MN8E-PAD back into his pocket and continues to walk and starts to say to himself in mind,

"I have to think this through, and today, not tomorrow. God what can I do? God, what can I do?" he said to himself as he passes an ATM machine and walks over to check his balance. MN80-M places his card into the machine; he shakes his head slightly from left to right, presses a button, and then takes his card out of the machine with some cash.

"Even if I wanted to go now, how can I when I don't even have enough to go to Egypt properly? And you know I am not allowed to use certain skills." he said to himself as he now continues to walk in the direction he was originally heading.

[MEANWHILE AT THE SAME TIME
IN A DIFFERENT LOCATION]

INSIDE LOCATION; AN EG MINISTRY 1
AUTHORITY HEAD OFFICE, CAIRO, EGYPT:
DAY 3:

A group of nearly fifty high ranking Egyptian specialists/ individuals are conversing around a very large round table without the minister. The FEMALE (50's) SENIOR EG MINISTRY 1 CONSULTANT speaks out in English, "Good morning everyone. As you all know . . . ." she said while drinking her coffee. "Today is another major day for us all in Egypt." she said again as she completed her sentence while taking another quick sip of her coffee, only this time, more of a longer gulp than a sip.

The table in the middle has a brilliant shine beaming off from the black color of the granite specially cut for the EG MINISTRY meeting rooms only. The high ranking Egyptian officials smile as they are nodding in agreement among one another and some now start to pour some of the hot tea from the metal containers, one container placed in-front of them, with a small empty plate next to some other more larger plates with several of the croissants and fresh Egyptian pastry placed neatly on. The atmosphere is not as tense as prior occasions, as if now everyone has more of a direction to focus on, more of a passion as one team working towards the greater-good. Everybody in the room continue to look at one another, this all being in a brief moment of silence as they all eat slowly the pastry and cakes while drinking the fresh Indian tea.

[MEANWHILE IN A DIFFERENT LOCATION]

INSIDE OF LOCATION: LONDON, ENGLAND, MN80M-UK-TEDDY-BEAR HOME; DAY 3: TIME: Unknown

MN80M-THE AMAZING ONE/MALE is sitting down on a half broken four legged chair in conversation with MN80M-UK-TEDDY-BEAR.
"MN80M why are you looking all stressed for? Just go out there. You got a job offer now; you have a valid reason, plus can make good money. So go." he said in a semi-sarcastic way as MN80M—THE AMAZING ONE/ MALE responds with,
"Yeah, but it is not about that is it!?!" MN80-M said.
"So what is it about then??" his friend says back suddenly.
A long moment of silence passes as MN80-M lifts his head to say, "Something bigger than we know is going on here. And on top of it all, even if I was able to, things could get nasty for my sister and others too. No one knows how this will turn out do they?" said MN80M
MN80M-UK-TEDDY-BEAR double looks at him before looking back in a more serious face asking,

"But how can this be a problem for her?" he said. MN80M smiles responding,

"Egypt is different to any country, and not saying I would make trouble, as just like most may do, I too want change for Egypt. And today this change, not tomorrow. But things can swing both ways here, and no one knows what is happening apart from probably a few. Trust me, I know what I say is true." MN80-M said with a smile, as they look at each other.

"Yeah but M, Look at you now you had a lot in Egypt and who stopped that!??! Money and the system, all the red tape you had to cut through drained you. And then with all the family issues that they did to you last year and more. They taking liberties" said MN80M-UK-TEDDY-BEAR.

"I know . . . I know . . . But without any money, how can I go?" MN80M-THE AMAZING ONE/ MALE said as he lifts his head up awaiting a response.

"If you want to find a way, you will find a way M."

"I know I will . . . I know . . ." MN80M—THE AMAZING ONE/MALE responded again, only this time in a much lower subtle tone and also nods his head in agreement.

A long pause of silence as the television sound starts to increase and MN80M-UK-TEDDY-BEAR presses the button on the remote control quickly, and then says out loud,

"So what you going to do MN80M?" he said with a smile on his face. MN80M—THE AMAZING ONE/MALE smiles back as he takes in a deep breath,

"God knows . . . God knows." MN80-M said.

[MEANWHILE IN A DIFFERENT LOCATION]

INSIDE LOCATION; AN EG MINISTRY 1
AUTHORITY HEAD OFFICE, CAIRO, EGYPT;
DAY 3:

A group of nearly fifty high ranking Egyptian specialists/
individuals continue in conversation. The FEMALE (50's)
SENIOR EG MINISTRY CONSULTANT 1 leading this
team in particular speaks out in English,
"So is everyone clear now on our assignments?" she said. The
group of specialists all simultaneously keeps nodding heads in
agreement at what is said and/or being asked. The FEMALE
(50's) SENIOR EG MINISTRY CONSULTANT 1 smiles
"Feel free to eat any and all fresh pastry and beverages here,
as well as any of the food in the other room ok. Bonne
Appetite." she said in English. The groups of specialists all
continue as they were.

[MEANWHILE AT THE SAME TIME
IN A DIFFERENT LOCATION]

INSIDE OF LOCATION; LONDON, ENGLAND,
MN80M-UK-TEDDY-BEAR HOME; DAY 3:
TIME: Unknown

MN80M THE AMAZING ONE/MALE continues conversation with MN80M-UK-TEDDY-BEAR as the TV
sounds continue in background.
"MN80M look at the news. Things kicking off big time."
said MN80M-UK-TEDDY-BEAR.
MN80M THE AMAZING ONE/MALE looks on towards
the television screen,

"I know. And look at this reporter, he is an unknown. I am telling you, they need people to report the news with better English. We at-least need a pure hearted Arabic Egyptian best-of-the-best correspondent that can do this job, that's all it is really. But like I said yesterday, they do not want me to say things the way I see them, they want to design the reports and control the correspondent. And as we all know, we cannot fight the media, they too strong apparently." MN80-M said.

MN80M-UK-TEDDY-BEAR looks up from his position to respond saying,

"M. You could be making more money than you know bro. What are you waiting for?" he said as he stares awaiting MN80M-THE AMAZING ONE/ MALE response of,

"It's not about the money though is it, not to me anyway." Said MN80M

MN80M-UK-TEDDY-BEAR stands up saying, "M. Stop making excuses." The Teddy-Bear says and continues to walk towards the mini kitchen area.

"Who said I am making excuses." MN80-M responded back to him as MN80M-UK-TEDDY-BEAR opens the fridge door and takes out a canned drink while picking up an empty glass from the sink area and walking back through the smoke filled air to his seated position. "M. It is Thursday now yeah. This all started when?"

MN80M THE AMAZING ONE/MALE looks at his hands as if counting on his fingers, and then says, "Tuesday the 25th of January 2011" said MN80M

MN80M-UK-TEDDY-BEAR sits down with drink in hand,

"Exactly!" he said.

"So what is your point Teddy?!" MN80-M asked.

MN80M-UK-TEDDY-BEAR smiles, "M. Is it more than that?"

"What do you mean?" MN80-M said in a curious asking tone.

"I think I know what it is with you M."

MN80M-THE AMAZING ONE/MALE eyes and mouth sort of come together in a scrunched up position, eagerly waiting to respond to the next words after asking,

"What do you think it is then?"

MN80M-UK-TEDDY-BEAR smiles and says back,

"Is it what happened last year? and how family members are dealing with things?"

MN80M THE AMAZING ONE/MALE lowers his head as MN80M-UK-TEDDY-BEAR persists asking, "It is, right!"

MN80M raises his head saying,

"Not really." he said in a kind of low tone childish kind of way.

"Don't lie M. I have known you for like how many years. And even if I have not seen you for most of it, I saw you most of last year, and things were difficult for you, especially when you found out what happened over there in Egypt." Said the MN80M-UK-TEDDY-BEAR.

MN80M lowers his head and then raises his head to say, "Look yeah. You and I know what I said happened. And yes, I still feel sick from everything. Especially not having any money to go back out there, and even when I do, I still need money. Egypt is a pay off with everything and anything. And dependent on the level you want to be on, you pay, you play. Simple." MN80-M said as if letting it all out in one breath.

"So you need a crew out there too. How are your contacts out there?" asked MN80M-UK-TEDDY-BEAR.

"I have my own links to do enough. But still, money is needed to get around and do things. Taxi's here and there."

MN80M. said as he nods his head in agreement to a silent pause as if both in contemplation mode for a brief moment before MN80M-UK-TEDDY-BEAR says,

"MN-80 M. You are just making excuses." he said in a bitter tone.

MN80M—THE AMAZING ONE/MALE in a jumpy way while moving around responds quickly with,

"How?" as MN80M-UK-TEDDY-BEAR moves his seated position slightly closer towards the television saying,

"Right now M, to get to Egypt, what do you need? Ticket?" he said aggressively.

MN80M THE AMAZING ONE/MALE remains still for a moment then responds with,

"Naaaa, I said I got that mate remember. My return ticket from when I came last year. And tried to use it in August but could not pay the £400 (Airline) was asking."

MN80M-UK-TEDDY-BEAR takes a gulp of his drink twice as he listens and then another gulp before asking,

"So what do you need now M." he said while placing the can down next to his side.

MN80M THE AMAZING ONE/MALE looks back and forth,

"What!?! Apart from me just wanting to go regardless of how to get there or not . . . Well . . . Basically, some more money to get to Heathrow Airport and some with me in case they ask me to pay an extra fee. I just more-or-less took out my last change from the bank. And to be honest, with all going on now, I think I need to get a proper smoke." MN80-M said as he sits back in the chair with his shoulders and back now straightened.

MN80M-UK-TEDDY-BEAR looks at him asking, "What type of smoke.? Your smoke or my smoke?" he said.

"Smoke. Smoke. Some green." MN80-M said back as MN80M-UK-TEDDY-BEAR laughs out loud twice, "But M. You need that change your saying to get to the airport." he said while his laughter tone decreased. MN80M responds,

"I think you and I know you need more than £10 or £20." he said as he scratches his head twice as both remain silent for a moment until MN80M-UK-TEDDY-BEAR continues; "So what are you going to do now?" MN80M smiles at the question, looks around, then answers,

"Nothing. I'm going to get a smoke, and go home. I already did my food shopping, and this is my life now, not Egypt anymore." he said as he moved back slowly.

MN80M-UK-TEDDY-BEAR lowers his head at hearing this response, but then decides to ask,

"Have you called him for a ting yet?" he said while raising his head to hear a response from MN80M—THE AMAZING ONE/MALE, yet he too shakes his head sideways in disagreement saying,

"No, not yet . . . I am about to do that now." said MN80M as he takes his ordinary phone out of his pocket and presses a couple of buttons. MN80M-UK-TEDDY-BEAR raises his head out of curiosity listening to MN80M-THE AMAZING ONE/MALE speak on the phone,

"Hello . . . yea its M. you live.?? OK. where about exactly? OK. see you then."

MN80M-UK-TEDDY-BEAR looks back at the television and then back to ask,

"What did he say?"

MN80M THE AMAZING ONE/MALE responds with, "She actually."

Both smile as the atmosphere all of a sudden seems more at ease. MN80M-UK-TEDDY-BEAR laughs responding sarcastically,

"She then."

MN80M continues to smile,

"She said come now if I want to green of strong hashish to smoke. She is at home, I may go over to see my soul sister 2 as her little ones asked me for some advice about film-making, and I think other sister and niece may be there, maybe both my sisters and my nephew may be staying there also, so I want to see them to make sure family is ok. So let me go and get this thing and come back to you later possibly if I can, all I do these days is smoke nicotine it is killing me, and I am doing best to stop smoking any green cannabis or strong hashish, you of all creations know that is all I smoke, I do not take any snow of class A illegal drugs, but this nicotine is a killer. Smoking one or two 20 packs a day is sickening, I have tried to stop, you know, cold turkey and stay without any cigarettes for days to weeks on end, many times this past year already, does not work, and I hope this year or next I can stop smoking in general, smoking kills, and I am supposed to be a role model, but, until then, I am addicted to nicotine, and the MN80M-SPECIAL SWEETS. Those I should be eating more of instead of smoking roll up tobacco and cigarettes, and to be honest, this Egypt issues I just want to forget." said MN80M.

"Go on then. I'm not going anywhere." MN80M-UK-TEDDY-BEAR said while making louder the volume on the TV news broadcast as MN80M then stands up and puts his jacket on before exiting the door.

The News correspondent commences speaking about Cairo, Egypt. MN80M exits the door.

[MEANWHILE AT THE SAME TIME
IN A DIFFERENT LOCATION]

EXTERIOR OF LOCATION; TAHRIR SQUARE,
CAIRO, EGYPT—
DAY 3: 27th January 2011—Tahrir, Cairo

Several explosions erupt in unknown locations yet close to the square. The sounds of dozens of helicopters above in the sky has increased as some commando helicopters appear and soldiers start jumping out onto the rope and down towards the skirmishes that continue. The crowds of thousands are running for their lives on one of the bridges leading into Liberation Square. Many thousands remain within and around certain parts of Tahrir Square, also known as Liberation Square. The now demanding and fuming Egyptian men and women within the square continue with others as the CROWD CHANTING "Down with the regime." and "(???Must fill in???) Continues as dozens of Police vehicles surround the bridge and force back thousands of civilians with water cannons, while hundreds of other people go down to pray on the floor with the water cannons persisting on them all to retreat. Hundreds remain standing and/or praying as they are.

[MEANWHILE AT THE SAME TIME
IN A DIFFERENT LOCATION]

EXTERIOR OF LOCATION; STREET, LONDON,
ENGLAND;
DAY 3 : 27th January 2011—London England

MN80M THE AMAZING ONE/MALE continues walking towards a house door on a somewhat peaceful street having only a few cars pass along up and down the road. As MN80-M approaches, he presses the white button and the door bell rings.

[MEANWHILE AT THE SAME TIME
IN A DIFFERENT LOCATION]

EXTERIOR OF LOCATION; TAHRIR SQUARE,
CAIRO, EGYPT—
DAY 3: 27th January 2011—Tahrir, Cairo

Skirmishes continue as the majority of the crowd is running for their lives while a couple of hundred brave Egyptian men continue to stand and/or pray on the bridge floor. MN80M-ALI is noticeable running fast past those running away from all the chaos towards the mayhem near those praying as hundreds of others continue with the main CROWD CHANTING, "(???????Must fill it in????????????)" continuing to intensify. The Police trucks surround the bridge and continue to force civilians back with water cannons. Several men can be seen running towards the water, yet an unnoticed female also stands her ground from afar, watching as the water cannons continue to pour out onto the Hundreds of men praying on the floor in an attempt to deter the police truck crossing over the bridge.

[MEANWHILE AT THE SAME TIME
IN A DIFFERENT LOCATION]

EXTERIOR OF LOCATION;
UNKNOWN HOUSE/ STREET,
DAY 3:—TIME: Unknown 27th January 2011—
London England

MN80M THE AMAZING ONE/MALE walks out from the house front-door and continues to walk towards the street and then turns right.

[MEANWHILE AT THE SAME TIME
IN A DIFFERENT LOCATION]

EXTERIOR OF LOCATION: TAHRIR SQUARE,
CAIRO, EGYPT—
DAY: 3: 27th January 2011—Cairo, Egypt

Skirmishes continue. The sounds of hundreds of screams can be heard simultaneously as thousands of others remain standing chanting, while hundreds are in battle as the Police trucks surround the bridge now assisted by a dozen of the EG Army tanks and continue to force civilians back with water cannons.

[MEANWHILE AT THE SAME TIME
IN A DIFFERENT LOCATION]

EXTERIOR OF LOCATION: BUS STOP/STREET,
LONDON, ENGLAND;

MN80M-THE AMAZING ONE/MALE is about to board a London bus allowing a few other individuals in front of him to board. MN80-M looks at the time on his phone and then up towards the sky before boarding the bus.

[MEANWHILE AT THE SAME TIME
IN A DIFFERENT LOCATION]

EXTERIOR OF LOCATION:. TAHRIR SQUARE, CAIRO, EGYPT

Skirmishes continue. MN80M-ALI and his 12 ASSO—CIATES are caught up within the battles as the CROWD CHANTING
"Down with the regime." and "(???Must fill in???) continues.

[MEANWHILE AT THE SAME TIME IN A DIFFERENT LOCATION]

INSIDE OF LOCATION: BUS, LONDON, ENGLAND;

MN80M is sitting on the bus looking out the window.

[MEANWHILE AT THE SAME TIME IN A DIFFERENT LOCATION]

EXTERIOR OF LOCATION: TAHRIR SQUARE, CAIRO, EGYPT

Skirmishes continue as the hundreds of people are running in different directions as thousands remain with the CROWD CHANTING,
"Down with the regime." and "(???Must fill in???) continuing to intensify with the heat of the day rising tension between all sides.

[MEANWHILE AT THE SAME TIME IN A DIFFERENT LOCATION]

EXTERIOR OF LOCATION: STREET,
LONDON, ENGLAND;

MN80M-THE AMAZING ONE/MALE is walking and turns a corner street to then walk an additional distance until he reaches MN80M SISTER N house located on the corner of a cross junction at the back roads behind one of the main roads and not that far from one of London's polluted air motorways. MN80M-THE AMAZING ONE/MALE walks to the front gate opening the latch on the wooden door-frame and walking on through making sure to close appropriately behind him the gate for karma reasons, and then moves on and knocks the main door three times. MN80M SISTER N voice sounds in the air out loud,

"Who is it?" she said.

MN80M THE AMAZING ONE/MALE

Takes two steps back saying, "It's me. MN80M."

The door opens and MN80M SISTER N says,

"MN80M is here." with a smile on her face an follows with, "Hi MN80M welcome, come in."

MN80M THE AMAZING ONE/MALE walks into the hallway past the front door allowing her to close,

"hi Sister, how are you? Are you ok?"

Both greet with cheek to cheek as MN80M walks into the house.

[MEANWHILE AT THE SAME TIME
IN A DIFFERENT LOCATION]

INSIDE LOCATION; AN EG MINISTRY 1
AUTHORITY HEAD OFFICE, CAIRO, EGYPT;

A group of consultants have remained behind after work hours to continue to support other individual assignments. The very large entrée tables are filled with exquisite snacks as well as pastries and hot beverages. The consultants come and go as they converse in a more relaxed and exciting environment.

[MEANWHILE AT THE SAME TIME
IN A DIFFERENT LOCATION]

INSIDE OF LOCATION; MN80M SISTER N HOME,
LONDON, ENGLAND; DAY 3:—TIME: Unknown
27th January 2011

MN80M-THE AMAZING ONE/MALE sit—ting on a chair at the dinner table is in conversation with his sister. The TV sounds low as MN80-M. SISTER N asks.

"So have you been watching the news MN-80—M.?" she said.

"Of-course I have. Who hasn't?" MN80M said as he smiles, allowing MN80M-SISTER N to continue on asking questions as if in a marathon and/or just a general desire to be kept up to date with any knowledge required. Some in the family have been known to know of her like one of the eldest elderly aunts, very short lady, that asks a million and one questions, and keeps all the antiques in life piled up like junk for no reason, as if a shrine, or maybe they have their own reasons that others do not understand.

"So what about our sister?" she says to MN80M-THE AMAZING ONE/MALE response of, "What about her?" he says, while taking in a deep breath looking at MN80M SISTER N for her reply.

"Her job . . . She just got it. What happens if the MN-80-
—THE EG PRESIDENT 1 leaves? Does everyone that has
a job in the government leave?" she asked passionately.

"I don't know. But if I was voting, I would want everyone
out. At least the main ones, and his or her close associates.
Otherwise everything remains the same for Egypt." he
said. MN80M smiles as he finishes his sentence, looking at
MN80M SISTER N as she looks at him in a moment of
silence before saying,

"Yeah but what's that got to do with our sister." she asked
again.

"I do not know what is happening. Or what can happen.
God knows." said MN80-M in a quick response as if to end
the questioning.

A moment of silence comes about as they look at the Television and then back at one another as if searching for the
words to say.

"Did you manage to buy any weed/cannabis? My boy is
not here; he went to spend time playing computer games
at soul sister 2 home to have fun, at-least we won't have to
smoke in the kitchen or outside. I'm going there later if you
want to come, we might spend the night." said MN80-M.
SISTER N. as MN80M THE AMAZING ONE/MALE
smiles again and says,

"Yeah, I just got some now. A quarter." he said with a massive
smile.

"Of-what? Green.?" she says and then smiles.

MN80M THE AMAZING smiles back saying,

"No. Not green. I got some strong-hashish for a change."

MN80M. pulls out a small zippy bag containing a small piece
of cannabis resin/hashish and continues saying, "Here You can
roll one if you like." while offering the mini bag with an even
bigger smile. MN80M SISTER N laughs,

"I already got high-grade weed earlier. It's in that box next to my marble pouch. Grab it for me please. The Rizla is in there too." she abruptly remarks as MN80Mpulls the small wooden box closer to them both.

"Here you go my sister." he said.

Both MN80M SISTER N and MN80M-THE AMAZING ONE/MALE take a sheet of Rizla and start to roll a joint each while continuing the conversation.

{EMPATHY LEVELS INCREASE}}

MN80M SISTER N puts her shoulder back and straightens her back as she says,

"Wow. This one is not easy to get. I have not had a smoke in ages." she said with a smile.

MN80M continues as is,

"Yeah, well I wanted a change, and all this going on in Egypt has my mind consumed. So I want to smoke."

MN80M SISTER N moves her chair closer to the table saying,

"Just forget about it. Nothing you can do M."

MN80M THE AMAZING ONE/MALE looks up at her with the same youthful face as when they were children,

"Yeah. I guess you are right. Nothing I can do." he said.

MN80Mlooks towards the TV as he and MN80M SISTER N continue to roll a joint.

[MEANWHILE AT THE SAME TIME
IN A DIFFERENT LOCATION]

INSIDE LOCATION; AN EG MINISTRY 1
AUTHORITY HEAD OFFICE, CAIRO, EGYPT;
DAY 3: NIGHT: 27th January 2011

Group of consultants continue with the individual assignments. MN80M SISTER F is in conversation with AN EG ASSOCIATE 1 next to the window overlooking the main street. MN80M SISTER F moves in closer to not have to speak loudly in Arabic.

"Do you think things will get worse than this?" she said. "Yes, unfortunately, of-course this will. Look at how earlier the fighting broke out along the bridge. Women were even bleeding severely." responded the EG ASSOCIATE 1.

MN80M SISTER F and AN EG ASSOCI—ATE 1 have a shock look on faces as they both look at each other and MN80M SISTER F asks in her Arabic,

"This is starting to get out of hand now. And I think my brother might be coming from London." she said as she takes in a short breath awaiting a response.

AN EG ASSOCIATE 1 responds in English, "Really, why?" she said.

MN80M SISTER F answer back in English saying,

"I am not sure exactly. But he did receive an offer from the media to be an extra news correspondent if and when required." said MN80M SISTER F as she wipes her forehead with a tissue.

"Really. That is interesting." AN EG ASSOCIATE 1 said as she places her hand on her chin slowly, now listening to MN80M SISTER F continue,

"So far he did not accept the offer, as he says they are only wanting people to report the way they want to, and not the truth in other ways." said MN80M SISTER F.

AN EG ASSOCIATE 1 continues listening while doing best not to keep eyes away for too long from the event taking place outside the window,

"Yes, that is always the way the media is though."

"Yeah, I guess so." said MN80M SISTER F. "Look . . . Look there. Police are fighting with civilians. Quickly, look." AN EG ASSOCIATE 1 said louder than her normal tone and now with left arm raised pointing out of the window, and MN80M SISTER F looking out of the window half sticking her head out to see in more detail that which happening exactly.

[MEANWHILE AT THE SAME TIME
IN A DIFFERENT LOCATION]

EXTERIOR OF LOCATION; STREET,
CAIRO, EGYPT:
NIGHT;

The Egyptian riot police are in battle with thousands of civilians on the street, while mini-police trucks and some mini EG ARMY tanks are noticeable spraying water out of cannons onto the demonstrators. MN80M EMPATHY TARGET NUMBER 4 is seen amongst the crowds wet as she stands strong. The sounds of water cannons and shouting continues aloud as some of the mini tanks are moving around the demonstrators in an attempt to block them all within one area. MN80M EMPATHY TARGET NUMBER 4 is trying to speak on her phone, shouting as the water sounds greater than her voice, "Yes, I can confirm. The police are forcing their way through the demonstration crowds smashing people's heads open with batons. The water cannons are pushing people back by force and the fighting continues." she said while reporting live on air via her mobile telephone.

The water comes gushing out from the mini-army tank past the Female News Reporter and others around her while police move in closer to MN-80 M. EMPATHY TARGET 4 while individuals close to her are beaten heavily. She speaks out again while on the phone,

"The police are beating us now, right next to me. I have to go now. Back to you all in the studios." she shouted out. MN-80 M. EMPATHY TARGET 4 presses a button on her phone, places it into her pocket quickly and then starts to run back fast away from all the crowd.

[MEANWHILE AT THE SAME TIME IN A DIFFERENT LOCATION]

INSIDE OF LOCATION; MN80M SISTER N HOME, LONDON, ENGLAND; NIGHT;

MN80M-THE AMAZING ONE/MALE is sitting on the chair next to the dinner table in conversation with MN80M SISTER N while MN-80—M. NEPHEW 1 has just walked in the door moments ago and rushes in to quickly watch television in the room joined with open doors. The TV sounds in background. MN80M—THE AMAZING ONE/ MALE smiles,

"I think I better get going now ok" he said.

MN80M SISTER N looks on saying, "You going home then?" as MN80M-THE AMAZING ONE/MALE responds with,

"Yeah. But maybe go to my friends first." he said while scratching his ear.

"Which one?" she asks.

"The one that lives just down the road, not far from here . . ." MN80M said as he stands up and picks up his jacket before he puts his MN80M-WOOLEN-HAT on his head and his MN80-M-SCARF around his neck and shoulders.

MN80M SISTER N smiles as she says,

"Oh, OK." she said sarcastically.

MN80M with jacket now on, makes way to the door, "No seriously, may pass there quickly then home. Anyway. Ok then. See you soon ok Insha Allah." he said.

MN80M SISTER N stands saying out loud,

"Say good night to your uncle"

NEPHEW walks towards them from the other room and speaks,

"Good night Uncle. Here, take this from me. You may be able to use them before I do." said MN80M NEPHEW 1 with a cheeky smile.

MN80M accepts the bag filled with cold

Marbles. MN80M greets both with a knuckle fist to fist with his nephew, and then cheek to cheek with his sister.

"See you soon then Insha Allah." MN80M said as he opens the door and departs.

[MEANWHILE AT THE SAME TIME IN A DIFFERENT LOCATION]

EXTERIOR OF LOCATION; STREET,
ALEXANDRIA, EGYPT:
NIGHT; 27th January 2011—
Alexandria, Egypt—Day 3

The Mediterranean Sea waves are crashing along the shore line from the major gust of wind moving south. Dozens of helicopters are in the sky as the Egyptian riot police are in battle with civilians on the streets of Alexandria, northern Egypt near the sea shore a few hundred meters north of the new futuristic Alexandria Museum. The sounds of water cannons and shouting are heard as more mini tanks are moving

around the demonstrators to create a border. The CROWD CHANTING,
"Down with the regime." and "(???Must fill in???) continues as the riot police are shooting rubber pellets into the crowd, as well as storming through with batons smashing on heads and body of any and all civilians standing.
Hundreds of civilians clash with riot police in a fierce manner as the CROWD CHANTING
"Down with the regime." And "(??Must fill in??)
Continues

[MEANWHILE AT THE SAME TIME
IN A DIFFERENT LOCATION]

EXTERIOR OF LOCATION; STREET,
LONDON, ENGLAND;
NIGHT; 27th January 2011—Day 3

MN80M-THE AMAZING ONE/MALE is walking along the street and crosses the first road and then waits for the signal to change as several cars pass before he crosses the secondary road. The green man/light signal starts flashing and MN80M-THE AMAZING ONE/MALE then crosses the road.

[MEANWHILE AT THE SAME TIME
IN A DIFFERENT LOCATION]

EXTERIOR OF LOCATION; STREET,
ALEXANDRIA, EGYPT:
NIGHT; 27th January 2011—
Alexandria, Egypt—Day 3

The Egyptian riot police continue in battle with civilians on the streets of Alexandria, Northern Egypt near the sea shore. The CROWD CHANTING, "Down with the regime. Down with the regime . . ." intensifies as does the anger from thousands more brave young Egyptians that come out of their home pouring onto the streets like the sea onto the shores, all in protest of the present day Government/Regime to step-down.

[MEANWHILE AT THE SAME TIME
IN A DIFFERENT LOCATION]

EXTERIOR OF LOCATION; MOUNTAIN AREA,
SINAI PENINSULA, EGYPT;
NIGHT; 27th January 2011—
Sinai, Egypt—Day 3

The Bedouin team up together with weapons in arms and jump into open back Jeeps, north towards the border crossing with Israel, and nation of Jordan. Thousands of stars remain in the sky as the Jeeps wheel-spin off towards the cemented road.

[MEANWHILE AT THE SAME TIME
IN A DIFFERENT LOCATION]

EXTERIOR OF LOCATION; STREET,
LONDON, ENGLAND;
NIGHT:

MN80M-THE AMAZING ONE/MALE is walking on route MN80M-UK-TEDDY-BEAR's HOME, he approaches the alleyway near MN80-M-STEPPING

STONE-MARBLE-AVENUE and walks towards and then rings the bell on the door. The Intercom sound buzzes and MN80-M walks in as the door buzzer sounds. MN80M walks through the winding corridors, up the spiral staircase, and through another door before reaching into the apartment of MN80M-UK-TEDDY-BEAR MN80M knocks on the door first, to hear a voice coming from behind the door within the room shouting out, "Come in, the door is open."

MN80M reaches for the door handle, opens the door and walks into the room filled with MN80M-UK-TEDDY-BEAR's 12 CHILDREN FRIENDS. The TV sounds in background as MN80M-UK-TEDDY-BEAR continues speaking and says before he asks,

"Ok now children, thanks for coming to visit MN80M-UK-TEDDY-BEAR today, you all have your assignments to show your mummy & daddies, now remember to come back for the next Outer-Space-Travel lessons next week ok. I have to speak with MN80M-THE AMAZING ONE/MALE right now about very important things." The 12 CHILDREN with massive smiles on their faces all smile, look at MN80M-THE AMAZING ONE/MALE, and walk out of the room silently.

MN80M-UK-TEDDY-BEAR waves them good bye, and then asks MN80M,

"Have you been watching the news in the past hour?"

"No"

MN80M and MN80M-UK-TEDDY-BEAR connect fists again to greet.

{{EMPATHY LEVELS INCREASE}}

MN80M-UK-TEDDY-BEAR continues to lay down on his bed watching the television opposite while speaking, "There was one Egyptian yeah, and she was in the middle of the demonstration at night, and then all of a sudden they were under attack." he said with a smile.

MN80M THE AMAZING ONE/MALE continues to walk around taking small steps while saying, "What do you mean under attack?" he said.

MN80M then takes a seat while taking his MN80M-SPECIAL-WINTER-JACKET off. Pulls out his packet of cigarettes and rizla, with the zippy bag containing cannabis resin and starts to roll a spliff while listening to MN80M-UK-TEDDY-BEAR continue.

"Watch on TV, it's probably going to come on again I'm sure. A repeat. But basically, while she was talking, the army tank was using water cannons to force the people away, and men were standing in front of it. The riot police rushed in and started beating everyone." said his friend.

A quick moment of silence comes about while MN80M-THE AMAZING ONE/MALE continues to roll the spliff asking MN80M-UK-TEDDY-BEAR, "How was her English?" said MN80M

MN80M-UK-TEDDY-BEAR looks back,

"English . . . What do you mean?" he said as if not hearing the question properly.

MN80M THE AMAZING ONE/MALE smiles back saying,

"Yeah. How was her English? Was it broken? Or like us?" said MN80M

MN80M-UK-TEDDY-BEAR looks back at the television screen.

"Sounded more broken, but very good American English. Why?" he said and then looks back at MN80M.-THE AMAZING ONE/MALE.

"I have just been noticing that they don't really have any one reporting properly yet do they. Like come on now, look at this guy on the TV news now." said MN80M

MN80M points towards the TV. A brief pause as they both look eagerly towards the screen to gain focus.

MN80M THE AMAZING ONE/MALE continues,

"His eye brows all shaved down to try hide that which he really is, plus his English is not good. Which means what for the British News Channel?" he said in a kind of chauvinistic way.

MN80M and MN80M-UK-TEDDY-BEAR both look at each other.

MN80M-UK-TEDDY-BEAR nods his head saying, "They need reporters." while MN80M.-THE AMAZING also nodding his head says,

"Exactly"

MN80M-UK-TEDDY-BEAR lifts his arms in the air and shouts back saying,

"So what the fuck are you waiting for M?" he said and then places his arms back down.

MN80M and MN80M-UK-TEDDY-BEAR look at each other as MN80M responds with a quick breath out of air from his mouth as if a silent sigh, and then,

"Nothing. I'm going to roll a spliff and relax. Nothing I can do. I don't have enough money, and like I said, it's not my fight any more. Whatever family I have in Egypt, and friends, I wish them the best. But after what I have been through out there, and what they did while I was here, I am not sure I want to even see Egypt for a looong time. They needed change they think they want now, many years ago.

And all of a sudden, when things start to boil over the hot pan, everyone wants to get up and speak once and for all. So you know what!!?? Good for the Egyptian people, but for me, seriously, I have had enough, and even if I was to do something, I also have to think about my Sister and her job. Don't forget she only got her job like twelve months ago, after leaving here to go marry, work hard and live there for the past ten years. If I go in now to report as these companies here and abroad want me to, then I would either get arrested and detained, and/or she would get into trouble may be." MN80-M said as he then takes in a deep breath of air to regain back that energy from what he just said.

MN80M-UK-TEDDY-BEAR looks towards the Television while saying to himself in his mind in English, "Oh shut up M . . ." he said to himself.

The sounds of the Television continue is the only thing heard, as MN80M and MN80M-UK-TEDDY-BEAR then look at each other and laugh at the same time. MN80M finishes rolling the spliff and lights it up, and smokes while saying,

"No, seriously . . . I am not joking. And even after all anyone has done to me. I do not think it would be good for me to get involved with this on my terms, as things may turn bad, and guess who will be getting the blame for it all?" said MN80M

MN80M-UK-TEDDY-BEAR quickly says, "You." the pause turns into a moment of dull silence as MN80M THE AMAZING ONE/MALE nods his head in agreement saying,

"Exactly." he said.

MN80Mand Friend look at each other again with a serious face.

"But M, at the end of the day. You know where her heart is?" said his friend.

"Who?", said MN80M

"Your sister. Even if she works for the government, her heart is with who really."

MN80M and Teddy-Bear look at each other with a serious face as MN80M-UK-TEDDY-BEAR says,

"The people." to MN80M-THE AMAZING ONE/MALE same response of,

"The people".

"Exactly. So go do what you have to M.", MN80M-UK-TEDDY-BEAR said as he presses the button on the remote control to higher the volume on the TV.

MN80M continues to smoke as MN80M-UK-TEDDY-BEAR continues speaking in English,

"Look at the Television M. The MN-80—EG PRESIDENT 1 of Egypt is making a speech." he said in a rapid moment of excitement as the television sounds continue and MN80M.-THE AMAZING ONE says,

"I think it is a repeat. I heard rumors he asked his cabinet to resign." said MN80M

MN80M-UK-TEDDY-BEAR sits up saying, "What! Seriously."

MN80M smiles, "Yeah." as MN80M-UK-TEDDY-BEAR continues saying in English,

"Wait a min. Ssssshhhh! let me listen." as he then presses the button on the remote control again and higher s the volume on the TV.

MN80Mcontinues to smoke as the TV sounds continue and the NEWS REPORTER speaks out saying the translation of Arabic into English,

"Dear citizens of Egypt, I have asked the Prime Minister, and Ministers to hand in their resignation. I have taken note of your frustrations, and all legal requirements shall be taken to make sure this process is dealt with in as sufficient manner as possible. My beloved nation, I have been your selected MN-80—THE EG PRESIDENT 1 for many years now, and I do consider your choice to be the best of choices." said the NEWS REPORTER translating the word into English from that which was just said in Arabic by the EG President.

The room is as silent as the sound of the television and all those possible billions of people watching around the World as MN80M-UK-TEDDY-BEAR half jumps up from his seated position laughing,

"Boooooooyyyyyyyyyy!! DON. Hahahahahahaha!" he said as he practically jumped from his position with laughter and joy.

MN80M smiles, as does MN80M-UK-TEDDY-BEAR as he continues to move around in a hyper and excited mode saying,

"The Egyptian, I mean MN-80—THE EG PRESIDENT 1 is not going anywhere . . ." said MN80M-UK-TEDDY-BEAR.

MN80M shakes his head saying. "Proud Pharaoh"

MN80M laughs and continues saying,

"Switch it over to another channel. I told you I heard this may happen."

MN80M-UK-TEDDY-BEAR presses the remote control and changes the channel as MN80M passes this spliff over to MN80M-UK-TEDDY-BEAR.

"You make me laugh M." he said as MN80M—THE AMAZING ONE/MALE smiles back with a cheeky response of, "Why?" as he half laughs to hear MN80M-UK-TEDDY-BEAR say back,

"Because think about it yeah. If he just asked his cabinet to step down, and not him, it means what?"

They both look at each other for a moment, MN80M looks a little unsure of the questions and scratches his head saying,

"What?

MN80M-UK-TEDDY-BEAR looks at him in a way as if shocked slightly, saying

"That includes the Minister of each ministry yeah!??" "I suppose so yes." said MN80-M in a quick response.

MN80M-UK-TEDDY-BEAR rubs his head from back to front,

"It's not I suppose so. It's yes." he said.

MN80M THE AMAZING ONE/MALE responds

"Ok, so what's your point . . . ?" he said as he looks at Teddy-Bear.

MN80M-UK-TEDDY-BEAR nods his head,

"That includes your sister too."

MN80M-UK-TEDDY-BEAR hands over to MN80M the rolled up cigarette as he blows out the smoke towards the balcony door that remains open. MN80-M. THE AMAZING ONE/MALE starts to smoke while responding to the question,

"May be so. I'm not sure yet. Everything is still up in the air." and then sits back as MN80M-UK-TEDDY-BEAR continues speaking out saying,

"No M. It is either she has her job, or she don't. End of!" he said.

MN80M is listening to what his friend has just said to him as he continues to smoke.

"Yeah, you are right." he said to MN80M-UK-TEDDY-BEAR now eager to get his point across,

"So what are you going to do about it MN80-M? Is that not personal enough for you??" he said.

MN80M THE AMAZING ONE/MALE takes in a breath of air before responding with,

"Yeah but if things swing the other way, It's not good for her then is it.!??! But you are right. This is personal anyway. And not just from that. But from everything that happened before, and now."

"What do you mean?" his friend said as MN80M-THE AMAZING ONE/MALE straightens his back as he sits up to say,

"Come on man. Look at this all. Tunisia first. Then Egypt, with the woman saying to me at that news company that others too are about to kick off. Media is playing up things for a higher reason, and I think certain countries may have a big interest in Egypt and to control Egypt. If they control the people, they control Egypt. And if you control Egypt. Believe it or not, but you control the majority of this World. Egypt is at the tip point of North Africa, and connecting to the Middle East. The Suez Canal is a major link and route for the world via seas. Blockage of this route could in time, for some, cause famine in the west. Ships would have to all go around South Africa, and as business says, time is money." MN80M said as if rehearsed with full confidence watching his friend nodding his head slowly in agreement.

"Forget about all of that M for now mate. You got a chance to make money here, and good money doing news reports. Plus, on the same side, you get to find out what happened last year." said his friend.

MN80M passes the spliff back to Tedd-Bear, he accepts and smokes.

"Yeah. You are right. And I did have similar in mind. but still." MN80-M said in an non encouraging way as MN80M-UK-

TEDDY-BEAR now finding his questions are also becoming the answers, continues with asking,

"Still what?" he said in a funny and sarcastic kind of way. MN80M—THE AMAZING ONE/MALE smiles saying semi-sarcastically back to his friend,

"Money to get to the airport tomorrow morning, and for a visa once I arrive in Cairo Airport." he laughs at the end of his sentence awaiting his friend to respond.

The room is silent for a long moment,

"How much would you need?" MN80M-UK-TEDDY-BEAR asks.

"Well, about £7 to £10 for travel card. £10-£15 for Visa." Says MN80M to a response, "So about £30-£50 then right!??"

MN80M THE AMAZING ONE/MALE starts nodding his head in agreement yet as if ignoring the questions,

"Yeah. And even as I mentioned, if I have it, I would still need about the same with me in-case of anything." MN80—M said in another sarcastic way as they both look at each other through the now smoke filled room that has a haze of layers looking like white clouds. MN80M-UK-TEDDY-BEAR smiles while blowing out smoke,

"Come to me in the morning MN80M if you don't have it all by then. I can get it for you, and just go, you need to go M." MN80M-UK-TEDDY-BEAR said as more smoke continues to come out of his mouth with a smile just about viewable.

MN80M THE AMAZING ONE/MALE lowers and then lifts his chin up,

"I know . . . I know . . ." MN80-M said as MN80M-UK-TEDDY-BEAR asks,

"That's your brothers and sisters out there init MN80-M?" he said as he points towards the Television broadcast of civilians clashing with riot police on the streets of Cairo. "Which ones??" MN80M-THE AMAZING ONE/MALE said as he looks on awaiting MN80M-UK-TEDDY-BEAR to respond.

"The ones I see on the news fighting the police." said MN80M-UK-TEDDY-BEAR "More than that . . ."

MN80M responds as he lowers his head. MN80M looks up lifting his head slightly higher as he continues,

"They are me. My blood.".

They both nod heads in agreement as they look across the room at one another in the eye as if speaking from the heart to surprisingly hear MN80M-UK-TEDDY-BEAR suddenly say,

"So what are you waiting for M? Organize and get out there. You lost more than money M. They took your man—hood from you. That is not right in any culture, and in London, that not right, and I think in your religion Islam you're supposed to be the man right.?? So go take it back M. This is your opportunity. This is your time. And I am not just speaking about this day and age either. I am speaking about over-all, and I know you have stopped certain ways in life, but you know as well as I do your life, and many more lives would, could, be a whole lot better than it is. You just choose this as ok for you. For us all . . ." said MN80M-UK-TEDDY-BEAR in a tone of disbelief as another moment of silence as MN80M THE AMAZING ONE/MALE takes in a deep breath before he responds,

"I wish many things you could know. Like many things I could know. Yet going back or forward to change things does not work, and you know this, it is better to evolve with time, and to this, yes, I think that maybe I shall, Insha Allah just stay here with my life in this day and age, if I choose to go to Egypt, then I should now . . . May be I will. I better get home now. Sort myself out, think for a moment . . . All this is giving me a headache and all of this has started from that time, and also that other time with what happened in 1920 in Egypt." said MN80-M while holding his head. MN80M-UK-TEDDY-BEAR eye brows raise, "Why!?! What happened in Egypt in 1920??" he says out of curiosity as MN80M-THE AMAZING ONE/ MALE responds in English,

"Don't worry about it. Long story . . ."

MN80M-THE AMAZING ONE/MALE said as his face is as pale white all of a sudden and as still as his green eyes glowing slightly from the light reflecting in through the balcony window.

CHAPTER EIGHT

105: Egyptian . . .

DAY 3: 27th January 2011
EXTERIOR OF LOCATION: TAHRIR SQUARE,
CAIRO, EGYPT;
NIGHT:

Helicopters remain high in the night sky while Egyptians continue clashing with police on the streets within and around Liberation square as the sounds of screaming combined with the sounds of tear gas being fired out of guns intensifies. Thousands of others screaming as they continue to run for their lives towards one of the bridge area entry/ exit points, while a few hundred men standing among some of the CROWD CHANTING,

"The People, and the Army, are one hand. "several times as night falls. The CROWD CHANTING,

"Down with the regime." and "(???Must fill in???) continues.

[MEANWHILE IN A DIFFERENT LOCATION]

INSIDE OF LOCATION: MN80M-THE AMAZING ONE/MALE APARTMENT, LONDON, ENGLAND; NIGHT:
DAY 3: 27th January 2011—

MN80M-THE AMAZING ONE/MALE is doing commando pushups in his apartment living room wall area. He lowers both legs slowly as he stands up and starts to shadow box with anger of what is happening in Egypt. You can see the aggression in his face as he moves around the room boxing alone around one candle on the middle of the room on a long stick. MN80M repeats up on the wall again and stops each five commando push up, gets down and is moving around the room, boxing and kicking around the candle light, and then goes down to do five pushups at a time on the floor. Then gets back up to shadow box as he says in mind,

"Why Masr? Why Masr?" he said to himself and continues moving around the room, and then goes down again to do five pushups at a time, and then gets back up to shadow box.

"Why Masr? Why Masr?" he said again.

MN80Mcontinues to shadow box, this time picking up pace as he moves around.

"Masr! Masr! Masr! Masr!"

[MEANWHILE AT THE SAME TIME IN A DIFFERENT LOCATION]

EXTERIOR OF LOCATION; TAHRIR SQUARE, CAIRO, EGYPT; NIGHT:
DAY 3: 27th January 2011

Egyptian civilians continue clashing with police on the street as the sounds of people fighting police and rocks being thrown in hundreds of pieces continue and combine to be the main source of what is causing the sounds of thousands more people scream. Hundreds are also screaming from the tear gas lingering in the air while hundreds more riot police men come chasing down one of the side roads towards the young Egyptian CROWD CHANTING

"Masr! Masr! Masr".

MN80M THE SPECIAL ONE/FEMALE (Unknown Age 20's/30) unharmed, is noticeable standing alone a far from the battle watching.

[MEANWHILE AT THE SAME TIME
IN A DIFFERENT LOCATION]

INSIDE OF LOCATION; MN80M's APARTMENT,
LONDON, ENGLAND;
NIGHT:

MN80M THE AMAZING ONE/MALE continues with the shadow boxing within the living room area near to the very good condition yet unusable fireplace right next to the double floor to ceiling window in the living room area.

"Why Masr? Why Masr?" he said.

MN80Mcontinues to shadow box alone.

"Move. Jab. Jab. Move . . ." he said as he boxes around the candle stuck on the stick in the middle of the room and then turns moving fast towards the living room door.

MN80M starts to punch the door several times.

[MEANWHILE AT THE SAME TIME
IN A DIFFERENT LOCATION]

EXTERIOR OF LOCATION; TAHRIR SQUARE, CAIRO, EGYPT; NIGHT:

The dark sky seems darker than usual as the smoke filled air from battles on the ground seems to have started polluting the sky above. The super humid temperature along with lack of water supplies is causing the majority of the demonstrators to dehydrate and fall back as the sounds of explosions starts to go off in the near distance several times as if one of the EG ARMY TANKS shot out missiles twice from the cannon. Panic starts to take place and apart from several thousand remaining standing strong fighting against the riot police, many thousands of people are now running for his or her life towards the bridge area entry/ exit points. An Egyptian civilian is in battle with a riot policeman. The young man is seen winning, as he punches the policeman several times, similar to how MN80M is seen boxing in his living room.

[MEANWHILE AT THE SAME TIME
IN A DIFFERENT LOCATION]

INSIDE OF LOCATION; MN80M-THE AMZING ONE/MALE's APARTMENT, LONDON, ENGLAND; NIGHT:

MN80M THE AMAZING ONE/MALE continues with the shadow boxing in an aggressive way as he says in English,

"Move. Move . . . Duck . . . Uppercut . . . Move . . . Duck back. Duck back. Now punch." he said while continuing with his jujitsu moves.

MN80M ducks, and moves back on his feet quickly and then unleashes a strong punch forward towards the centre of the living room wooden door.

[MEANWHILE AT THE SAME TIME
IN A DIFFERENT LOCATION]

LOCATION: TAHRIR
SQUARE, CAIRO, EGYPT;
NIGHT:

Egyptian civilians are clashing with police as the CROWD CHANTING in Arabic continues louder than before, "Masr! Masr! Masr! Masr!" is said simultaneously by tens of thousands of brave young Egyptian men and women.

The male civilian continues fighting hand-to-hand combat with a police man. The civilian does not duck back or move from his standing position. The civilian is then rushed by several other armed police coming from aside and battered him to the floor with batons repeatedly. Other young Egyptian civilians rush to assist the young man and fight, yet they too are beaten to the ground by the heavily armed police force. MN80M-ALI and the 12 ASSOCIATES are noticeable in combat from afar winning. MN80M-ALI and ASSOCIATE number 8 both with faces covered by a bandanna, run back a few meters and use sling shots to fire rocks back at the police. The chanting continues around them and Thousands of individuals disperse as well as move to different locations around the main area of fighting and mayhem from the centre of the square towards one of the main bridges. MN80M

THE SPECIAL ONE/FEMALE (20's/30) is in a battle mode among her 12 ASSOCIATES against riot police on the bridge. THE SPECIAL ONE/FEMALE (20's/30) takes out her special sling-shot, kneels to the ground and picks up a rock and places inside her weapon before release. The rock continues from the sling-shot fast until impact on riot police man face. THE SPECIAL ONE/ FEMALE, quicker in her MN80M-FEMALE-BOOTS on her feet then some of her 12 associates are on their MN80M-SPECIAL-ROLLER-BLADES, runs on through a crowd leading her 12 ASSOCI-ATES as she continues to run straight into the direction of the riot police man that is now wounded from the rock attack. The same rock attack that has now placed the police man in a daze as he remains standing next to the other police men beating the man to the ground with batons and several fist punches to the face of the young man bleeding heavily on the floor screaming for them to stop, and/or someone to help. MN80M—THE SPECIAL ONE/FEMALE barely touching the floor as she runs super fast, leaps into the air positioning her feet in a jujitsu fly-kick position directed towards the heads of two police men.

"In the name of God." She said tree times, the first two times she whispers in the Arabic language while flying in the air and just as she connects with a double kick to both policemen faces and then lands on her feet to then quickly do a round-house kick to disable the policeman still in a daze from the rock attack. She then says it the third time. "In the name of God." MN80M-THE SPE—CIAL ONE/ FEMALE said in English.

"Move. Move . . . I am trying . . . . Duck . . . Uppercut . . . Move . . . Duck back. Duck back. Punch. Punch . . ." She said to herself silently while now in a fighting mode punching several police men.

Quick on her feet and with a left fist like iron, MN80M THE SPECIAL ONE/FEMALE releases three combination kicks, and a punch straight into the chest of two riot police men three times her size and height and weight. MN80M THE SPECIAL ONE FEMALE does the exact same moves as she senses inside of her somehow and continues to speak in English in her mind as her jujitsu techniques are no match for those heavily armed policemen around her that she is now disabling one-by-one.

"In the name of God . . . . OK now . . . Duck back. Duck back. Punch, I'm trying . . . . Help . . ." she said to herself.

[MEANWHILE AT THE SAME TIME IN A DIFFERENT LOCATION]

INSIDE OF LOCATION; MN80M's APARTMENT, LONDON, ENGLAND; NIGHT:

MN80M THE AMAZING ONE/MALE continues with the shadow boxing as he speaks his mind in English.

"Why Masr? Why Masr?" he said to himself.

MN80Mcontinues to shadow box around the candle in the middle of them room and then comes to a halt placing both hands on top of his head.

"God. Why Masr? Why Egypt?" he said.

MN80M stops shadow boxing and stands looking at a picture on the mantel piece above fireplace in living room of him and his dad in Egypt. The picture is in an unknown location. MN80M picks up the picture, takes a moment, and then looks at the TV while taking in a deep breath as the TV News broadcast at the bottom of the screen comes up as the TV remains on silent. The NEWS BROADCAST reads,

"Egypt update; US, UK and International News Agencies have started to send in their best news correspondents to report on the uprising in Egypt."

MN80Mcontinues to look back at the picture,

"They want to take Masr. They want Egypt I Know it. And have known it for many years. The want Egypt . . ."

MN80-M said as he takes in deep breaths to catch back some lost air from the shadow boxing.

MN80M lowers his head, takes in a couple more deep breaths, smiles slowly and then continues speaking his mind alone,

"Ok. I am coming God Willing. I am coming Insha Allah ya Masr."

MN80M looks at the time on his phone and then turns slowly towards and walks out of the room.

[THE FOLLOWING DAY]

INSIDE OF LOCATION: MN80M-THE AMAZING ONE/MALE APARTMENT, LONDON, ENGLAND;
DAY 4: 28th January 2011—TIME: Friday, 7:45am (GMT)

The morning light shines brightly through the floor to ceiling Victorian Windows onto MN80M-THE AMAZING ONE/MALE face as he is fully dressed and ready to leave his apartment with his two small bags at the side. MN80M goes into the living room area, picks up his fish bowl, and empties the two fishes into a plastic bag. "Bism Allah. Come on Schilachi, and Baggio. Insha Allah you will be ok with MN80-M-UK-TEDDY-BEAR for a week or so." He said as he picks up two DVD's and also places them into another plastic bag with the now empty fish bowl/mini bucket, and then picks up his phone pressing a button to make a call. "Good morning. Yeah, I am on my way. You home? Ok, see you soon." he said quickly.

MN80M walks over to set the alarm before he walks out the front door.

[MEANWHILE IN A DIFFERENT LOCATION]

EXTERIOR OF LOCATION: STREET, LONDON, ENGLAND;
DAY 4: TIME: Friday 7:47am (GMT)

MN80M-THE AMAZING ONE/MALE is walking along the street towards MN80M-UK-TEDDY-BEAR's home. He holds a plastic bag in his hand containing the two fishes and two DVD's.

MEANWHILE AT THE SAME TIME
IN A DIFFERENT LOCATION]

INSIDE OF LOCATION: MN80M-UK-TEDDY-
BEAR's HOME,
LONDON, ENGLAND; DAY4:

MN80M-UK-TEDDY-BEAR is speaking to a female Teddy-Bear, blonde-hair, and slim figured, that is in his bed undressed.

"Stay here I need to do something." He said.

"Do what?" the female teddy responded as she moves around in the bed slowly.

MN80M-UK-TEDDY-BEAR smiles,

"Just something for MN80-M." he said and then he walks across the room picking up things and placing them into his pocket.

"When are you coming back to bed?" she said as she moves around in the bed slowly awaiting MN80M-UK-TEDDY-BEAR as if he will jump into the bed with her. "Soon . . . Just relax your sexy teddy-body."

Both smile as the Telephone intercom/buzzer rings. MN80M-UK-TEDDY-BEAR answers, "Yeah M . . . Ok, I am coming down." he said.

MN80M-UK-TEDDY-BEAR looks at the naked Female-Teddy-Bear in the bed, putting the intercom phone back onto the machine, and then picking up a dark blue pouch from the table and a pair of MN80M-SPECIAL-GLOVES. He opens the door and departs placing the pouch inside the MN80M-SPECIAL-BACKPACK.

[MEANWHILE AT THE SAME TIME
IN A DIFFERENT LOCATION]

EXTERIOR OF LOCATION; STREET,
LONDON, ENGLAND:
DAY 4:

MN80-M is standing outside awaiting MN80M-UK-TEDDY-BEAR to come out and meet him. The door opens, "MN80M, come in for a minute." a voice said.

MN80M then starts to walk towards the door holding the plastic bag and enters asking,

"How are you? Ok?" as he holds the door while MN80M-UK-TEDDY-BEAR moves back inside saying,

"Yeah. But it's early M . . ." Both smile.

"I know." said MN80M

MN80M-UK-TEDDY-BEAR walks into the hallway towards the laundry room area.

"One minute M, I will be with you ok." he said as MN-80—M. has already started to walk up the stairs.

[MEANWHILE AT THE SAME TIME
IN A DIFFERENT LOCATION]

INSIDE OF LOCATION: MN80M-UK-TEDDY-BEAR's HOME,
LONDON, ENGLAND: DAY 4:

MN80M-THE AMAZING ONE/MALE is walking through the corridor, and towards MN80M-UK-TEDDY-BEAR door, and then opens the door and walks into the room to be surprised as the now naked Female-Teddy-Bear is still in the bed under the covers with her legs hanging off the side. MN80M-THE AMAZING ONE/MALE looks away. "Oh. Excuse me Female-Teddy-Bear. I am sorry. I did not mean to disturb you." MN80-M said quickly as if embarrassed that he did something wrong, just as the Female-Teddy smiles.

"That's ok. M." She said as she moves her legs around slowly while blushing.

MN80M THE AMAZING ONE/MALE does his best not to take a peek at her as he walks towards the kitchen area.

"I am just going to leave this plastic bag here on the floor ok." he said as he places the bag on the floor containing the fishes and the DVD's. Before continuing to say, "Ok then. Have a nice day. Bye." he said while turning towards the door.

The Female-Teddy smiles showing more teeth than a normal person would as she waves the one hand that is above the covers and says out loud twice,

"Bye bye. M. Bye bye . . ." she said while still waving her hand.

MN80M opens the door and walks out of the room slightly embarrassed for intruding, continues downstairs until he reaches MN80M-UK-TEDDY-BEAR. "Where did you disappear to M?" MN80M-UK-TEDDY-BEAR said as he starts laughing. Awaiting his friend to say,

"I never knew you had company. You make me laugh Teddy, seriously, if it is not the MN80-M-SPECIAL 12 CHILDREN you always have around you for teaching lessons, then it is a Female-Teddy-Bear or two . . . Hahahahaha . . . Anyway Teddy . . . I put my two fishes upstairs and two DVD's. Brave heart and something else." said MN80M both laugh before exiting the building.

"So you decided to go then yeah!?!"

Both smile as MN80M-UK-TEDDY-BEAR continues in English,
"Let's walk . . ."

[MEANWHILE AT THE SAME TIME
IN A DIFFERENT LOCATION]

EXTERIOR OF LOCATION; STREET,
LONDON, ENGLAND:
DAY 4:—TIME: (Unknown)

The grey clouded sky shields some of the sun light for a moment as MN80M THE AMAZING ONE MALE and MN80M-UK-TEDDY-BEAR are walking in conversation just past the special alleyway.
"What is life to you?" MN80-M said surprisingly quickly.
"What do you mean?" MN80M-UK-TEDDY-BEAR responded as they continue to walk.
"Life. Look at us all here. What is this all about to you my friend?" MN80-M asks again as MN80M-UK-TEDDY-BEAR looks back at him,
"Nothing." he said with a straight face.
MN80M THE AMAZING ONE/MALE smiles, quickly responding with,
"Exactly . . . And to me. Without Egypt. I can never feel alive." he said.
MN80M lifts his head up high as he continues in English,
"Do you now understand?" he said slowly.
MN80M-UK-TEDDY-BEAR puts his head down for a brief moment, and then up high.
"Yes." he says as he then pulls out his wallet and takes out some notes.

"We do what we have to-to survive. Here is £30 M. I wish I could have given you more." said MN80M-UK-TEDDY-BEAR.

MN80M smiles. "God is the Greatest, always."

{{EMPATHY LEVELS INCREASE}}

Both embrace a knuckle punch as MN80M-THE AMAZING ONE/MALE continues speaking,

"Stay strong brother. God willing, I am back soon." he said with a smile.

They both continue walking.

"have you told anyone you are going yet?" MN80M-UK-TEDDY-BEAR asks with a smile.

"No. not yet. Let me get to the airport first and see what they say about my ticket I have from last year. God willing everything works out." said MN80M

"Give them hell MN80M Give them hell . . . Show them who you are. and take these special gloves, and my marble pouch too. You may be able to use it while there, and also this lighter. Special one, only special people can use it if you are smart enough to get around the child safety, so use it if you need to, and only if you must. Give them hell MN80M. Be you." said MN80M-UK-TEDDY-BEAR as he lifts his chin up high.

A long moment of silence as MN80M-THE AMAZING ONE/MALE smiles thinking of a response, "Insha Allah I will. But what is this? Why give me a pouch of marbles for?" MN80-M said as he accepts the pouch.

"I got them from the Caribbean remember. May be we can have a game when you get back home ok. I know you do not like to play games and have no time for games, but. Just make sure you use them wisely if you play, and remember to hit one strong for me ok."

MN80M THE AMAZING ONE/MALE smiles saying, "Insha Allah I will. Peace" Both touch fists.

{{EMPATHY LEVEL INCREASE}}

MN80M walks to the corner of the road, places his head phones on and crosses over to the bus stop.

[IN A DIFFERENT LOCATION]

INSIDE OF LOCATION: BUS,
LONDON, ENGLAND;
DAY 4

MN80M-THE AMAZING ONE/MALE is sitting on a seat alone on the bus.

[LATER IN A DIFFERENT LOCATION]

EXTERIOR OF LOCATION: MN80M-THE
AMAZING ONE/MALE's APARTMENT
LONDON, ENGLAND;
DAY 4

MN80M-THE AMAZING ONE/MALE has his keys in hand and is walking into his apartment.

[LATER IN THE SAME LOCATION]

INTERIOR OF LOCATION: MN80M-THE
AMAZING ONE/MALE's APARTMENT
LONDON, ENGLAND;
DAY 4

MN80M-THE AMAZING ONE/MALE is picking up his belongings, puts his rucksack on his back, walks over to set the alarm, and walks out of the front door.

[LATER IN A DIFFERENT LOCATION]

INSIDE OF LOCATION: LONDON
UNDERGROUND TRAIN ENGLAND
DAY 4: 28th January 2011—Friday, 11:55am

MN80M-THE AMAZING ONE/MALE is on the Blue-Line on route to Heathrow Airport.

[MEANWHILE AT THE SAME TIME
IN A DIFFERENT LOCATION]

EXTERIOR OF LOCATION; TAHRIR SQUARE,
CAIRO, EGYPT;
DAY 4: 28th January 2011—Friday, 11:55am (EET)

Egyptian civilians continue clashing with police. MN80M-ALI and the 12 ASSOCIATES are noticeable among hundreds of thousands of other brave Egyptians.

[LATER IN A DIFFERENT LOCATION]

INSIDE OF LOCATION; LONDON HEATHROW
AIRPORT, ENGLAND:
DAY 4:
MN80M-THE AMAZING ONE/MALE is standing at the British Airways check in desk. MN80M walks away from the desk and starts to speak on his phone. "Hello. it's me. Yes! Me!" he said abruptly.

MN80M continues to walk until he is outside the entrance. "I am in a little bit of a situation. I know you are in Dubai, and have more important things than to hear me ask for a favor. And you know I never would unless urgently need to. Long story short . . . £70 is needed to pay the extra fee to get to Egypt on the ticket I have. No I am not getting into any funny business. What's your problem? No, I have not told anyone yet. But you should know, I have been offered a contract, and work is available, there are no reporters now out there and you know this. Yes I have seen the news and the fires happening. I am asking you for your card, if you can help great, if not, forget about it. Ok. Send it to my phone, or call them direct from you. I shall send you a sms /text now with my reservation number. Thank you!" MN80M-THE AMAZING ONE/MALE presses a button on his phone as he takes in a deep breath from all he just said over the telephone. He then starts to send a message on his phone, while taking a cigarette out to smoke.

[MEANWHILE AT THE SAME TIME IN A DIFFERENT LOCATION]

EXTERIOR OF LOCATION; TAHRIR SQUARE, CAIRO, EGYPT; DAY 4:

Hundreds of brave young Egyptians continue clashing with police and remain doing so under heavy fire now of tear gas and sounds of weapons are being fired in the air.

[SLIGHTLY LATER IN A DIFFERENT LOCATION]

INSIDE OF LOCATION: LONDON, HEATHROW AIRPORT. ENGLAND; DAY 4

MN80M-THE AMAZING ONE/MALE is standing at the British Airways check in desk but then walks away from the desk and starts to speak on his phone.

"They said it did not work too from here. Do not worry about this all anyway. Forget about it. It is late anyhow. They saying now flights to Egypt are cancelled from today. So I will just have to wait and see what happens. Thanks Anyway." he said.

MN80Mquickly presses a button on his phone before he places it back into his pocket and walks back to the check in desk. The CREW MEMBER AT DESK calls out loud while curling her hair with her fingers.

"Next person please." she said.

MN80M approaches the desk in a somewhat nervous way.

"Hi ya, it's me again. I need to know what the rules and regulations are in regards to when an incident like this occurs. Am I not supposed to at least get a refund from my ticket, so that I could put towards another ticket? or at least also swap flights to Egypt another way?" He said with his arms now up on the counter in-front of her.

The CREW MEMBER AT DESK smiles.

"I am not sure about that sir. We do have our managers in a meeting right now actually. And once they come out with an update, we can see what to advise you. Is that ok sir for you yeah?" she said in one of those airport worker tones.

MN80M—THE AMAZING ONE/MALE now annoyed looks around in frustration.

"Sir, may be if you like, you could save time and go to the customer services main desk in the other terminal, I think our customer service manager is there." She said again with a smile as she notices him continue to look around. MN80-M smiles and walks away.

[MEANWHILE AT THE SAME TIME
IN A DIFFERENT LOCATION]

EXTERIOR OF LOCATION; OLD CAIRO, EGYPT;
SUNSET: DAY 4:

MN80M-ALI and the 12 ASSOCIATES are all together in conversation outside the TRADITIONAL FOOD RES—TAURANT. Hundreds of people run around the street area in a panic going home while others prepare to protect the street and barricade roads and prepare for battles.

[MEANWHILE AT THE SAME TIME
IN A DIFFERENT LOCATION]

EXTERIOR OF LOCATION; TAHRIR SQUARE,
CAIRO, EGYPT;
DAY 4:/NIGHT/SUNSET:
28th January 2011—Friday,

Egyptians continue clashing with police within and around Tahrir Square, Cairo, Egypt. The dark sky and lots of smoke in the air is the only things most individuals within the clashes can see as most are being trampled over in a panic rush as hundreds more police dressed in plain clothing come as reinforcements to those already battling the civilians.

[MEANWHILE IN A DIFFERENT LOCATION]

INSIDE OF LOCATION; LONDON
UNDERGROUND TRAIN,
DAY 4: NIGHT

MN80M-THE AMAZING ONE/MALE is on the Blue-Line on route back to his apartment.

[MEANWHILE AT THE SAME TIME
IN A DIFFERENT LOCATION]

EXTERIOR OF LOCATION; TAHRIR SQUARE,
CAIRO, EGYPT;
DAY 4: NIGHT:
28th January 2011

Egyptians continue clashing with police. MN80M-ALI and 12 ASSOCIATES come together as groups clash in battle.

[MEANWHILE AT THE SAME TIME
IN A DIFFERENT LOCATION]

INSIDE OF LOCATION; LONDON
UNDERGROUND TRAIN,
LONDON, ENGLAND:
DAY 4: NIGHT;

MN80M THE AMAZING ONE/MALE is sitting on a seat on the train, a Blue-line on route back to his apartment looking seriously confused or upset. His headphones on his ears while his bag on his lap.

[LATER ON IN A DIFFERENT LOCATION]

INSIDE OF LOCATION; LONDON BUS
DAY 4: NIGHT;

MN80M-THE AMAZING ONE/MALE is on the bus on route home, his phone rings and he answers speaking in English.

"Yes Mum. Ok mum. No mum. Mum, I do not remember saying that, if I did I am sorry for being rude, and you even said to me that I do not have to tell you everything do I? This is my life too you know, and my choices? This is something I have to do. Imagine me then, I have a headache too mum." MN80—M said.

A long silent pause as he continues in English,

"Hello. Hello. Mum. Mum . . . What the hell. For Christ sake man why is she putting the phone down in my face for??? I am 30 years old now, not a baby." he said.

MN80M puts phone back into his pocket and then looks out of the window.

[LATER ON IN A DIFFERENT LOCATION]

INSIDE OF LOCATION: MN80M-UK-TEDDY-BEAR's HOME, LONDON, ENGLAND: DAY 4: NIGHT;

MN80M-THE AMAZING ONE/MALE is sitting opposite MN80M-UK-TEDDY-BEAR in conversation.

"What happened M?" Teddy asked.

MN80M THE AMAZING ONE/MALE looking sad has a massive smile on his face,

"Missions, missions, missions, firstly they wanted £70." MN80M said as he raised his eye brows. Both raise eyebrows.

MN80M-UK-TEDDY-BEAR nods his head, "Ok. Go on." he said.

"Then, when I tried to get assistance that never worked, then, all of a sudden all flights are cancelled to Egypt. I managed to speech the manager in the end at another terminal to exchange my ticket for a compensation ticket. And use that to get to Egypt via Egypt Air if tomorrow is cancelled." said MN80M

"Did it work?" MN80M-UK-TEDDY-BEAR asked.

"Insha Allah. They have me booked on the 7:30 am flight tomorrow." said MN80-M with a massive smile on his face. MN80M-UK-TEDDY-BEAR jumps for joy. "Yes. I told you that you are blessed M. And I been watching on the news, the Egyptians have taken over the police, they burning down buildings and police stations. And everything is hectic now." said MN80M-UK-TEDDY-BEAR full of excitement.

Both smile as MN80M-THE AMAZING ONE/MALE says, "Not too quick though. That flight may be cancelled too."

"Yeah, but at least God open the way for you now." Said MN80M-UK-TEDDY-BEAR as they both smile and Teddy-Bear continues, "Go for it M. Go for it." he said.

MN80M THE AMAZING ONE/MALE smiles taking in a deep breath and letting the air out slower than he breathed in. "Insha Allah. Insha Allah. Anyway, I better get going now, I want to see my sister and nephew before I depart." Both smile.

[MEANWHILE AT THE SAME TIME
IN A DIFFERENT LOCATION]

EXTERIOR OF LOCATION; TAHRIR SQUARE,
CAIRO, EGYPT;
DAY 4: NIGHT;
28th January 2011

Egyptians continue clashing with the few police remaining within and around the square. The majority of the helicopters have disappeared as the majority of the police force has started to retreat into side road.

[SLIGHTLY LATER IN A DIFFERENT LOCATION]

EXTERIOR OF LOCATION: MN80M. SOUL
SISTER 2 HOME / LONDON, ENGLAND
DAY 4: TIME:??:?? (GMT)

The night came quick as MN80M approaches the door walking fast, stopping only to as he reaches the door and knocks twice. He looks up at the dark cloudy sky awaiting the door to open as a gentle cold breeze of air passes him and he smiles at the silence of the street. The door opens, he enters.

{MEANWHILE AT THE SAME
TIME IN SAME LOCATION}

INTERIOR OF LOCATION:
MN80M SOUL SISTER 2 HOME
LONDON, ENGLAND
DAY 4: TIME:??:?? (GMT)

MN80M THE AMAZING ONE/MALE is sitting in conversation with his sister and MN80M SOULS SISTER 2 FRIEND 1 (20's/30 Years old) about the recent events in Egypt. The television sounds continue in the background as the three of them sit on chairs next to the dining table while MN80M THE AMAZING ONE/NEPHEW walks out of the room and up the stairs to the second floor bedroom.

The lights in the room are slightly dimmer than usual as the three adults start smoking cannabis and hashish while in conversation.

"You seem all ready to go MN80M. But why go? what for M?" MN80M SOUL SISTER 2 FRIEND 1 said.

"Because I have to go . . ." MN80-M replied.

"You don't have to. You just choose to."

MN80M. SOUL SISTER 2 said as if throwing in her piece of mind as usual.

"But M. I do not even know what is happening exactly there, but I can sense you truly want to go; But, Why?"

MN80M SOUL SISTER 2 FRIEND 1 said, as if wanting to go with him.

"This is not just an uprising as we see the news on the television in the United Kingdom here say to us all, you know this right, and at times, they, the media, are saying this is a revolution. So you know what yeah!??! This is a revolution, and hundreds of millions of people around the World are about to see, either via TV or with their own eyes this global revolution, that is truly, an Evolution. Most people just do not see it yet." MN80-M said as he then takes in a deep breath to continue. "An Evolution I want to be part of, and not just by watching things unfold via the TV or Radio like billions of people will be doing very soon, or taking part only on-line via the Internet like Millions of people already do . . . This is a revolution I want to be part of, physically, in every way possible." MN80-M said as he smiles. "In hope, I can bring positive vibrations and Equilibrium to the situation(s) at hand. Peace is needed here with not just one person, but with like a billion people. If that makes any sense . . ." he said.

The smoke filled room has an atmosphere of peace, yet the feeling of some-what uncertainty from the two females in the room at what MN80-M has just said.

MN80M SOUL SISTER 2 FRIEND 1 responds again in English saying,

"It's ok, I understand what you mean MN80M Just be careful ok. But yes, I know the feeling when you get you have to do something, then you just do." she said with a small smile.

"Insha Allah I will. I just have a gut feeling I have to do this and go." MN80-M said back in English.

MN80-M SOUL SISTER 2 puts her arms across the table and now has a grip of the massive candle, pulling it closer to the middle of the table saying,

"Let's all go over and sit on the sofas, why we sitting in this section for all the bloody time, I think he has gone up to sleep or play the MN80M-GAME-STATION already. Yalla, let's move." said MN80-M SOUL SISTER 2 as she stands and walks over towards the other room.

MN80M SISTER N smiles as she picks up the ash-tray containing her spliff and also continues walking into the other room.

"Ok, let me just go upstairs for a moment to the toilet, be back in a minute." MN80-M said as he continues smoking and blows out some smoke, leaving his spliff in the ash-tray next to him on the table as he walks towards and up the stairs.

INTERIOR OF LOCATION:
SECRET BEDROOM/ HOME/
MN80M THE SPECIAL ONE/FEMALE
HELIOPOLIS {KORBA} CAIRO, EGYPT.
DAY 4: TIME: Unknown (EET)

Wearing her special handmade MN80M-PINK-PAJAMAS, and her MN80M-SPECIAL-GLASSES at the tip end of her nose, MN80M THE SPECIAL ONE/ FEMALE is sitting down on her bed speaking her mind to herself and her female pink MN80M-SPECIAL-BUNNY-TEDDY-BEAR while taking off her MN80-M-SPECIAL-EYELASHES and the MN80M-SPECIAL-BUTTERFLY-HAIR-CLIP while then combing out the static and last few knots in her hair with her Japanese *Ikemoto* Hair Brush and her MN80M-STATIC-HAIR-BRUSH looking at her reflection in the mirror at the same time.

"Why God? Why?" she said.

MN80M THE SPECIAL ONE/FEMALE continues finishing up with her hair, places her brushes back inside the MN80M-SPECIAL-BOX and moves a few things around in the special orange colored Japanese Style Box with five of her other Anti-Static Hair Brushes, on the side table next to her bed. She then moves down onto her knees with elbows now on her bed close together, in a praying mode.

"Please God. Please show me a sign." she said with her eyes now closed.

MN80M THE SPECIAL ONE/FEMALE moves over a few steps with her knees still firmly on the ground. Well, technically, the MN80M-PERSIAN-RUG beneath her knees that has thick layers as if cushioning her soft skin. "Please God. Please show me a sign. All these years of devotion, all the divine, please God. Please. I cannot do this alone, not this time. and even my twelve associates are yes all beautiful and talented with skills like me, but hay, even with all our weaponry, might and power, and finally finding out who MN80M-THE AMAZING SECOND/ONE was for real, and all of his skills combined regardless of him telling me he loves me on-line, this still all feels different, and forgive me God for saying this, but, this is not that I am being selfish and ungrateful for all blessings, especially my mother, father, family and now also a super blessing with finding MN80M-THE AMAZING SECOND/ONE in my life . . . but . . ., this all may be too much for us all, even if my skills superseded their skills and all. I am honest enough to say all of this to you, and only you alone God. From my deepest part of my heart and soul, as much as I do feel completeness, honestly, I do not feel complete totally. Not yet. Not yet. Please show me a sign, send an angel to help. Something . . . Anything please . . . This is very difficult for me and my beloved nation of Egypt, all of my family, especially my mother and father. My people need help. We are just too proud to ask for it in this day and age, that's all. But God, please. Please make things as peaceful as can be." MN80M THE SPECIAL ONE/ FEMALE said while whispering out in a semi loud tone the last sentence in a short breath onto her hands that are still held together in a prayer mode close to her lips and face with her eyes tightly shut. MN80M THE SPECIAL ONE/ FEMALE opens her hands slowly and moves her right hand towards the necklace around her neck holding it in her hand. "Please. Make your suffering be enough for this World already. Jesus. Please. Please. If God wishes for any more suffering and pain, then crucify me, leave all to be. Please . . . please." said MN80M THE SPECIAL ONE/ FEMALE as her eye sheds one tear rolling down her cheek.

She then leans over and presses a button near the side table next to her bed, the lights turn off. She presses another button next to it, the lamp sitting on top of the table light flashes on. MN80M THE SPECIAL ONE/ FEMALE jumps onto her bed leaping high into the air and landing perfectly into position as she floats down with a smile in a slow, yet fast motion. A quick gentle breeze of fresh air comes in through the open window. THE SPECIAL ONE/FEMALE looks out towards the night sky with the moon in the near distance. She smiles.

"In my heart, I know. Regardless of all, everything is going to be good." she said.

MN80M THE SPECIAL ONE/FEMALE smiles again as she moves her head around now on the duck feathered massive pillow that takes up half of her bed size. She takes in a deep breath, smiles letting out the inhaled air slowly, making a sigh, as if relief has over-come her spirit. A faded white beam of light, as if directly from the moon shines through the window down into the room towards MN80M. THE SPECIAL ONE/FEMALE as she lay now beneath the silk feathered double duvet. The stunning Golden body of Jesus Christ necklace now showing around her neck starts to glow, as if flickering many times, and then all of a sudden, a shine and continues to shine bright, and then brighter, she smiles more as she continues to move her legs around under the covers in excitement as well as to adjust herself in the double Queen sized bed. She takes in a deep breath and smiles again closing her eyes as if to make a wish, she then lifts her right hand slowly towards her necklace and touches it while opening her eyes and looking out towards the moon. The special multi-colored, MN80-M. SCARAB BEATLE RING on her pinky/small finger on her right-hand starts to flash in all the different colors of the Rainbow, and then glows together with the necklace. The MN80-M. ANCIENT CERULEA RING on one of the fingers of her left-hand starts to glow-white, and slowly starts to open/blossom like a flower. The MN80M-SPECIAL-FEMALE-WATCH on her hand starts to flash-pink-lights. She smiles as she closes and opens her beautiful brown eyes slowly. "Thank you Jesus . . . Thank you God . . . I know he will come, and truly believe it, and in my dream that he has the MN80-EG ANCIENT SPE-CIAL RING with those initials engraved on them that glows blue. "O"—"M"—"B". yet what does it mean? Or is it like my MN80M-SPECIAL-ANKLE-BRACELET and initials glow randomly for separate reasons? I guess in time you shall show me the mystery. I want one like he has though, with his powers, like my MN80M-BUTTERFLY-HAIRCLIP is supposed to be able to do, or like a toe ring that can help me vanish to the moon to be alone like he does and God knows what else . . . But Anyway . . . back to main point here, just wanting to say again . . . Thank you Jesus. Thank you God . . . Thank you! I think I sense love. Real love . . . Thank you God . . . Thank you!" said MN80-M THE SPECIAL ONE/FEMALE.

{MEANWHILE AT THE SAME TIME
IN ANOTHER LOCATION}

INTERIOR OF LOCATION:
MN80M SOUL SISTER 2 HOME
LONDON, ENGLAND
DAY 4: TIME:??:?? (GMT)

MN80M THE AMAZING ONE/MALE is washing his hands in the wash-basin in the upstairs toilet and splashes some water onto his face before turning the tap off and dry-ing his hands and face. MN80M takes two steps out of the toilet area and turns left towards the first bedroom door and then taking two steps towards the door frame.

"Son, are you ok? Are you sleeping or playing computer games?" MN80M said.

"I am still awake uncle." replied MN80M THE SPECIAL ONE/NEPHEW.

"Can I come in please." asked MN80M

"Yes. Ok." MN80M THE SPECIAL ONE/ NEPHEW said as MN80-M enters the room.

"You ok boy." MN80-M said.

"Yes, I am ok thanks." MN80M THE SPECIAL ONE/ NEPHEW replied as he remains laying down in his bed pretending to sleep.

MN80M THE AMAZING ONE/MALE continues to walk into the room, taking a moment to stand next to the glass window and have a quick glance out towards the moon far up high into the night sky.

"I have to make a journey now." MN80-M said in a low tone.

"Why?" his nephew asked.

"I just have to." MN80-M replied.

"You have my marble pouch yeah uncle . . . ?"

"Yes, I do. Thank you!" MN80-M said as he sits down on the bed, more closely to the feet angle of his nephews' body. "I have something for you to keep boy."

"What is that then uncle?"

"This sling-shot, this is my UK one. Keep hold of it for me please. And on the 2nd of February 2011, at around between 3pm exactly your time here, I want you to take this sling-shot, and the one marble I leave for you, and I want you to hit that marker on your garden wall outside here, do you understand what I have just said to you son." MN80M THE AMAZING ONE/MALE said while looking straight at his nephew.

The bedroom is a small room; with the only light now on visible to be the mini black table lamp on the desk next to the laptop.

"I understand uncle. I will do it. But can I ask you a question please uncle??" he said.

"Yes my nephew, go on, ask?"

"Which marble will you leave me? And why? And can I bring some friends to watch?" MN80M THE SPECIAL ONE/NEPHEW asks while half laughing at the last six words he just expressed sarcastically to his uncle.

"No. How many times must I tell you, this you cannot share ok. Either you do, or you do not. so which one you choose boy?" MN80-M said to his nephew in a stronger tone of voice as if the questioning games are over now.

"No uncle. You answered my questions. Thank you." MN80M THE AMAZING ONE/MALE takes out from behind his back something wrapped in cloth, and then from his side pocket, a pouch.

"This is my sling-shot, guard it with your life boy ok." MN80-M said.

"I can keep it under my pillow, it's safe here." MN80M THE SPECIAL ONE/NEPHEW said while laughing and trying to keep his voice down at the same time.

"I said with your life boy, do you understand??" MN80-M said seriously.

"Yes uncle, ok. I'm just joking with you. I know what you said, and on the 2nd of February 2011, at around 3pm exactly my time, I will fire the one marble only towards the orange target at the end of our garden here . . . Is all this I say right uncle?" He said reassuringly and confidently.

"Yes my nephew that is all you have to do, and then, around 7pm, I want you to place this sling-shot, into the earth over-there, in the corner where I showed you last time ok. Then turn anti-clockwise when pushing it down into the earth. Anti-Clockwise. This is all you have to do my hero. I love you ok. Stay strong for mummy and all, and remember to keep this secret safe please. We cannot use my blessed skills and talents freely in this day and age, and I know this is frustrating for you, as it is I, and everything else linked to me that know and all of those that do not know of my true Skills/Ohako." MN80-M said in English as he places his hand on his nephews head and continues speaking.

"Stay happy and true to you ok." MN80-M Said while kissing the top of his nephews head and walking towards the door and down the stairs.

"Love you too Khalu . . . Good-night."

MN80M THE AMAZING ONE/MALE comes to a halt at the staircase and comes back into the room wishing his nephew a good night while also taking another glance outside of the window towards the moon.

"Uncle, can I have the ring then until you come back? At-least then I can have some skills and some power. You can fly without it I have heard, and yet I never in my life seen you fly Uncle like I see Super-Hero's or even Neo in the film Matrix . . . Why do you not use your invisible stealth mode, or flying, or any of your other special powers, I hear you have every special power ever created, and more that Humans, I mean people do not know about. Let me just have the ring please Uncle?" asked his Nephew with a massive smile on his face.

"You watch too much Television and films habibi on the TV and Cinema. Flying is only a myth, and even if I could, no one would know, not even you . . . Plus, Is it not enough I leave you my MN80-M SPECIAL SLING-SHOT!?! And the MN80-M SPECIAL CARIBBEAN-POUCH, I made that with my bare hands adding in my MN80-M SPECIAL SPACE MARBLES, and MN80-M SPECIAL CHINESE MARBLES that I won in battles over seas when MN80-M-UK-TEDDY-BEAR and I met for the first time in the finals of the street fighting universal battles over there in Costa Rica and Brazil!?! I shared my winnings equally with him, as I do with everyone. You have a power there and you don't even know it . . . Seriously boy/son, you teenagers these days do not appreciate much, or anything . . . You have another power too, all of us, especially from birth as children we are very special in the World, but the majority of us, especially you kids just don't' all really know how to use the power, and because you, as the majority, were nurtured and conditioned that way, as if you are not as special as you all are, as we, as Humanity all are. I know how you feel. And just like when you were two years old, I shall say it again now, as like I always do, and that's never to smoke cigarettes please, or anything. Do not smoke. It's bad . . . Do you remember me saying that to you yeah? It's bad boy, don't do it, and I would pretend to hit you, while you ran off in your nappies, until today when you sit here being rude running off your mouth to your mum and being rude to her all the time making her go mad. Don't do it anymore. You are a teenager now. She has enough to worry about. Just focus on your studies, staying in school is the best walahy, better grades, leads to better jobs, better pay, better life. Plus, if you continue being bad, not only will you lose your MN80-M EMPATHY POWER CREDITs', but we die slowly when we do bad things, do you understand son!?? Smoking kills. I wish I was not addicted to nicotine since I was a teenager like you . . . and yes, I know your big enough to understand this world and life around you more than you did before, yet so much you and even I, do not know. and at times you've seen me smoke many cigarettes, and even role cannabis and hashish spliff, but this is no good boy, you understand this ok. I repeat it, smoking kills, and decreases Human fertility, you know,, no more sperm would mean no more any of us. So not only do we kill ourselves softly. We cut off our sperm. Now you don't want that with any of your future girlfriends, fiancé's and future wife now do you?? No!! You want to produce later, someone strong wise and handsome as you boy, or if you blessed with a baby girl, then so be. Yet always keep in mind, smoking kills. Plus, if I ever hear you try smoking, then you will not just be hearing my loud voice. I will just ignore you, and not teach you how to use your special powers. Plus Habibi, you have the MN80-M SPECIAL BOOTS, the MN80-M SPECIAL HAT, the MN80-M SPECIAL TOOTHPICK-80-PACK, and the MN80-M SPECIAL TOOTHBRUSH, and what else have I given you are as gifts with skills since birth to just name a few, you even have the MN80-M SPECIAL MOON SKATEBOARD-Level7 and the other level skate-boards, and you have the MN80-M SPECIAL FOOTBALL, the MN80-M SPECIAL BASKETBALL, all to name a few son . . . and just because you are not allowed to use your MN80-M SPECIAL TOOL PACK like I have and do, and Ohako/skills until you are 18 years old, does not mean we cannot use some powers until then, or have fun, you must learn to have fun more you are still young, ok.!??! it just means you have to be patient with the special powers we have, and the ones you may learn to have. Especially when you stay in school to learn more skills, school is very important ok. I wish I listened to my mum more and done my best with everything when I was your age, it is not good to be rude to our parents or the elders, and I feel like I lose my MN80-M EMPATHY CREDITS when rude or negative to my mum. I wish I never started smoking, or let anyone influence me to smoke when I was young, but I chose to do so, and it was wrong. Smoking is bad for the health, and smoking kills. Learn from my mistakes, do not do the same. Please be good boy, well, you are a young man now ok, start to act like one then, and be an adult, I keep saying it to you, we cannot share our true 'Ohako/special skills' with anyone ok. This is very important . . . Otherwise you can just give back all the MN80-M SPECIAL TOOLS just mentioned to you, and I ask your mum to give you her MN80-M SPECIAL RED SLIPPERS and her MN80-M SPECIAL BATHROBE and her MN80-M SPECIAL DAYTIME FEMALE HAT. Then you only will have three MN80-M SPECIAL ITEMS to use until you are 18. And believe me when I say this to you, as a man, you do not want any of the MN80-M SPECIAL FEMALE ITEMS, we men, us, we have enough MN80-M SPECIAL MENS ITEMS to think about, let alone utilize for peace making. Ok. So please appreciate and respect the special sling-shot . My MN80-M. SPECIAL SLING-SHOT!?! and this responsibility . . . So my answer is 'No'. you know this was given to me for the reasons the Universe chooses, not man-kind. May be when you are a man you will understand ok. Just please do as I asked and we see how the future goes Insha Allah. Is that ok?" responded MN80M.

"Yes Uncle, I will do what was asked and will try my best to be humble while learning from you in the future. Thank you Khalu." said his nephew with a straight face.

"See you soon Insha Allah ok. See you soon. One day I hope we are blessed to live together, may be then I can teach you how to fly, with, or without the ring. See you soon. Salam." MN80-M whispered while still looking out towards the moon, and then back towards his nephew as he then continues walking down the stairs towards the living room area. MN80-M turns left into a room noticing MN80M SISTER N sitting alone on the sofa in her pink female MN80-M-SPECIAL-NIGHT-ROBE and matching slippers and fiddling with her MN80-M-SPECIAL-BUTTERFLY-HAIR-CLIP on her head as she is watching television.

"Where did your friend go to all of a sudden?" he said.

"Oh, she has gone home already." she said.

"What!?! Just quickly like that?? I only went up to the toilet quickly." MN80-M said as if he wanted to share more information with MN80M-SISTER N FRIEND 1 about Egypt before she had gone.

"Yeah well she does that some times, just vanishes and we don't see her for days. Why? What's up!?! Did you want her to give you a lift home or something?" she said.

"No. I just wanted to finish our conversation. It's ok, another time Insha Allah." MN80-M said in a reassuring way as he walks over towards a single sofa.

"I better make a move then myself too. I guess I see you when I see you my sister Insha Allah ok. I will send your love to our sister in person, even though you will probably speak to her over the phone before I get there. Anyhow, stay safe ok. Love you all, and try to go easy on him upstairs, I know he breaks the rules at times, but you remember what it was like when we were his age." MN80-M said while now walking towards the front door.

"Yeah well, I try with him day and night, he don't listen to anyone, and he never does his home-work or course-work, I don't know what to do with him anymore, we may as well send him to boarding school or to live with our sister in Egypt at-least then he can learn manners and true life, and if you are out there, he can learn from you too, you are the like the closest man in his life since he was born and this is all too much for me, but I will speak to you about that when you get back ok. You have a safe journey and stay out of trouble." MN80M SISTER N said as she gets up from her seated position with her night-gown wrapped around her walking towards the front door to greet MN80M

"Just be safe ok." she said in English. "Insha Allah I will." he replied in English.

MN80M THE AMAZING ONE/MALE now walks towards and opens the door.

"Salam." he said.

"Salam to you too brother." she replied back.

MN80M THE AMAZING ONE/ MALE continues walking out the front door as they embrace with a hug and kiss from cheek to cheek first. MN80-M continues walking, turning slightly left, and straight up the street towards the main road.

[LATER IN A DIFFERENT LOCATION]

EXTERIOR OF LOCATION; MN80M—
THE AMAZING ONE/MALE'S APARTMENT,
LONDON, ENGLAND;
DAY 4: NIGHT;

MN80M-THE AMAZING ONE/MALE has his keys in hand and is walking up the few steps into his apartment.

[MEANWHILE AT THE SAME
TIME IN SAME LOCATION]

INSIDE OF LOCATION; MN80M-THE AMAZING
ONE/MALE'S APARTMENT,
LONDON, ENGLAND;
DAY 4: NIGHT; 28th January 2011—Friday

MN80M-THE AMAZING ONE puts down his belongings, walks over to switch off the ringing alarm and then walks into the living room and switches on the TV.

[MEANWHILE AT THE SAME TIME
IN A DIFFERENT LOCATION]

EXTERIOR OF LOCATION; TAHRIR SQUARE, CAIRO, EGYPT:
NIGHT; 28th January 2011

The Government Party building is on fire burning heavily and quickly with every floor ablaze. The Egyptian Museum is located near and in-sight of the same building. A YOUNG MAN (20's) is standing in front of an army tank firing water out of a cannon. Egyptian civilians are running havoc on the streets repeating one another's brave recent stories of bravery while the police are either running, or nowhere to be seen as the violence has now over escalated with millions of brave young Egyptian men and women taking to the streets in every city across the entire Egyptian nation.

[MEANWHILE AT THE SAME TIME
IN A DIFFERENT LOCATION]

INSIDE OF LOCATION: MN80M's APARTMENT
LONDON, ENGLAND
DAY 4: NIGHT; 28th January 2011

MN80M-THE AMAZING ONE/MALE is sitting watching the news on TV in his living room. The TV news broadcast sounds as MN80M is rolling a hash spliff and watches the news. MN80Mpicks up his phone to make a call.
"Hello uncle. How are you?? Yes, I am good thank you uncle. Listen, uncle. Long story short here, I am going to Egypt ok, and am stuck right now needing to get to the airport. To save money, can you help me by dropping me there into the

early hours of the morning please? Ok, thank you. See you then Insha Allah. Salam." MN80-M said.

[MEANWHILE AT THE SAME TIME
IN A DIFFERENT LOCATION]

EXTERIOR OF LOCATION; TAHRIR SQUARE,
CAIRO, EGYPT:
DAY 4: NIGHT; 28th January 2011

The Museum has been deserted with no security and no police presence in sight as people can be seen running around the outside entrance. More Egyptian civilians are noticed standing, or running in groups in both directions while the police are either running in the opposite direction, or nowhere to be seen. Fires continue in several places within and around the Square. Sounds of glass smashing and rocks hitting metal can be heard throughout the night as the day ends the worst ever with the early hours of the morning being the same in extreme chaos and mayhem.

[THE FOLLOWING MORNING]

INSIDE OF LOCATION; HEATHROW AIRPORT,
ENGLAND:
DAY 5:—TIME: (Unknown)
29th January 2011—
Saturday. London, England.

Hundreds into thousands of travelling passengers and workers come and go freely at the airport. MN80M-THE AMAZING ONE/MALE is at the checkout desk at British Airways shaking his head at what the Female in-front of him sitting behind the desk is saying. MN80M. looks at his watch; accepts the paper the female hands him, and starts walking towards the airport cafeteria with a voucher in hand.

[BRIEFLY AFTERWARDS]

INSIDE OF LOCATION; CAFETERIA,
HEATHROW AIRPORT, ENGLAND:
DAY 5: 29th January 2011—Saturday, London, England.

The atmosphere sound is soothing as soft tones are heard from the near one hundred people, some travelers, as well as other loved ones eating breakfast together. MN80M-THE AMAZING ONE/MALE is sitting alone looking over the menu as the WAITRESS is standing awaiting his order.
"Good morning Sir. Can I take your order please?" she said in an up-beat and joyful tone as she smiles at MN80Mwho also is looking at the waitress with a smile.
"Just give me a moment to read over and collect my thoughts" he said as he scratches his head and continues speaking, "Feel free to get me a coffee for now please. Oh, and milk and sugar please." he said with a smile.

The waitress writes on her note pad with her orange tip pen. "Anything else for now?" she said.

"No, that would be it. Thank you!" he replied.

The waitress walks away as MN80M looks around him at all the other passengers in the restaurant/cafeteria, eating breakfast.

"I wonder how many here even know what is happening now in Egypt." he said to himself.

MN80M continues to look around as other passengers and guests continue with life freely. The waitress passes by and catches eye contact with MN80M

"Ready for that order Sir?" she said.

MN80Mlooks at the menu again as if undecided, "Yeah. sure. Umm. Give me the morning special with spinach. Does that sandwich contain egg??. As I am not too fond of eggs recently." he said as the WAITRESS moves closer saying,

"Yes Sir, spinach, egg, and cress, with a touch of honey and lemon. The bread is from France. Fresh." she said.

MN80Mface looks uneasy.

"Umm . . . Sure. Why not! Go for it. And my coffee." he asked. The WAITRESS smiles saying out to him with a smile, "On its way Sir. Would you be paying by cash or airport voucher?" she said.

MN80M pulls out the voucher given to him from the airline assistant and hands over to the waitress.

"Here you go. The Airline voucher." he said. The waitress accepts.

"Thank you! And which flight would you be departing Sir?"

MN80M—THE AMAZING ONE/MALE opens his passport with ticket inside,

"Was British Airways 7:30 this morning. But that's can—celled because of the civil unrest in Egypt. They have trans—ferred us to another airline now. I think the only flight flying out to Egypt today, and that's all for this afternoon." said

MN80-M as he looks around at the passengers now seated near to his table.

The waitress stands focused in-front of him looking into MN-80—M.'s eyes and says silently in her mind in hope no one can hear.

"You have such beautiful green eyes." she said.

THE WAITRESS smiles and says out loud in English,

"I am so sorry to hear that Sir. I hope your journey is blessed safely and that you go and come in peace. Until then, I will go over now and see where your coffee is. Three or two sugars right!??" she said with a smile.

MN80MSmiles.

"Yes. Three sugars please. Thank you!"

The waitress smiles back and walks away. MN80M-THE AMAZING ONE/MALE continues to look around him with a smile slowly uttering,

"She looks nice as well." he said while still watching the waitress.

"Ok M. Are you ready now?? Do you have everything you wanted? Yes and no . . ." he said to himself as he pulls out his wallet, looks at a picture inside that no one else can see and then pulls out a £20 note and some change from his pocket. "Alhamdulillah". He said with a smile.

"What else M? What else?? Did you bring that new costume MN80M-UK-TEDDY-BEAR said I should take."

MN80M smiles as he continues speaking in mind, "With a pair of MN80-M-SPECIA-GLASSES to look conspicuous." he said laughing. MN80M smiles, pulls his bag closer to his legs, and takes out his head phones. The waitress walks over with the hot coffee and places it on the table in front of MN80M As she pushes the sugar closer to him,

"Here you go Sir. And the food will be with you shortly. Would there be anything else I could help you with?" she said as she continues to keep eye contact.

MN80Msmiles. "Thank you!" he said.

MN80-M then places his headphones on as the waitress walks away with a smile. MN80Madds more sugar into the coffee before tasting.

[LATER ON IN A DIFFERENT LOCATION]

INSIDE OF LOCATION: WAITING-HALL
TERMINAL 3/ HEATHROW AIRPORT
ENGLAND: DAY 5:

MN80M-THE AMAZING ONE/MALE is awaiting with other passengers to board the Egypt Air flight to Cairo. MN80M walks closer to the 52 inch wide-screen television at one corner of the waiting area while passing several passengers in the waiting hall. The 52 inch television is showing the live news of Cairo demonstrations, and some scenes of polices firing tear gas onto civilians on one of the bridges as some clash with police officers and hundreds of others are noticed praying on the bridge floor. MN80M stops next to the TV and attempts to put the volume up manually, yet fails. Others come closer to watch the news updates as the volume is set on a very low level. MN80M stands for a moment, and then walks away, and finds a chair to sit on while nearly everyone else in the waiting hall are focused on the news broadcast on the TV. A female is sitting next to MN80M with her child. MN80M looks at the mother and child and smiles. MN80M.

-THE AMAZING ONE/MALE makes a funny face by sticking out his tongue and rolling his eyes at the same time and whispering,

"Everything is ok, and everything will be ok now Insha Allah." He said out in enough of a tone for those seated in-front of him to hear.

The little girl and mother smile together. MN80M maintains his smile as many passengers start walking through towards the entry door/gates boarding the flight. MN80M stands and walks towards them all.

[SLIGHTLY AFTERWARDS]

INSIDE OF LOCATION;
INSIDE LOCTION: AIR-FLIGHT / PLANE
HEATHROW AIRPORT / ENGLAND
DAY 5:—TIME: (Unknown)

The Egypt Air flight is about to depart. MN80M-THE AMAZING ONE/MALE is sitting down looking out of his window seat as other passengers continue to board the flight and sit around him. MN80M looks at the time on his mobile phone.

[MEANWHILE AT THE SAME TIME
IN A DIFFERENT LOCATION]

EXTERIOR OF LOCATION; TAHRIR SQUARE,
CAIRO, EGYPT;
DAY 5: NIGHT/SUNSET:
29th January 2011—Saturday, Tahrir Square, Cairo, Egypt.

Thousands of brave Egyptians continue clashing with police regardless of the tear gas being directed at civilians as well as gun fire. Gun shots can be heard as civilians are running in every direction.

[MEANWHILE AT THE SAME TIME
IN A DIFFERENT LOCATION]

INSIDE OF LOCATION; AIR FLIGHT/ PLANE;
HEATHROW AIRPORT: ENGLAND:
DAY 5:-TIME: {Unknown}

MN80M THE AMAZING ONE/MALE remains seated as the plane takes off/departs to Cairo, half full of passengers and crew members. MN80M looks at the time on his phone at the same time looking out of the window at the land below.

[MEANWHILE AT THE SAME TIME
IN A DIFFERENT LOCATION]

INSIDE OF LOCATION; MN-80—THE EG
PRESIDENT 1 PALACE,
SHARM EL SHEIKH, EGYPT;
DAY 5: NIGHT/SUNSET: 29th January 2011

MN-80—THE EG PRESIDENT 1 (80's) is sitting in his chair alone silently looking out the window to the clear dark blue sky containing thousands of stars glittering bright.

[MEANWHILE AT THE SAME TIME
IN A DIFFERENT LOCATION]

EXTERIOR OF LOCATION: TAHRIR SQUARE,
CAIRO, EGYPT—
DAY 5: 29th January 2011

The majority crowd and riot police are now clashing with
one another in serious battle.

[MEANWHILE AT THE SAME TIME
IN A DIFFERENT LOCATION]

INSIDE OF LOCATION; MN-80—THE EG
PRESIDENT 1 PALACE OFFICES,
SHARM EL SHEIKH, EGYPT;
DAY 5: 29th January 2011

The fourteen Supreme Military Council members are in
conversation amongst one another privately and near
silently. Everyone in the room looks in shock, yet confident as
the faces of each of the Military Council members is bold with
chins up high as the door opens, and MN-80—THE EG
PRESIDENT 1 is about to walk into the room. All fourteen
of the men, the Military Council members, including the
General stand to their feet to salute MN-80—THE EG
PRESIDENT 1 as he enters, and continue to stand in same
position until given the order to do so by MN-80—THE
EG PRESIDENT 1 himself.

The MAN IN SUIT walks into the room first and takes a
look around from left to right and then towards the General
and his side weapon, that, unlike the others in the room, is

not holstered properly, before looking up at the General in his eyes, then around the room again saying,

"Everything is clear Mr. MN-80—THE EG PRESIDENT 1." The Man in Suit continues to look around and closely at each of the Military Council members, including the General, and then continues to speak in Arabic this time saying out loud,

"His Excellency, MN-80—THE EG PRESIDENT 1 of the Arab Republic of Egypt."

The Military council all salute simultaneously. MN-80 —THE EG PRESIDENT 1 walks into the room in a bold way with his chest and head raised high, dressed in one of his brand new dapper MN80-M-1960's-CLASSY-SUITS and separate specially tailored one of a kind, MN80-M-BOSSALINO hat placed perfectly on his head.

[MEANWHILE AT THE SAME TIME
IN A DIFFERENT LOCATION]

INSIDE OF LOCATION; FLIGHT:
AIR/ OVER THE ATLANTIC:
NIGHT:

MN80M-THE AMAZING ONE/MALE is just walking out of one of the toilets and makes his way along the isle towards his seat. As MN80M reaches his seated area, he leans up towards the above baggage compartment area to get one of his bags down, pressing the button, the compartment opens, and he brings down one of his bags positioning it on the seat in-front of him. MN80-M looks around with a smile as he opens the zip on the bag and taking out a few MN80M items, pens and paper, a book, and throws them down onto his chair while slowly pulling out from a hidden zip inside the bag a MN80-M-1960's-GREY-BOSSALINO-HAT, with cream trimmings along the side. MN80-M smiles and then places the Bossalino hat back into the secret compartment of his bag, closing the bag, and lifting it back up into the over-head compartment. MN80M-THE AMAZING ONE/MALE sits down on his seat and takes the note pad to write on, and then places the headphones connected to the on-board film on his ear to listen as he starts to write.

CHAPTER NINE

105_2b: Egyptian . . .

INSIDE OF LOCATION; PRIVATE CHAMBERS/
MN-80—THE EG PRESIDENT 1 PALACE,
SHARM EL SHEIKH, EGYPT;
NIGHT;
DAY 5: 29th January 2011

MN-80—THE EG PRESIDENT 1 (80's) is sitting on his chair calmly looking out of the palatial windows overlooking the garden area. He stands and walks towards the balcony to open the door. He does so, and opens the balcony door and exits, walking outside towards a very large bird cage and then stands next to the cage and looks at the creature inside.

[LATER IN A DIFFERENT LOCATION]

INSIDE OF LOCATION: FLIGHT/ OVER THE
ATLANTIC OCEAN
NIGHT: DAY 5:

MN80M THE AMAZING ONE/MALE is being served dinner by the AIRHOSTESS. MN80M accepts the hot readymade meal and a drink and sits back with his food in front of him just above his lap on the mini table that comes out from the seat in-front acting as a dinner table. His headphones now on, MN80M Starts watching the TV screen in front of his eyes as he can finally start to relax. MN80—M inhales deeply, breathing in twice, and then smiles.

[MEANWHILE AT THE SAME TIME
IN A DIFFERENT LOCATION]

INSIDE OF LOCATION; PRIVATE BALCONY/
MN-80—THE EG PRESIDENT 1 PALACE, SHARM
EL SHEIKH, EGYPT; NIGHT;

MN-80—THE EG PRESIDENT 1 is standing next to a bird cage containing a stunning looking Egyptian Eagle that is double the size of an ordinary Egyptian Eagle. MN-80—THE EG PRESIDENT 1 picks up a mini sack/ pouch of food hung next to the cage containing baby rabbits. MN-80—THE EG PRESIDENT 1 places a special glove on his hand and opens the cage and places his hand inside. The Eagle willingly moves onto his wrist with ease. MN-80—THE EG PRESIDENT 1 takes out one of the earlier slaughtered rabbits from the mini sack/pouch with his other hand, and lifts it close to the Eagle. The Eagle quickly takes hold of the rabbit with ease while remaining on MN-80—THE EG PRESIDENT 1 wrist and staying as still as a rock. MN-80—THE EG PRESIDENT 1 speaks out In-Arabic,

"In the name of God." MN-80—THE EG PRESIDENT 1 said as he gently touches the head of the Eagle and continues in speaking out in English,

"Look at how beautiful you are? Creation of Allah"

MN-80—THE EG PRESIDENT 1 continues to gently touch the head of the Eagle.

"Do they honestly think I would let them take Masr? I would gladly give Egypt up to the people, but only, the Egyptian people. But not all of those others that want to attempt to take our beloved land for his or her benefit. And even my own council does not know of the deals the west and east have been begging us for years. But I refuse to sell Egypt for what they want. And all of this and none of my people know. May be I should tell them the truth about the deals I refused that is causing all these problems and more. May be then they will wake up and understand I love them more than they know. This is my country too. But . . . How . . . ." said the President as he looks up and down at the Eagle.

The beautiful clear sky with a gentle southern wind breeze brings a moment of silence as MN-80—THE EG PRESIDENT 1 smiles and gently touches the head of the Eagle with his hand and looks up at the night sky.

"Now look at all the trouble they have caused with all those social networks and media non sense. that is not true life. We are Pharaohs. Not PC'oas. What do they think I am? Stupid??. I had the Honorable Anwar Sadat as a teacher back in the day among many more. He started the Whole Peace process between close nations . . . And now, look at us. Peace for 30 years." MN-80—THE EG PRESIDENT 1 said as he continues to gently touch the head of the Eagle while looking out towards the stars in the sky.

"I am not perfect, and have my sins too, God knows the truth, and I pray God has mercy on me on the Day of Judgment for all and any bad decisions I personally made." He said as he takes in a deep breath letting out the air from his mouth slowly.

"Only such a blessed creature and lover of this land, that is already living, or flying over this land looking down from above can understand. The love of thy creator of all things is great, and the people are the land, Masr, able to speak, or do, for the dignity of Masr. Only God can judge me, just like only God can judge you. Such beautiful creation, I know Allah (swt) will keep us safe, and send blessings in abundance Insha Allah. But for now, Egypt remains the same as she was before I came and after I depart from this World Insha Allah by the will of God, and God's will only. For now though, you are free my beloved bird. Fly. Fly like the Eagle you are for Masr and keep an Eye from the sky for me, and for us all, Insha Allah." MN-80—THE EG PRESIDENT 1 continues to gently touch the head of the Eagle as the rabbit remains in beak. MN-80—THE EG PRESIDENT 1 raises his right hand, and the Eagle fly's off from his wrist and into the sky. MN-80—THE EG PRESIDENT 1 smiles.

"Let us pray this evil force against Masr has some goodness in them to make them see sense. Otherwise they will feel an Egyptian force never felt before in the history of Mankind. And by the will of God they would all feel the wrath of my fully trained and ready Egyptian present day army. We are one hundred million warriors. Men and Women." the president said to himself in a bold manner.

The Eagle continues in motion flying away into the night sky. "Salam" MN-80—THE EG PRESIDENT 1 says while raising arm as if to send regards to the Eagle now in flight far up into the dark night sky.

[MEANWHILE AT THE SAME TIME IN A DIFFERENT LOCATION]

INSIDE OF LOCATION; FLIGHT: AIR/ OVER THE ATLANTIC: NIGHT:

MN80M-THE AMAZING ONE/MALE has finished eating and is writing into his notepad in English, but speaking his mind in Arabic.

"Bism Allah—In the name of God." he said.

MN80M takes a sip of the water in the plastic cup in front of him.

"Ok M. Start to plan properly now; what is your primary objective? I cannot remember most things these days, especially with my dreams; it's as if everything is like a dream. Think M. Think!" said MN80Mas he takes another sip of the water in the plastic cup in front of him.

"Ok M. First; Find sister make sure she is ok and then after a day or so, get keys for home and go settle into your own space. Second: Find out what happened last year August during Ramadan times? And then Third; locate others I know In Egyptian Media? Fourth; Locate others sent or already working as news agents and disable with empathy levels if needed? And then what else!?!! What else.!?!? And then, Fifth . . ."

MN80Mtakes another sip of the water in the plastic cup in front of him and looks out of the air plane window on his right hand side looking out towards the night sky with a smile.

"Number five on the list"

He said as the plane starts descending towards the runway at Cairo airport.

[MEANWHILE AT THE SAME TIME
IN A DIFFERENT LOCATION]

EXTERIOR OF LOCATION; TAHRIR SQUARE
LIBERATION SQUARE, CAIRO, EGYPT:
DAY 5: NIGHT:

The main political party building is burning down near to
the Museum. The police are no longer seen and the army
tanks have rolled into the square among the tens of thousands of demonstrators remaining. Some minor skirmishes
continue, yet more or less the streets are emptier as no more
police management control Liberation Square.

[MEANWHILE AT A DIFFERENT LOCATION]

INSIDE OF LOCATION; PLANE: AIR:
CAIRO, EGYPT:
DAY 5: NIGHT; Saturday the 29th January 2011

The plane has just landed, and MN80M prepares himself
to depart with the others already boarding off of the plane.
MN80M-THE AMAZING ONE/ MALE looks at his
MN80-M-SPECIAL-SWISS-WATCH for the time and
then his MN8E-PAD secretly while pulling out his ordinary phone then picks up his MN80M-SPECIAL-BAG and
makes his way down the aisle towards the exit door, and then
exits the plane doors to then walk down the steps towards
the coach awaiting to take the remaining passengers to the
terminal.

[LATER ON]

INSIDE OF LOCATION; IMMIGRATION DESK/
EGYPT INTERNATIONAL AIRPORT,
CAIRO, EGYPT:
NIGHT;

Hundreds of arrival passengers await immigration procedures inside the terminal as a bus pulls up outside an entry door and more passengers exit. Another bus arrives behind, and MN80M-THE AMAZING ONE/MALE exits, walking towards and then into the terminal among other passengers. He then walks over to start filling out his immigration form while standing with others in the smoking room waiting area. Once finished his cigarette, MN80-M walks out of the room. The newly built airport is now filled with thousands of passengers and others awaiting transit, yet the police are not visible, only a couple of immigration officers. MN80M-THE AMAZING ONE/Male walks over until he reaches the bank section to purchase a visa and then on towards the immigration desk. While standing, MN80—M is requested to move forward to the bank teller by a passenger waiting behind him, so he does, and then says in English,

"Hello. One Visa please . . ."

MN80M hands over the money and the bank teller gives MN80M a visa (sticker) and some change. MN-

80—M. accepts the visa sticker and places it into a page within his passport while walking towards the immigration desk. MN80M starts walking towards the immigration officer and hands over his passport and immigration card before saying in English and Arabic,

"Hello. Peace and blessings onto you. Happy New Year." he said with a smile as the Immigration officer looks up at MN80M-THE AMAZING ONE/Male with a straight face and then back down at his passport photo while flicking

through the pages. MN80M smiles back as the IMMIGRA-
TION OFFICER asks in Arabic,
"MN80M" said the officer.
"Yes, this is me." MN80M-THE AMAZING ONE/MALE
said in English as he keeps his smile. The IMMIGRATION
OFFICER looks back at the passport and then back up at
MN80-M asking him in English.
"is this your full name you have written?" "Yes." said
MN80M
The Immigration officer convinced with what MN80-M
has presented, picks up the stamp, and presses down with
the visa stamp onto a page in the passport before handing it
to MN80M A moment of silence as the IMMIGRATION
OFFICER looks around from left to right and then says in
English,
"Welcome to Egypt!"
MN80M Smiles responding, "Thank you!"
MN80M accepts his passport into his right hand and walks
on toward the luggage area.

[MEANWHILE AT A DIFFERENT LOCATION]

EXTERIOR OF LOCATION:
EGYPT INTERNATIONAL AIRPORT/CAIRO
DAY 5: NIGHT: Saturday the 29th January 2011

MN80M-THE AMAZING ONE/MALE is exiting the
airport exit with his bag/suitcase. Thousands of passengers
are both sitting on the floor, or in a sleeping position or
standing as the curfew has been implemented and everyone
in the airport including the country is at a stand-still.

MN80M THE AMAZING ONE/MALE takes a look from left to right at all of the passengers waiting in-transit to depart from Cairo awaiting in the entry check—in area, as well as Hundreds of those looking to attempt to get from the airport out into Cairo. MN80M walks over to a group of men he noticed on the same flight from London and decides to walk over to them.

"Excuse me. Can someone tell me what is happening here please?" said MN80M

MN80M THE AMAZING ONE/MALE comes closer to one of the men. The Egyptian MAN 1 IN GROUP responds in Arabic,

"There is a curfew now." the man said.

MN80M-THE AMAZING ONE/MALE eye brows come together as he asks in English, "What do you mean?" as another one of the men in the group listening comes in closer and responds in English,

"Curfew. No one is allowed out."

"What do you mean "no one" is allowed out? How?" MN80-M. said as he looks around from left to right.

The Egyptian MAN 2 IN GROUP says back in English, "Curfew. There is no more police in Egypt from today. Some say from yesterday night. No more police. The Army has a curfew and we all have to stay inside our home or like us here, inside the airport." the man said.

Another moment of silence as MN80M—THE AMAZING ONE/MALE continues to look around and then says in Arabic, "How can no one be allowed out?" asked MN80M.

The men in the group smile as the Egyptian MAN 2 IN GROUP says back in Arabic,

"This is Egypt." said the man as he laughs out loud.

MN80M is listening to what the kind men have just said an looks around from left to right again as the Egyptian MAN 2 IN GROUP continues in English,

"We must stay here until eight-o-clock in the morning." said the man.

MN80M looks around from left to right again before responding in Arabic,

"Thank you!" he said in a subtly tone as he takes out his packet of cigarettes, his lighter, and places a cigarette in his mouth and ignites it before he walks away alone towards a foreign couple and two men.

A dozen vehicles are parked up and down the one road that Hundreds of passengers standing outside are trying to nego-tiate with for the possibility of an exit from the airport while thousands more remain inside the airport waiting. The hot air at night is a change in climate for MN80M's usual English weather. He continues walking slowly towards the couple and speaks out asking in English.

"Hello . . . . Excuse me, quick question please. Are you all going into Cairo?" MN80-M said in a soft tone.

The JAPANESE WOMAN standing next to him smiles and responds in English,

"Yes." she said as The JAPANESE GIRL a much younger identical version of her, standing next to her, turns around and says at the same time in English,

"We are trying to go to central Cairo. This man here help-ing us." she said with a smile.

MN80M Looks at the two men standing as the FRENCH YOUNG MAN smiles and says in English,

"Hello. We are trying to secure a taxi, but they say no one is going out right now until the morning. We need to go towards Tahrir Square." said the FRENCH YOUNG MAN.

MN80M smiles while speaking to himself first in his mind as the young French man is speaking and he looks at him as if listening to each word.

"Tahrir Square. What the hell are you coming into Egypt today for and going straight towards the battle zone in Tahrir Square???" said MN80M to himself in his head.

MN80M THE AMAZING speaks out in English.

"Hello. Nice to meet you too, I think getting out of the airport right now is not permitted. I think we can do it though, but it will be difficult. Have you tried speaking to these taxi drivers?" MN80-M said out loud enough for the group of Egyptians next to them all to hear.

The FRENCH YOUNG MAN nods his head as if in agreement then responds in English with,

"Yes. We try. But everyone saying same thing until now. But some taxi's we have seen take people out, so we keep asking." he said in a broken English dialect.

MN80M looks around from left to right again and then says,

"I see over there some cars. Let me go and ask them for us." MN80M then walks over in the direction of a couple of taxi drivers in conversation with other passengers.

[MEANWHILE AT THE SAME TIME
IN A DIFFERENT LOCATION]

EXTERIOR OF LOCATION; TAHRIR SQUARE,
CAIRO, EGYPT:
DAY 5: NIGHT;

Buildings continue burning down. The police are nowhere to be seen and the army tanks are in the square among thou—sands of demonstrators remaining vigilant. The thousands of people are doing the same so that their demands and passion to protect one another's dignity and remain in control of the square properly for the first time continues as they start to form road blocks on the main entry exit points.

[MEANWHILE AT THE SAME TIME
IN A DIFFERENT LOCATION]

INSIDE OF LOCATION; TAXI/ EGYPT
INTERNATIONAL AIRPORT, CAIRO, EGYPT:
DAY 5: NIGHT;

MN80M-THE AMAZING ONE/Male and the other three passengers get into the taxi. MN80M is now in the taxi with the two JAPANESE FEMALES and the FRENCH YOUNG MAN on route towards central Cairo, out from the airport.

"We sure are lucky. But are you all sure it's ok if I come along the journey." MN80—M said asking out in English towards The FRENCH YOUNG MAN now sitting in the front passenger seat.

"Yes. Thank you for your assistance." said the FRENCH YOUNG MAN in his broken English dialect. The JAPANESE WOMAN DAUGHTER says in English, "Thank you!" with a smile as she waves at MN80—M. MN80M— THE AMAZING ONE/MALE smiles and says back in Japanese

"You are welcome. Thank God."

The Japanese women double looks at MN80M in shock that he spoke Japanese.

MN80M smiles as the car starts motion. The Egyptian TAXI DRIVER speaks out in Arabic,

"Please sir, make sure they prepare the money from now."
MN80M—THE AMAZING ONE/MALE responds in Arabic,

"Yes no problem. But I still think 500 is too much, and you know it." he said quickly as if still in a negotiation mode with the driver from moments before getting into the vehicle with the other passengers.

The vehicle is silent as the Egyptian TAXI DRIVER then says back in Arabic,

"Sir you know how it is now. No one is going out onto the streets. The army can take my license, and how will I work. I have a wife and four children, and we look after my mother in-law as well, she is very sick. Please, let us not debate about this now when we already did."

MN80M THE AMAZING ONE/MALE smiles saying in Arabic,

"Like I said to you, no problem, but you know as well as I do. From here to Ramses, and then Tahrir, is not even 100. But God knows everything."

Another moment of silence before MN80M—THEAMAZ-ING ONE/MALE continues to say in English towards the others in the vehicle,

"The driver was just asking me kindly to pay him from now, because he is worried that the army might stop him and take his license."

MN80M puts his hand into his pocket and takes out his wallet. The FRENCH YOUNG MAN does the same. The JAPANESE WOMAN DAUGHTER says in English,

"Ok. Here you go, as we agreed. 300 Egyptian for the two of us"

The JAPANESE WOMAN DAUGHTER hands over to MN80Mthe money cash. The YOUNG FRENCH MAN says in English.

"One hundred and fifty from me too, thanks."

MN80M THE AMAZING ONE/MALE responds with,

"Fifty from me, totals 500. Here you go. You give it to him." MN80M said as he hands the cash money over to the YOUNG FRENCH MAN in the front passenger seat next to the driver.

The Egyptian TAXI DRIVER eagerly waiting with a smile places out his hand saying in English,

"Thank you! Thank you!"

The Taxi Driver then looks in his rear view mirror at MN80-M. and smiles. MN80M notices and stares back for a moment. The JAPANESE WOMAN DAUGHTER speaks out in Japanese in an attempt to defuse any tension, "You speak Japanese good. How comes?" she said in a joyful tone.

MN80M-THE AMAZING ONE/MALE says back in Japanese.

"Forgive me. I wish my Japanese language skills were good. I only know one or two words. oh. And my name is MN80-M. Pleased to meet you. Both of you, Welcome to Egypt." said MN80M

The JAPANESE WOMAN DAUGHTER smiles. MN80-M. smiles at her and then looks back at the driver saying to him in Arabic,

"Make sure you drop me off where we agreed on before I got into the vehicle." said MN80-M in a more serious tone.

"But sir. I may not be able to now, the road closes up ahead, and I have to go around. Would it be ok if I drop you off before we go up on the bridge." the Egyptian TAXI DRIVER said in Arabic nervously.

MN80M THE AMAZING ONE/MALE pauses for a moment and then says in Arabic,

"That is not what we agreed on. I told you my sister lives in Heliopolis and/or New Cairo if you can drop me off to the closest area. I hope this is the road. Go on then. Drop me off there then God willing." he said as the Egyptian TAXI DRIVER sarcastically says back in English,

"yes sir. Thank you!" he said as he continues to drive out from the airport security gates.

The long moment of silence allows the YOUNG FRENCH MAN the opportunity to ask in English,

"Is everything ok?" he said in a more understandable English tone.

MN80M THE AMAZING ONE/MALE responds in French,

"Yes." said MN80-M and then smiles.

The YOUNG FRENCH MAN then quickly asks back in French,

"You speak French too.?? How many languages do you speak?"

MN80M smiles and responds in English,

"Just one or two. My French is limited to a few words. Yes and no." Both laugh as MN80M—THE AMAZING ONE/MALE continues in English,

"Will you all be ok on your own? Please take my email address and contact number." said MN80-M as he places his hand into his jacket pocket in search of a pen.

The JAPANESE WOMAN AND DAUGHTER also starts looking for a pen and paper in bag. The YOUNG FRENCH MAN sitting next to the driver is already writing on a piece of paper as the JAPANESE WOMAN DAUGHTER says in English,

"Yes. We will be ok. When do you have to leave?" she said.

MN80M—THE AMAZING ONE/MALE looks at her

with a smile before he says back in English, "Before we reach to the bridge."

The JAPANESE WOMAN DAUGHTER responds,

"Ok. Here you go. This is our contact information. Thank you!" she said.

MN80M smiles accepting, "Thank you!" he said.

MN80M smiles as the car starts to come to a halt. The Egyptian TAXI DRIVER speaks out in English.

"Sir. I am sorry, but I will have to drop you off here, is that ok."

The YOUNG FRENCH MAN suddenly Says,

"Here, take my information before you go."

MN80M-THE AMAZING ONE/MALE says in Arabic to the driver,

"Yes, this is ok, thank you."

MN80M smiles and continues in English while looking at the other passengers.

"Thank you. And if you need anything, please email me ok." The YOUNG FRENCH MAN now seated has fully turned around in his chair and responds in English. "Ok. It was a pleasure meeting with you. Thank you again M." he said.

MN80M-THE AMAZING ONE/MALE says back in English,

"The pleasure was all mine."

MN80M then looks at the JAPANESE WOMAN and her daughter, smiles and says in Japanese,

"Thank you for your kindness. I wish you a safe journey." The JAPANESE WOMAN smiles and MN80M smiles back at her and her daughter as the car comes to a halt. MN80Mexits the door as the JAPANESE WOMAN says out in Japanese,

"Always remember the inner soul . . . The inner soul within you. Your greatest Ohako is true."

MN80M THE AMAZING ONE/MALE glances back taking in a deep breath as he glances into her eyes as if they had met before. He now has a smile while closing the door softly and watching the Taxi drive off towards the bridge.

[MEANWHILE AT THE SAME TIME
IN A DIFFERENT LOCATION]

EXTERIOR OF LOCATION: CAIRO,
EGYPT: Tahrir: DAY 5: NIGHT;

Only two helicopters hover in the night sky as buildings continue to burn down while the thousands of demonstrators have taken control of Tahrir Square, known as Liberation Square in Cairo, Egypt.

[MEANWHILE AT THE SAME TIME
IN A DIFFERENT LOCATION]

EXTERIOR OF LOCATION:
NEW CAIRO, EGYPT:
DAY 5: NIGHT;

MN80M-THE AMAZING ONE/MALE is walking on the right hand side under the bridge area and crosses the road with his rucksack on his back. The entire street and whole area is deserted, and minimal to no one is on the streets. MN80Mhas a long walk on the road ahead of him, yet he is on the right track and continues. The near enough star-less dark blue sky and the silence of the city roads seem surreal as MN80M-THE AMAZING ONE/MALE continues to walk alone. A mile ahead of him a group of army tanks approach. MN80M-THE AMAZING ONE/MALE speaks his mind, "Shit. is that army tanks?? Fucking hell man . . . What the fuck is going on!!??!!" MN80M said as he continues to walk along the side walk in the direction of the oncoming tanks. The Egyptian Army tanks are soon closer to MN80-M. then he could have imagine, yet the tanks continue past MN80-M, as he continues walking forward on the deserted road. MN80M looks up into the night sky as he continues to speak to himself in mind,

"Oh my gosh . . . So this is what they mean by Curfew?" he said as he continues to walk as the army tanks pass him on the other side of the road heading in the opposite direction. MN80M continues walking until he notices a group of individuals a couple hundred meters away.

[MEANWHILE AT THE SAME
TIME IN SAME LOCATION]

EXTERIOR OF LOCATION;
NEW CAIRO, EGYPT:
DAY 5: NIGHT;

GROUP OF YOUNG MEN (Forty or so of them) holding machetes and sticks are standing on the corner of a road while some are placing more objects into the road block they created out of vehicles and tires, with a burning fire. One of the individuals notices MN80M walking towards them with his bag on his back from afar. He waits for MN80M to approach closer before saying anything to anyone else.

[MEANWHILE AT THE SAME
TIME IN SAME LOCATION]

EXTERIOR OF LOCATION;
NEW CAIRO, EGYPT:
DAY 5: NIGHT;

MN80M THE AMAZING is still walking towards the
GROUP OF YOUNG MEN along the deserted street of
Cairo. MN80Mreaches one hundred meters nearer to the
GROUP OF MEN and one individual starts to approach.

[MEANWHILE AT THE SAME
TIME IN SAME LOCATION]

EXTERIOR OF LOCATION;
NEW CAIRO, EGYPT:
DAY 5: NIGHT;

GROUP OF YOUNG MEN (One individual) holding a
machete walks towards MN80M
"Say your name and where you are from exactly?" The
YOUNG MAN WITH MACHETTE shouted out in Ara-
bic as the young man holds up his machete towards his side
hip level.

[MEANWHILE AT THE SAME
TIME IN SAME LOCATION]

EXTERIOR OF LOCATION;
NEW CAIRO, EGYPT:
DAY 5: NIGHT;

MN80M-THE AMAZING ONE/MALE continues walking towards the YOUNG MAN. MN80M reaches twenty

meters nearer to the YOUNG MAN and can hear what he has said, yet ignores and continues to walk towards him and all the others silently.

[MEANWHILE AT THE SAME TIME IN SAME LOCATION]

EXTERIOR OF LOCATION;
NEW CAIRO, EGYPT:
DAY 5: NIGHT;

GROUP OF YOUNG MEN (One individual) holding a machete walks towards MN80M, this time faster and the YOUNG MAN WITH MACHETTE shouts out in Arabic,

"I said. Say your name and where you are from exactly?" The Young man said as he holds up his machete towards MN80M

The group of men now start to become weary and gather around together as MN80M-THE AMAZING ONE/MALE continues walking towards and through/past the YOUNG MAN and the GROUP OF YOUNG MEN without answering them or saying a word.

MN80M reaches five meters and walks towards the YOUNG MAN WITH MACHETTE that now continues shouting out in Arabic,

"Are you stupid? or can you not hear me?" The YOUNG MAN WITH MACHETTE said while raising the shiny silver blades he holds in his hands.

MN80Mcontinues to walk closer to the young man responding this time, in English,

"Hello. How are you?" MN80M said with a smile.

The YOUNG MAN looks confused next to another YOUNG MAN WITH MACHETTE. One then approaches slowly from behind with others running towards MN80M's direction in a now apparent attack mode. The YOUNG MAN WITH MACHETTE 2 shouts out in Arabic,

"Who is he?"

MN80M THE AMAZING ONE/MALE hears what he said and quickly speaks out first in English, "Hello. How are you? My name is MN80M. I am going home to my sister's home. She lives here on this road. I just came from England, to be with the people, to be with all of you."

MN80M smiles as a YOUNG MAN WITH MACHETTE asks in Arabic,

"What is he saying?" he said.

THE YOUNG MAN swings his machete at MN80M-THE AMAZING ONE/MALE as some of the other men at the same time attempt to rush towards and jump on MN80-M.

MN80M-THE AMAZING ONE/MALE takes two steps forward, now closer to his first target, quickly grabbing the one arm holding the shiny silver machete, and with the other arm, now at a closer distance to his target within inches of THE YOUNG MAN, a quick movement in his wrist allows MN80M-THE AMAZING ONE/MALE to produce enough energy force needed, and with wrist now in a horizontal axis and knuckles facing out, in a rapid movement, MN80-M unleashes a one-inch-punch straight to the chest of THE YOUNG MAN, connecting as his wrist moves up striking hard with the bottom two knuckles forcing THE YOUNG MAN to start flying a few meters up into the air and eight meters back, and then down onto his back on the cold floor as if just hit by a truck. GROUP OF YOUNG

MEN stand in awe at what MN80-M has just done and are in shock for a moment.

MN80-M quickly moves around to feel his bearings as the other men surround him now while at the same time continuing to stand in awe.

"You are good fighter I can see . . ." A YOUNG MAN said in Arabic.

"I get better . . ." MN80-M said back in English.

Three men quickly move in with weapons to attack MN80—M as he moves out of the way from one attack attempt and quickly switches techniques on each individual, Jujitsu techniques to disable all of the young men within seconds, while at the same time Jeet Kune Do techniques making sure each one of them starts dropping all weapons to the ground and causing only minor injuries before talking to them.

"DO YOU BELIEVE ME NOW." shouted MN80-M in Arabic. "Please, I am not allowed to fight anyone, especially any of you. Please. Let me just go on my way in life and you stay with your way of life." MN80-M said again, but this time in the Japanese language as he continues looking around cautiously at each individual.

The YOUNG MAN WITH MACHETTE 2 holding his chest and trying to catch his breath shouts out in Arabic to the two men attempting to stand on their feet while the others continue laying down on the ground wounded,

"Ok, Ok . . . He is from England. He is going to his sister's home. I believe him now, let him go before he breaks all of our legs." The YOUNG MAN WITH MACHETTE 2 said while wounded on the floor speaking out to the others around him.

MN80—M smiles as he now walks slower while listening, yet continues forward, away from the fighting. The YOUNG MAN WITH MACHETTE 2 shouts out in English, "OK! Ok! Welcome to Egypt. Go, it's ok. Go. You Prince" MN80M continues to walk, this time picking up his pace as he passes many of the GROUP OF YOUNG MEN on the floor that were holding machetes. The YOUNG MAN WITH MACHETTE 2 then says in Arabic, "Everyone. He is from England. Let him to pass. Let him to pass." he said still in a wounded tone of voice.

The GROUP OF YOUNG MEN all watch as MN80M continues to walk past each one straight ahead on the main road. MN80M smiles while walking the same long dark deserted road. He continues on forward towards his sister's home not looking back once.

[MEANWHILE AT THE SAME TIME
IN A DIFFERENT LOCATION]

INTERIOR OF LOCATION:
MN80M SISTER F's APARTMENT,
CAIRO, EGYPT
DAY 5: NIGHT;

MN80M SISTER F is sitting alone working on the laptop and speaking on the phone. All the doors locked and a bag and her hand-bag ready by the door with her jacket. The dog's are sitting next to her as the Television is on very loud with the TV News broadcasting in background as MN80M SISTER F is speaking in English on the telephone, "I know mum. But what can I do? The whole country is on curfew now. Mum, even now on the news is saying the air—port closed. A flights were cancelled, MN80M is lucky he found one. They will probably stay at the airport until the morning. I know mum. But what can I do!!?? It would be impossible for anyone to come out, so I do not think he will be coming to me tonight mum. Yes mum. Ok mum. As soon as he comes to me, I will call you." she said as she then presses a button on her phone and then places it next to her and one of the dogs on the sofa.

The TV NEWS BROADCAST continues in English in the background.

"This reporting live from Tahrir Square right now, the situation has worsened, and it is apparent that the police are no longer to be seen."

MN80M SISTER F higher s the volume on the Television as the TV NEWS BROADCASTER continues in English,

"The situation at Cairo Airport as we know it remains the same. Flights since yesterday afternoon coming Egypt have been cancelled. And apparently one or two international flights have started to arrive, yet this is curfew time, and no one would be permitted out of the airport." said the broadcaster.

MN80M SISTER F looks on attentively as she types on the laptop.

[MEANWHILE AT THE SAME TIME
IN A DIFFERENT LOCATION]

EXTERIOR OF LOCATION: NEW CAIRO, EGYPT:

MN80M-THE AMAZING ONE/MALE has located the street that MN80M SISTER F has her apartment within. MN80M encounters several road blocks of individuals holding sticks and/or machetes, none of which ask MN80M who he is as he continues to walk slowly in the shadows of the

trees coming onto the streets a few meters apart. MN80-M
continues alone past them all and the fires that are alight
on the street. MN80-M. looks around him while searching
for the exact road to turn into as he passes each GROUP OF
YOUNG MEN. MN80M-THE AMAZING ONE/MALE
speaks out in Arabic, "Peace and blessings onto you all." The
GROUP OF YOUNG MEN respond in Arabic, "Peace and
blessings onto you too." as they look at MN80-M. wearily as
he continues to walk and notices the road he needs to turn
into, and does so. But just as he passes another GROUP OF
YOUNG MEN with machetes and sticks at the beginning of
his sisters road, starts calling out to MN80M-THE AMAZ-
ING ONE/MALE as he continues to walk into the road
towards his final destination.

"You! I said you there. Where are you going?" shouted out
The YOUNG MAN in Arabic.

MN80M continues to walk into the road, now only
200 meters from his sisters' apartment, The YOUNG MAN
shouts out again in Arabic,

"Where you are going?"

MN80M just heard what the young man had asked, yet
continues to walk as the YOUNG MAN runs over to his
friends to alert them as he runs towards MN80M

"We have an intruder . . .

We have an intruder. Hurry! Hurry! Come quickly."

The YOUNG MAN signals with his stick in the air as more
of the GROUP OF YOUNG MEN start to join in running towards MN80M knowingly hearing them, continues
to walk, now only 100 meters away from his destination.
Another YOUNG MAN 2 shouts out in Arabic, "Quickly,
get him now . . . ." as he throws from a far his machete in
the direction of MN80M while he continues to walk slowly.
MN80—M turns around quickly and catches the machete

with his left hand without those on coming runners even noticing as they continue shouting out words and running towards him in a panic. MN80-M quickly throws the machete under one of the parked vehicles quickly without anyone noticing. MN80M-THE AMAZING ONE/MALE speaks to himself for a moment in English,

"Either I break their bones, or talk them out of this, which one M . . . Which one . . . ." he said.

MN80-M then says out loud in English,

"Hello. Salam. I am just going to my sister's home."

Several of the GROUP OF YOUNG MEN are now closer to MN80M The GROUP OF YOUNG MEN shout out in Arabic,

"We have an intruder. Get him . . ."

The GROUP OF YOUNG MEN start charging towards MN80-M yet MN80M remains calm and stands still saying out louder than before in English,

"Hello. I am from England. My sister lives here." and then he continues in Arabic,

"My sister lives here. I just came from the airport from Eng— land. I live here. Come and see." he said.

The brave GROUP OF YOUNG MEN stop running as they get closer to MN80M-THE AMAZING ONE/MALE. The YOUNG MAN 2 says in Arabic to the others around him that await eagerly to fight,

"He is not from here. He is from England."

MN80M-THE AMAZING ONE/MALE smiles and says in English, "My sister lives here. You can come with me if you like." said MN80-M with a smile on his face looking into the eyes of each of the brave young men. MN80M continues to walk, looking over his shoulder. The YOUNG MAN 2 signals with his stick in hand to the GROUP OF YOUNG MEN. The YOUNG MAN 2 says in Arabic to his friends,

"Come. Leave him. He is going to his sister's home. Let's go back to the road." The YOUNG MAN 2 said.

MN80M continues to walk to the entry doors of MN80M SISTER F's apartment building now only yards away. The GROUP OF YOUNG MEN all turn back and start walking towards the road entrance again. MN80M walks up to the door and through the entrance to the main door of MN80M SISTER F's apartment. THE MN80M SISTER F CARETAKER is standing with his sons at the entrance. MN80M-THE AMAZING ONE/MALE smiles and places his hand out to greet saying in Arabic, "Peace and blessings onto you. My sister lives here. Her name is . . ." said MN80-M as the caretaker and sons follow behind MN80-M now walking together with him as he approaches and knocks on the door.

{MEANWHILE AT THE SAME TIME
IN SAME LOCATION}

INTERIOR OF LOCATION: MN80M SISTER F's
APARTMENT, CAIRO, EGYPT;
NIGHT;

MN80M SISTER F is typing on her laptop. The dog starts to bark once hearing/sensing the footsteps close to the door. The sound of the door knocking alerts the dog even more as she moves fast to run.

"Who is it?" MN80M SISTER F said in
Arabic while startled, as she is not expecting anyone.

The door knocks again, only this time twice more as MN80M-SISTER F speaks out again in Arabic this time louder,

"Who is it?" she shouted out.

MN80M-THE AMAZING ONE/MALE voice can be heard saying back in English,

"It's me SIS. MN80M Open up. Everything is ok. It's me." he said from behind the door standing with the caretaker man and his youngest son.

MN80M SISTER F looking startled responds in English,

"MN80M" she said as she turns the keys in the door to unlock and then open the door. The door opens with the continuing and increasing sounds of the barking as MN80M-THE AMAZING ONE/MALE is standing with his two bags, one on his shoulder, and the other in hand with a smile. MN80M says in English, "Hello sister. I made it." MN80Msmiles as does MN80M-SISTER F as she says, "Come in M . . ."

The CARETAKER asks out in Arabic while standing in the background, "Is everything ok?" MN80M SISTER F responds in Arabic,

"Yes thank you! My brother came like I said to you all." she said.

The CARETAKER rubbing his eyes from sleep deprivation says back in Arabic,

"Yes. Good to see him. Welcome, if you need anything just call for me or my sons."

MN80M SISTER F smiles while responding to what he just said with,

"Ok. No problem. Thank you!" she said.

MN80M walks into the apartment with the dog blocking his entry from excitement yet allowing him to pass through so she can have more space to jump up onto him in hope that his attention would be on her and her only first. MN80M SISTER F closes the door behind MN80M

The both embrace with a hug. MN80M-THE AMAZING ONE/MALE then says,

"Good to see you my sister."

"Good to see you too brother, so you made it then from the airport ok?" she said.

MN80M-THE AMAZING ONE/MALE responds in Arabic saying, "Yeah well. You know me."

Both smile. MN80M SISTER F,

"Come in and put your bag down. Relax. Let me put the kettle on." she said happily.

The dog is still jumping around in excitement as MN80-M. walks in through the hallway area into the bed—room. MN80M SISTER F walks into the kitchen to put the kettle on and takes her phone out of her pocket to make a call.

{MEANWHILE AT THE SAME TIME
IN ANOTHER LOCATION}

EXTERIOR OF LOCATION: CAIRO, EGYPT: Tahrir:
NIGHT;

The political party building is burning down while some individuals are running towards the entrance direction of the Egyptian MUSEUM.

[MEANWHILE AT THE SAME TIME
IN A DIFFERENT LOCATION]

INTERIOR OF LOCATION: (BATHROOM) MN80M
SISTER F APARTMENT, CAIRO, EGYPT; NIGHT;

MN80M-THE AMAZING ONE/MALE is washing his face with water and completing (wuduu/ washing) his wash for prayers. He speaks out whispering in Arabic as the water falls from his face,

"Dear God. Accept my wash for my prayers. Thank you for allowing me a safe journey into Egypt, and to find my sister safe. Thank you Allah thank you God. Thank you."

MN80M SISTER F comes to the door to speak to him. The door knocks and MN80M-THE AMAZING ONE/ MALE responds in English, "Yes" he said.

MN80M SISTER F says back in English, "The kettle has finished boiling, shall I make us a cup of tea."

"Coffee if you have it please. I am just washing to pray, will be with you in a short minute Insha Allah. OK!?!"

MN80M SISTER F still standing at the bathroom door says back,

"OK! will be in the sitting room when you ready OK. Thanks." she said as she turns to walk away slowly.

MN80M-THE AMAZING ONE/MALE continues to wash his face while saying,

"OK. Thank you." and then continues to wash his face, arms, head and then feet as he performs washing ritual for prayers,

"In the name of Allah, Most gracious, Most merciful."

{MEANWHILE AT THE SAME TIME
IN ANOTHER LOCATION}

EXTERIOR OF LOCATION: TAHRIR SQUARE,
CAIRO, EGYPT:
NIGHT;

The Egyptian MUSEUM is deserted from inside and out. Some individuals are seen climbing the fire escape in an attempt to break into the landmark location filled with priceless artifacts.

[MEANWHILE IN A DIFFERENT LOCATION]

INSIDE OF LOCATION: (BEDROOM) MN80M-
SISTER F's APARTMENT
CAIRO, EGYPT.
NIGHT

The door is closed and MN80M-THE AMAZING ONE/ MALE has finished praying. MN80Mcontinues speaking in English to himself silently while all alone in the bedroom, "Thank you God for everything you have given me, and about to give to me. Thank you god for everything you have given my family and about to give my family. My safe journey here, and God willing home once I have dealt with all that is needed here and find out what happened last year exactly before I deal with any of the situations happening now." MN80M-THE AMAZING ONE/MALE said calmly as he stands and walks to open the door.

{MEANWHILE AT THE SAME TIME
IN ANOTHER LOCATION}

EXTERIOR OF LOCATION: CAIRO MUSEUM:
EGYPT:
NIGHT:

A GROUP OF MEN DRESSED AS THUGS are on the roof top and preparing to break into the Museum from the glass area. A MAN DRESSED AS THUG is whispering loudly in Arabic to many others around him also suited in unnoticeable dark clothing,

"Quickly, hurry up now. Smash the glass and give me the rope." he said.

A MAN DRESSED AS THUG then signals with his hand to others around him.

"Quickly."

[MEANWHILE AT THE SAME TIME
IN A DIFFERENT LOCATION]

INSIDE OF LOCATION: MN80M SISTER F
APARTMENT,
CAIRO, EGYPT; NIGHT;

Now dressed in MN80M-SPECIAL-TRACKSUIT track-suit, MN80M is sitting with his sister in the living room drinking a hot beverage and in conversation while the Dog is in a calm mode laying on the sofa. The TV sounds on low in background as MN80M-THE AMAZING ONE/MALE asks in English,

"So how is everything with you my sister?" he said.

Both smile. MN80M SISTER F responds with, "Hectic as you can see. I'm surprised they let you out of the airport." she said calmly with a smile. Both smile.

MN80M-THE AMAZING ONE/MALE responds,

"God is the Greatest. Plus, I could not leave you all alone here tonight could I."

Both smile.

MN80M SISTER F says. "It is late. Let's call mum." and then picks up her phone and presses a button. MN80—M.

watches the TV broadcast as MN80M SISTER F is now speaking in English on the phone,

"Hi mum. Yes he made it. Here he is."

MN80M. looks at MN80M. SISTER F, and accepts the phone,

"Hello mum. I made it safely ok. I am sorry for shouting or being rude mum. I love you ok. I just have to do this for me mum, be the man I have to be ok. I am sorry Mum ok. and please do not be upset with me, my MN80-M EMPATHY LEVELS lower each time you or anyone I love do. And please do not take away from me the MN80-M. MUMS SPECIAL STRAWBERRY JAM. I promise I am trying my best to be good mum ok, I even cut down on smoking nicotine, and smoking the strong hashish or cannabis is nearly in my past, the nicotine is the main killer, and smoking kills I know, but this is not easy to stop, especially with all this stress and death pains I feel, and being around people who smoke cigarettes all the time has to stop soon too, God willing it shall as soon as possible, even if it takes me two years to stop, I am trying my best here. Smoking two twenty packs of cigarettes a day, now down to one pack a day, is better than increasing smoking nicotine, this is my struggle, and should not be a concern to any one, or be anyone's business. But you upset me when you just keep getting involved when it's not about you, and you upset me when you give most, if not all of the MN80-MUMS STRAWBERRY JAM away for free, it's like everything grows on trees for free or something and you near enough always give the MN80-M SPECIAL FOOD PACK away free. I would not mind if just the MN80-M SPECIAL FOOD PACK 3, but you give away the MN80-M SPECIAL FOOD PACK 1 as well, and that has the MN80-M SPECIAL MILK, and MN80-M SPECIAL WATER inside with all the other MN80-M

SPECIAL FOOD ITEMS and the MN80-M SPECIAL SUPER HOT SAUCE attached with the MN80-M SPECIAL8TOOTHPICK PACK. All which I must add, come from the MN80-M SPECIAL COMPANY SOURCE, the same source that has to milk the MN80-M SPECIAL COWS, and this is not all free. Please mum, don't upset me, and I will not react this way, I am showing you what upsets me, and yet you still do what you do, mainly for your own benefit to benefit others. Stop it, please mum, you only have one son. Always remember this. And if anything, give for free the MN80-M SPECIAL PRAYER PACK 1 & 2. Or the MN80-M SPECIAL HEALTH PACK 1 & 2. There is MN80-M SPECIAL WATER inside those packs too you know with MN80-M SPECIAL BREAD and MN80-M SPECIAL FRUIT & VEGI's. Please mum, we must think of the future more, nothing is free anymore in life like it used to be, and you know this mum, even though we add extra into the MN80-M SPECIAL PACKs' for free, from love, but adding the extra MN80-M SPECIAL RICE and things like MN80-M SPECIAL RAISEN & DATES is not free, it costs us mum. Humanity remember . . . . This a main reason I shouted at you earlier, mum, you have always done things the ancient ways, and I love you for this natural-nurture. But thank you Mum. I love you Mum. Sorry mum. Ok mum, yes mum I have with me the MN80-M SPECIAL PACKS and more. Yes Mum. I got the MN80-M SPECIAL CHOCOLATES and MN80-M SPECIAL COLA BOTTLES and most of the MN80-M SPECIAL SWEETS & SPECIAL CAKES. Yes mum. Ok mum. Yes mum, I got for her the MN80-M SPECIAL HAIR-DYE you wanted her to have, and the MN80-M SPECIAL FEMALE HAIR EXTENSIONs', and the MN80-M. SPECIAL FEMALE EYE LASHES, and the MN80M. SPECIAL WEDDING

DRESS. Ok mum. Yes mum. I got the MN80-M SPECIAL MUMS SPINACH inside one of the packs remember. And I have with me the MN80-M SPECIAL GLASSES. But I do not have the MN80-M-SPECIAL-CHINESE-MEDICINE-PACK or the MN80-M(SCP) SPECIAL COMMUNICATIONS PAD, or the MN80-M. SPECIAL GLOVES, but I have another pair of special gloves, it's just not the same, so I am limited to help everyone mum, but you and I do not need that now do we . . . It's just, I have to be here to help out mum . . . I have to do this as a man, and for Humanity in general, plus it's not my fault the other six or seven are practically rotten apples, I can only do my best. Even if it kills me, God forbid. Ok mum. I am sorry mum. Ok mum. Yes mum.Ok mum. Yes mum . . ." MN80M. smiles as he continues,

"Yes mum. ok mum. I will mum. Thank you mum. ok mum. As soon as I know. Ok mum. Love you mum. ok mum. bye mum. here she is." he said as he passes the phone back to MN80M SISTER F and she accepts phone with a smile,

"Ok mum. He is staying here anyway. He is welcome or he can go home, it's up to him. Ok mum. bye mum." she said as she presses the button on phone and puts the phone next to her side.

MN80M-THE AMAZING ONE/MALE asks,

"So what's the latest news? What's happening?"

"As you can see obviously. No more police. Just army." she said.

The room is silent for a moment as the sounds of the Television remain.

"I do not understand . . . How can there be no more police? And why are there men outside with machetes and sticks.?? What's all that about." MN80-M asked.

MN80M SISTER F then responds saying, "That is all from last night and into today. The police have been taken off the streets, no longer working. The army is in control now of the street in major areas, and everyone else is left to defend his or her homes. All those you see outside, and all over Egypt the same, is people who live on each street protecting his or her area. Unless you live here, and get home before the curfew, then no one is allowed in or out of any road. You are very lucky to have come out of the airport." she said as if in disbelief still of his arrival.

MN80Msmiles as he turns to look at the TV broadcast and then back towards MN80M SISTER F while saying to himself in Arabic in mind.

"God is great!"

He said as he takes in a deep breath and then says out loud in English,

"Thank God. I am happy to have arrived back to Egypt. So what's the latest with all the family stuff? What's happening with what happened last year?" asked MN80M-MN80M SISTER F looks away and back again before she responds with,

"Nothing is happening. Everything is the same as I last said to you. Plus, how can anything get done now with all that is happening these days?" she said wearily.

MN80M-THE AMAZING ONE/MALE sits up straight from his position to respond to her,

"This should not be a concern to what is happening. Who do I need to speak to them about this all?" he said as MN80M SISTER F responds quickly with, "No one. Who can or will do anything anyway?? If you want to speak to the uncles involved, then that is up to you." she said.

MN80M-THE AMAZING ONE/MALE now looking slightly annoyed at what he just heard her say placing his hands on his face,

"Yeah but what about my and MN80M SISTER N paperwork? You still have not helped with that have you!??! No! So what is it happening with that then? How comes you don't want to use a freedom-wasta-pass on us then??"

"Nothing. Like I said before, we need to ask the right people the right questions." she said quickly.

"What do you mean the right people the right questions?? This has been nearly two years now, and what do I have for it all? Nothing!!!! Only headache, becoming sick, and even more Grey hairs while I return to London the poor person." MN80-M said out loud forcefully as MN80M SISTER F takes in a deep breath and blows out the air quickly, yet slows the pace down slowly through her now semi-closed mouth and pouted lips as if about to boil over like a kettle.

"What you talking about.? stop being stupid." she said back in an attempt to hold back the anger in her tone.

MN80M-THE AMAZING ONE/MALE notices this and decides to quickly respond with,

"It's the truth. You were OK to get all of your paper work done after I handed you the final piece that we needed, and what did you do!!?? You get it for yourself, and not for us." said MN80-M as his face changes into an upset and aggressive look.

"I told you that we are still trying to ask the right people the right questions so we can do it the best way. I am still working on it OK." she said.

MN80M-THE AMAZING ONE/MALE smiles and says,

"How many times in 24 months do I hear you say the same thing? And every two months or so, you say the same or similar thing."

MN80M—SISTER F lowers her head for a brief moment to what he just said and then smiles back saying, "Because that is the truth." she said innocently.

"Yeah God knows . . ."

"What is that supposed to mean?" she says back at him as they quickly go back and forth as if in a fast argument.

MN80M-THE AMAZING ONE/MALE then quickly says,

"It means, what it means. Anyway . . . Tomorrow I can visit the uncles and aunties and see what they say about what happened last year without my knowledge or approval." MN80M SISTER F raises her eye brows and responding with,

"Good. See what they say." she said as if challenging manner.

MN80M-THE AMAZING ONE/MALE smiles while nodding his head as if in agreement in the conversation.

"Insha Allah I will. And find out the truth once and for all God willing . . . . Anyway . . . on another positive note, what's the channel number for that action channel with films on, I've had enough of watching news, and a I really do miss Egyptian television, even if I watch English channels mainly, I still love it here . . ."

The outside sounds of screaming and shouting all of a sudden surprisingly shocks both as well as many outside as the dogs start barking and jumping around near the Balcony door area.

"What's that??" MN80-M said,

Both rise to feet and MN80M SISTER F in a semi-shocked tone of voice says out as if whispering,

"I don't know. I don't know . . ." and then she looks at MN80M.

The outside screams continue in the background as MN80—M. SISTER F continues speaking,

"Someone is trying to get onto the street and the boys and men have caught them." she said as she moves towards the Balcony door.

The sounds of others running past on the street outside the apartment balcony combined with a sound of a woman screaming clearly shows the severity of this now extreme hazardous environment MN80-M has come into, and especially at this stage. MN80M-THE AMAZING ONE/MALE eyebrows curl in as he looks around,

"What the Fuck is that!!????" he said.

Both look at each other with a serious look. MN80M SISTER F moves closer to the balcony door area to double check she has locked it,

"This is what it has been like since last night. Once curfew is over then everyone has to stay inside. If not, they are considered an intruder and/or a thief, as news reports show many shops, homes, and other places looted in a major way. It's OK. Let's just go to sleep now, and hopefully in the morning we can talk more." said his sister as MN80Mnods his head in agreement saying, "Ok. Just rest for now, everything is ok Insha Allah." he said and smiles as MN80M SISTER F sits back down on the sofa, and takes/pulls the duvet to cover over her body. The dog calms down and join her on the sofa. MN80M looks at the TV.

"Good night my Sister." he said.

MN80M SISTER F responds,

"Good night MN80M Thank you for coming." she said in a more calm and relaxed tone as MN80M lays down on the sofa opposite, switches off the lights next to him and looks at the TV as he rests his head on the pillow unable to sleep. He picks up his phone to check the time and date and reads out in his mind silently,

"Sunday 30th January 2011—New Cairo, Egypt 2:52 AM must be day six now, get some rest M. Day six is going to be very interesting, and fruitful to some God willing. Whatever you do, keep calm and do not use any of your skills unless you need to defend yourself M, and your family too first. Just don't get involved in this all, and find out first what happened last year. Thank God you made it here now, Egypt. Where this shall all begin Insha Allah, again . . ." MN80M said as he smiles.

{THE FOLLOWING DAY SAME LOCATION}

INSIDE OF LOCATION: MN80M SISTER F
APARTMENT,
CAIRO, EGYPT:
DAY 6; Sunday 30th January 2011—New Cairo, Egypt
8:57 AM

The sun has started to sine though the window and MN80M-THE AMAZING ONE/MALE is waking up slowly. MN80M SISTER F is already awake and walking around the apartment. MN80M stands from his laying down position,

"Good morning." he said.

MN80M SISTER F has a smile on her face as she asks,

"Morning M. Did you sleep good?" she replied.

MN80M starts to walk towards the bathroom area. "Yeah, ok thanks. Not too bad." he said as he continues walking. "The kettle has boiled if you want to make a cup of tea or coffee?" MN80M SISTER F shouted back while standing in the kitchen area. MN80Msmiles. "Thanks I will. Let me pray first though, and then I want to go home before I speak to the Uncle and Aunties."

"Well MN80-M, have breakfast first. And I can come with you." she said.

"Breakfast sounds good to me. and that's up to you if you want to come with me home."

"Ok. Just get ready and I can prepare breakfast for us. I may come, I may not, I have work to do. Will try to find out now ok." she said as MN80M-THE AMAZING ONE/MALE starts nodding his head in agreement,

"Ok, thanks. But make sure you get the keys ready for me anyway. You said you changed the locks. So I need a key." MN80Msaid as he continues to walk towards the bath—room area. "What time is it anyway my sister?"

"It is near enough nine O clock." "Thanks."
MN80M walks into the bathroom area. MN80M SISTER F
takes her phone out of her pocket and presses a button then
lifts the phone to her ear.

{MEANWHILE IN ANOTHER LOCATION}

EXTERIOR OF LOCATION: TAHRIR SQUARE
CAIRO/EGYPT
DAY 6: Sunday 30th January 2011—9:27 AM

The square is filled with Hundreds of Thousands of demonstrators in large groups. Some army tanks are noticeable
as some form of law and order has appeared, yet remains at
a standstill. Many buildings have been burnt down and/or
are still burning to the ashes.

{MEANWHILE IN ANOTHER LOCATION}

EXTERIOR OF LOCATION: STREET
NEW CAIRO, EGYPT
DAY 6: Sunday 20th January 2011—New Cairo

MN80M-THE AMAZING ONE/MALE is walking alone
in search of a taxi along the main road nearest to MN80M
SISTER F apartment. Dozens of cars are constantly passing
on both sides of the main road. MN80M-THE AMAZING
ONE/MALE pulls out his mobile phone from his pocket,
takes off the back cover, and removes the battery and then
sim chip, placing inside a new Egyptian sim while then putting back the battery and back cover and presses a button to
switch it on and make a call. The early morning sun is hotter
than MN80-M is used to compared to the recent weather in

the United Kingdom. Many people are walking around in an early morning rush to go where-ever they needed to before the curfew time. MN80-M notices the phone now come on as he continues to walk and look back for an available white taxi. He presses the button on his phone while placing the phone to his ear and waiting for a moment.

"Hello, Estabina, peace and blessings onto you my brother, yes, the eagle has landed, where are you and everyone. Ok, Old Cairo, well then assure the brothers to stay strong brother ok, I am here to join you all. Yes brother, we do have much to catch up on, and I hope to hear and share with you soon ok I just have to take care of something very important quickly and I shall be with you. Yes, I am coming God willing. I am coming." MN80M Said as he smiles and then presses the button again while putting the phone back into his pocket, taking in two deep breaths as he speaks his mind while attempting to stop a taxi.

"I am coming . . . and thank God, there is a Taxi, I see one coming. Shall I take this one." he said to himself as he lets out a huge amount of the air that he breathed in moments ago. MN80M puts his hand out signaling the taxi to stop. The Taxi pulls up and stops right next to MN80M and he asks the driver a question in Arabic,

"Nasr City?" he said while trying to remember if his Arabic words said were correct and in an attempt to get his bearings of the city from his standing location.

The Taxi driver nods his head in acceptance and places his cap bearing an EG FLAG onto his head. MN80M opens the back passenger seat door and gets into the taxi slowly but first takes a look at the sun rising within the early morning clean breeze that now passes gently across his entire body. MN80-M smiles as he then enters the taxi. The taxi drives off.

MN80M-THE AMAZING ONE/MALE places his special mp3 player on and presses the button, French rap music comes on, MN80M Smiles as he nods his head slightly up and down looking out of the window as the taxi continues driving and he changes the song to some English Hip-Hop Music.

"I'm coming." he said as he whispers and continues looking out of the window towards the streets of Cairo. "God willing, I am coming."

{MEANWHILE AT THE SAME TIME
IN ANOTHER LOCATION}

EXTERIOR OF LOCATION; TAHRIR SQUARE/
CAIRO/EGYPT;
DAY 6: Sunday 30th January 2011—Egypt
9:44 AM

The atmosphere is alive with an uproar of voices as Hundreds of Thousands more brave young Egyptian men and women demonstrators continue pouring into the square in large groups into and within and around Liberation Square in support of the regime change and to put a halt to the extreme police brutality and corruption within the system. Some army tanks remain at a standstill while banners are being erected by supporters in support of the change. MN80M THE SPECIAL ONE/*FEMALE* (Unknown Age Possibly 20's to 30 Years Old) is notice—able among the crowd alone, with her EG bandanna still wrapped around her face as she looks from left to right at every one slowly like a hawk to prey. Her MN80-M-88-High-Carat-White-Golden Necklace lights up bright orange under her special attire, yet no one notices as the Demanding CROWD CHANTING in Arabic,

"Egypt!" "Egypt!" "Egypt!" "Egypt!", continues. MN80-M THE SPECIAL ONE/ FEMALE starts to walk towards and into the heart of the Egyptian crowd with her head held high. "Please Jesus, show me a sign. Please God. Show him to me. We need him more than his special ring. Please God. Let my dreams come true . . ." Said MN80M THE SPECIAL ONE/FEMALE while looking up into the sky at the Egyptian Eagle in flight above as she continues to walk into the next crowd chanting with the sounds intensifying louder than ever,

"The People & the Army are one hand . . ." "The People & the Army are one hand . . ." "The People & the Army are one hand . . ."

"Masr!" "Masr!" "Masr!" "Masr!" Said the brave young Egyptian demonstrators as MN80M THE SPECIAL ONE/FEMALE vanishes into the Hundreds of Thousands of people within Tahrir Square.

THE END; {to be continued.}

Part
2

THE
LAST EGYPTIAN
STANDING:
The Great Egyptian

CHAPTER (BEFORE)ONE ZERO NOW IT BEGINS . . .

INTERIOR OF LOCATION: UNKNOWN /
DAY:??—TIME:??:?? (GMT)
MONTH: FEBRUARY—YEAR: 1996

MN80M-THE AMAZING ONE/MALE (16 Years Old) is standing in a special room on his own next to the MN80-M-DRAGON-TEDDY and the seven or eight tubes coming up from the ground to ceiling with flashing pink and blue colors. Writing coming up from the tubes is read by MN80-M. and the room remains silent.

[Information taken out for book 2 or 3]

MN80M-THE AMAZING ONE/MALE smiles and says, "In the name of God. Yeah! I heard the MN80M-RE-DRAGON-TEDDY keep saying it. 'MN80M-MN80M-MN80M' how many times do you have to communicate this to me? I keep telling you as well, it sounds like the DRAGON-TEDDY is saying, 'MN8E', and not MN80M . . . Can you give me another clue please as to what you already asked of me to do. Where am I exactly please, is this Mars? Or is this the other location deep under the ocean like last time? And why am I not allowed to speak to anyone about anything apart from the Teddy-Bears you have said to me I would meet in my life, because I have only located two of them, and one is in the UK, and the other one is in EGYPT I think or BRAZIL or CHINA . . . . You all said I am not allowed to use any of my special powers unless approved, and only until I locate MN80M-LEO-THE-LION-TEDDY-BEAR will I be able to use more of the MN80M-SPECIAL EQUIPMENT. I have not been able to do so yet, and why me? From every creation, why pick me? Who can I speak to then if I cannot speak with any other Human? Who? You said family and special others always help, and you can pass messages on through them. And apart from the MN80M-SPECIAL-COMMUNICA-TIONS-EQUIPMENT you have already given to me to use secretly many years ago at-least to unload information, yet you all rarely answer my questions, plus, how am I supposed to use this MN80M-SPECIAL EQUIPMENT? Most of this technology is not even out for twenty or so years, people are bound to notice I am more advanced then they are, the only thing I can see so far I can hide, is like only eleven special items, the rest is too obvious. The best one for me is my MN80M-TV-CONTACT LENSES, what are these, made in China or Japan, these lenses are too perfect, even plasma Televisions are not even out, how am I supposed to keep a secret like this, like all of the secrets I have to keep, why??" asks MN80M-THE AMAZING ONE/MALE as he takes a step back to read the in-coming message.

[MN80M-SPECIAL WORDS SCROLLS UP THE GLASS TUBES]

MN80M-THE AMAZING ONE/MALE starts to read the hieroglyphic writing as the pink and blue lights continue to flash and glow in the room and words scrolling up the glass tubes from floor to the ceiling.

{{MN80M-MSG::::::::: THE MN80M-UK-TEDDY-BEAR may assist you; then, later, seek MN80-M-THE SPECIAL ONE/FEMALE-BUNNY-TEDDY-BEAR; and then later the MN8EM-SUPER-SPECIAL-TEDDY-BEAR:::::::::::MN80M-MSG completed . . .}}

The writing stops.

[Information taken out for book 2 or 3]

MN80M-THE AMAZING ONE/MALE smiles as he raises both arms slowly. The blue and pink lights in the room start to brighten, and the MN80M-SUPER-SONIC-LIGHT appears, and MN80-M vanishes with the light.

CHAPTER ONE

ZERO⁇⁇—NOW IT

BEGINS . . .

INTERIOR OF LOCATION: UNKNOWN /
DAY:??—TIME:??:?? (GMT)
MONTH: FEBRUARY/MARCH
YEAR: 2012

MN80M

(Quoted)

Imagine a true story, a miracle, with real events, in our life-time . . . and/or, then turn that into a fantasy film while reading with your own imagination this book. The real life event(s) finally written herein, has real people/CHARACTERS written in BOLD with the names changed for the book(s), but nearly all the real words, and actions, said and done in the past now, to be true here in writing. The present day already complete heartfelt story allows all to free the minds, and from this, I believe I am ready now to take the World by storm, to just be me, because yes, *"If you understand the languages of the World, you understand the stage . . . ."*

A Dedicated Poem: Title; "Author House"
Written by Author

— Allowing me to reach perfection.
— Untold corrections.
— This company & team allowed this progression.
— How can I thank them all enough, an expression.
— Or wait a minute. This is the blessing . . .
— Read the letters downwards for my icing.

— How can one express something amazing.
— Outer-Space is the way things look.
— Universal writer like those in centuries shall talk.
— Such a miracle poet they all lived with, and took.
— Energy taken for granted, then shook, one look at book.

A Dedicated Poem: Title; "Author House"
Written by Author
Date: 27th September 2011
Location: London, England, United Kingdom

Thank you all for your time, and most importantly, your energy with me and reading. Please do remember, this inspired by true events story, also has a super-fantasy added to create chemistry between the characters and readers on a global scale within the 2011/2012/2013 global market trends, this does not mean that any real life characters have special skills like those mentioned. Author accepts no responsibility for any misunderstandings that any reader may have, and would recommend that a medical consultant or a general practitioner is consulted if any issues may arise. Thank you!

Any inspirational characters that have inspired emotional written characters this book and storyline are kindly thanked by the Author for all of their kind energy and support. All should know in their hearts and minds; this could not have been completed without you!! So for the least, and for the record now, this is all you shall receive from Author, nothing more, nothing less. Empathy Levels Increase. This second edition is considered a work in progress still, as many parts {??Must fill in??} has been left out on purpose, in order to allow readers around the globe to participate in 2012 and 2013 with the Author via Universities and Colleges around the World, to assist with their thoughts and emotions of what should be best to be added, especially for the scenes in Egypt during the Egyptian Revolution. Author welcomes all Egyptians to take part, through a system organized via Authors' public relations teams, and one that is available for requests of the Author to make University and College visits for reads possible from 2012 and 2013 in order for Book 2 and Book 3 that area already completed, to be more complete once as many Egyptians and non-Egyptians have his or

her say in what we all feel is best for the [Must fill in parts]
Thank you all!

& to MN8E . . . . "I miss you"

Best regards

Mo Nassah

A NEW CHAPTER
LOCATED IN THE FUTURE BOOKS

INTERIOR OF LOCATION: UNKNOWN / CAIRO, EGYPT
DAY:??—TIME: 12:47 AM (EET)
MONTH: FEBRUARY [11th] YEAR 2011

MN80M
(Quoted saying on-line)

"Happy we are ALL peacefully on our way to be the number 1 nation without violence towards one another Insha Allah :) slowly but surely . . . Let us pick what seed we want to plant TOGETHER as ONE."

"All we have to do now is pick." Mango tree

Orange tree
Nectarine tree
Apple tree
Satsuma tree
Apricot tree
Date tree
Olive tree

Any good tree Insha Allah . . .

Let's start to think what we like to see grow. For our future Insha Allah

Printed in the United States
By Bookmasters